2

35
3″
3′

'I have a proposition to put to you, Lord Stainton, that may benefit both of us.'

'Mrs Brody, the last time you had a proposition to put to me it was to apply for the position of nursemaid to my children. What is it this time?'

'Well—I—I would like to ask you—in all humility—to marry me.'

'What?' He was incredulous. The startling pale blue eyes swept over her face. 'Mrs Brody, I think you must have taken leave of your senses.'

Eve straightened up and walked towards him. 'Please have the good sense to take me seriously.'

'I do,' he ground out, angry now, and insulted. 'And the answer is no.' It was an instant response. Unconsidered. Automatic.

Eve met his eyes. This man was sharp, intelligent, and he was observant. 'The marriage would merely be a business arrangement. You need someone to look after your children and financing. I need a home for myself and my daughter. It will be a marriage in name only—an affair of convenience.'

Lucas gazed at her unblinkingly—a sudden interest seemed to appear in his eyes, and then it was gone.

Helen Dickson was born and still lives in South Yorkshire, with her husband, on a busy arable farm, where she combines writing with keeping a chaotic farmhouse. An incurable romantic, she writes for pleasure, owing much of her inspiration to the beauty of the surrounding countryside. She enjoys reading and music. History has always captivated her, and she likes travel and visiting ancient buildings.

Recent novels by the same author:

THE PIRATE'S DAUGHTER
BELHAVEN BRIDE
THE EARL AND THE PICKPOCKET
HIS REBEL BRIDE
THE DEFIANT DEBUTANTE
ROGUE'S WIDOW, GENTLEMAN'S WIFE
TRAITOR OR TEMPTRESS
A SCOUNDREL OF CONSEQUENCE
WICKED PLEASURES
   (part of *Christmas by Candlelight*)
FORBIDDEN LORD
SCANDALOUS SECRET, DEFIANT BRIDE

FROM GOVERNESS TO SOCIETY BRIDE

Helen Dickson

MILLS & BOON®
Pure reading pleasure™

FROM GOVERNESS TO SOCIETY BRIDE

Chapter One

1820

The young woman paused to look around. It was early morning and most people were still abed. There was not a sound in this great London park, shrouded in the kind of thick fog the city was famous for. It was as if she were alone in the world. This was the time of day she loved best.

But then, somewhere in the distance, she could hear the pounding of a horse's hooves. She could almost feel the ground tremble beneath her feet. She resented the sound, that anyone should disturb her solitude. Turning full circle, she strained her eyes, listening to the thundering crash coming ever closer, when suddenly a sharp shout rent the air and a huge black shape of a horse and rider descended on her.

She cried out for him to stop and threw herself to one side, landing on the grass in a tumbled heap.

The rider jerked at the reins and the beast reared, its hooves flashing like quicksilver, its coat glistening as the muscles beneath it rolled and heaved. Flared nostrils and blazing eyes gave him the look of a demented dragon. It missed her by mere inches.

The woman saw the man as if through a long tunnel. A small cry came from her throat as she saw the black apparition swing himself from his mount in one quick, effortless bound. With his cloak flying wide behind him he resembled a huge bat swooping down toward her. Seized by terror, she scrambled to her feet; brushing down her skirts she glared at him, her heart pounding fit to burst.

'You damned fool,' he roared. 'What the hell are you doing on the track? I could have killed you.'

'I beg your pardon?' she retorted sharply, setting to rights her bonnet, which had been knocked sideways, and trying to smooth away the mixture of terror and anger that had taken hold of her. He was so tall she was forced to look up at him, and she found herself confronting pale, snapping eyes. Black hair accentuated lean cheekbones and a resolute jaw, and his mouth was compressed into a stern arrogant line.

'If you had been any closer you could have been trampled to death. Is there no room in that brainless skull of yours for common sense?'

'Why, how dare you?' She was incensed, her

face pink with indignation. 'And will you please not wave your crop about like that as if you were going to thrash me.'

The stranger slapped the offending weapon to his side without relinquishing her eyes. 'I am sorely tempted. Don't you know not to walk on the track? It's for horses, not ladies to stroll on.'

She raised her chin belligerently. 'I do know that, but I didn't think anyone would be foolish enough to be out riding with the fog as bad as this. And I was only following the track so that I wouldn't become lost.'

'Which is a dangerous thing to do at the best of times.' Abruptly the man interrupted his tirade to say with a touch of concern as a thought occurred to him, 'Are you hurt?'

She glowered at him accusingly, her face showing no sign of softening. 'No—no thanks to you. If you had been riding with more care and attention, this would never have happened—or perhaps your horse got the better of you and you haven't taught it who is master.'

'I assure you he knows who is his master.' He looked at her closely, seeing a gloriously attractive young woman whose whole manner spoke of fearlessness, of her need to let him see that she was afraid of no one, and certainly not of him. Even if she had not jumped out of the way as she had done, he would not have run her down. He was too good a horseman for that, but it had been a close shave. He smiled lazily. 'What a firebrand you are. Are you sure you stumbled and didn't just swoon at the sight of me and my horse?'

His hollow chuckle held a note of mockery. A flush of anger spread to the delicate tips of the woman's ears and icy fire smouldered in her deep blue eyes. 'Why, you conceited, unmitigated cad. You are arrogant if you believe I would ever swoon at your feet. Thank God I'm not afflicted by such weakness.' She stepped away from him, finding his closeness and the way he towered over her a little intimidating. 'Good day to you, sir.'

Not yet ready to be dismissed, he touched her arm to delay her. 'At least let me escort you to your home.'

Her chilled contempt met him face to face. She slapped his hand away. 'Do not touch me. I am quite capable of taking myself home. Go away and take that vicious beast with you,' she snapped, glancing irately at the black stallion that had begun to snort and stamp impatiently, its vigorous temperament reminding her so very much of its master.

'Aren't you taking a risk? You might be set upon by footpads or worse. Anything could happen to a young woman walking alone at this hour.'

'It just did, and I'm of the opinion that I'm in less

danger of being set upon by footpads than I am from you. At least they may have better manners.' Turning her back on him, with her head held high she began to stalk away.

He sighed in feigned disappointment, slowly shaking his head. 'Such ingratitude.'

She spun round. 'Ingratitude?' she gasped. '*You* call me ungrateful? You almost trample me to death and I am supposed to be grateful?'

His eyes gleamed with amusement. 'Have it your way.' He set his tall hat securely on his head and swung himself back in the saddle on his prancing beast. 'Good day to you.'

He kicked his horse into motion. His laughter drifted back to her, his mockery infuriating her yet further. She stamped her foot and glared after him, muttering all kinds of threats under her breath. She had never met a man who had irritated her as he had just done and it chafed her sorely to consider his flawless success.

It was a glorious spring day. The sun had risen out of a broad expanse of opal mist, and scraps of cloud floated like spun gauze in the sky. Ash and sycamore, cherry and lilac trees were bursting into full flower, and trumpet-headed daffodils and clusters of primroses filled beds and borders. The air had a trace of freshness in it, a breeze blowing across Hyde Park from the river beyond. The park was quiet, save for a skylark singing high above and a few people taking an early morning constitutional, including a young woman walking aimlessly along the paths with two small girls trailing behind her.

Seated on a bench watching her five-year-old daughter, Estelle, running happily between the flower beds pursued by Jasper, a Labrador pup that was a recent addition to the Seagrove household, Eve sighed and looked down at her hands in her lap. Why did she feel so despondent? What was the matter with her? Why did her life seem to be so limited? She had her health. She had a good friend in Beth Seagrove. She was not unattractive and, thanks to her dear deceased father, eventually she would have more money than she would know what to do with. She was reasonably clever and had a broad base of interests. Everyone was always telling her how lucky she was to have Estelle, whom she adored. That should really be enough for anyone—but it wasn't. There had to be more that she could do with her life, something else to absorb her time and energies.

Tonight she was to attend a private party at Lady Ellesmere's house in Curzon Street. These affairs where most of the faces were familiar were more to her taste than the more established venues, and she really did enjoy attending them with Beth and her husband. However, Eve was determined to find something to do to earn her keep until her father's money was made available to her and she could look for somewhere else to live.

Turning her head, she looked at the young woman with the children. She was perhaps eighteen or nineteen. Her clothes were of good quality, but plain grey and unadorned—the same clothes a nursemaid would wear. Her face was pale and dark rings circled her eyes—she really didn't look at all well. She was seated on the bench adjacent to Eve's and her head was lowered on to her chest. Her shaking shoulders indicated that she was weeping very quietly.

The two little girls, her young charges, stood in front of her and stared at her. Their faces showed confusion and they were clearly anxious and frightened. The youngest child picked up on her mood and started to cry and shrank into the girl next to her.

'Don't cry, Sarah,' the eldest girl said to the woman on the bench. 'It will be all right.'

Her words seemed to calm the young woman, not because she was able to believe them but because of the sweet unselfishness of the child uttering them. Raising her head, she smiled at the child but her shoulders remained drooped in dejection.

Eve stood up. Fishing a handkerchief out of her

pocket, she went to the unhappy trio. 'Can I be of help?' she asked, directing the question at the woman while bending down and smiling at the weeping child. 'Here, let me wipe your face.' Gently she dabbed at the tears of the child, who was looking up at her with solemn light blue eyes that reminded her of a wounded puppy. 'What are your names?' she asked.

'I am Sophie,' the older girl replied politely, 'and this is my sister Abigail. Abigail is three, nearly four, and I'm five.'

'Is that so? Well, I'm pleased to meet you both,' Eve said, thinking what pretty children they were. Both had heart-shaped faces and glossy dark brown curls and were dressed in identical blue dresses. Looking towards where Estelle was playing, Eve waved her over. 'Estelle, while I sit and talk to…?' She looked enquiringly at the young woman.

'Sarah, Sarah Lacy,' she provided quietly.

'While I talk to Miss Lacy, why don't you take Sophie and Abigail to play with Jasper—would you like that?' she asked the two little girls. They nodded, looking shyly at Estelle, but not moving until Sarah had given them her permission.

'It's all right, children. You can go. I can see you from here.'

Typical of Estelle, who was accustomed to playing with Beth's two boisterous boys, she held out her hand to Abigail, and the three of them chased over the grass after a staggering Jasper, who stopped suddenly and sat down in a heap of tumbled legs.

Smiling, Eve sat next to the young woman. The poor girl was obviously not well. Her skin was pale and her soft grey eyes had a wild, almost desperate look about them.

'I hope you didn't mind me suggesting that your charges play with my daughter. The puppy is quite harmless.' The young woman shook her head. 'My name is Eve Brody, by the way.'

'No, I don't mind. I'm their nursemaid. It's good for them to be with other children. They so rarely are, poor mites.' Lowering her head, she stifled a sob. 'I'm sorry…' she began, then broke off miserably.

'It's all right, Sarah,' Eve said, moving closer to her. 'Are you ill?'

Unable to meet the kind stranger's eyes, Sarah looked down at her fingers twisting her handkerchief in her lap. 'I've just got a bit of a headache, that's all,' she answered shyly.

'Have you seen a doctor? Perhaps he can give you something that will help to make you feel better.'

Sarah shook her head and sniffed. 'I'll be all right. I feel better than I did.'

'Then why are you crying? You look quite distraught.'

'To tell you the truth, miss, I've been at my wits'

end these past weeks. I don't know what to do. Really I don't.'

'Why is that?'

'Mark, my young man, lives and works as head groomsman at a big house in Surrey. He's asked me to marry him, but it would mean leaving my job—and the children.'

'What's so terrible about that? Surely there is someone else to care for them—their mother?'

'They have no mother. My master, Lord Stainton, the children's father, is in the middle of closing down the house, which is why I'm out with them so early—to get them away from the upheaval. Workmen are all over the place and his lordship isn't in the best of tempers. Apart from myself and the housekeeper, most of the servants have been dismissed, and very soon we are to move to Lord Stainton's country estate in Oxfordshire. I haven't told Mark yet and I'm dreading it. He doesn't understand, you see, the bond I have with the children.'

'If your position means so much to you, then why doesn't your young man go with you?'

'Lord Stainton can't afford to take on more staff. His lordship's affairs really are in quite a bad way, which is why he has to sell his London house.'

'Even so, his problem is not yours, Sarah. Lord Stainton must find someone else to look after his children. It shouldn't be too difficult. I'm sure there are lots of young ladies with the right credentials who would jump at the chance.'

'I know—but there has been so much heartache in their young lives that I hate the thought of deserting them. They've been in my charge since Abigail was a year old. I can't bear to leave them. It will break my heart—and theirs—but I know I must.'

'Your concern is commendable, Sarah, but you do have to think of yourself.'

Estelle's laughter came to them from across the grass. Eve's eyes were drawn towards the sound, seeing her daughter rolling on the grass with Jasper on top of her licking her face, while Sophie and Abigail looked on, reticent to join in, but smiling none the less. Concerned, she fixed her attention on the young woman by her side.

'You really do look quite poorly. Perhaps you should go home and lie down for a while,' Eve suggested.

Sarah shook her head. 'That's impossible, although I really should be getting back.' She stood up, putting one hand to her head and the other grasping the back of the bench as she swayed slightly. 'Oh, dear. I do feel quite dizzy.'

Standing up, Eve took her arm. 'Come, I'll walk back with you. I can't let you go by yourself.'

'Oh, no. You've been very kind, but I've imposed on your time long enough.'

'I insist. Besides, I have nothing better to do. Where do you live?'

'Not too far away, just across the park in Upper Brook Street.'

'Then it is not far from Berkeley Street, which is where I live. Come, children,' Eve called. 'Estelle, you must carry Jasper.' She smiled as she watched her daughter bend down and pick a wriggling Jasper up off the grass and tuck him beneath her arm.

Stainton House was certainly in a state of upheaval. Workmen swarmed about all over the place and furniture was being either covered with dustsheets or loaded on to wagons in the street. Holding the children's hands, Eve and Sarah went inside. The size of the house surprised and impressed Eve. With its white-and-gold décor, she could well imagine how elegant it must have looked before the workforce moved in.

Eve was about to say her farewells to Sarah and the children when Jasper broke free of his captor and landed on the floor. Excited by the new environment and noise, the little dog bounded yelping loudly up the broad sweep of the staircase rising gracefully from the centre of the hall.

'Don't worry,' Sarah said, having recovered a little from her earlier discomfort. 'I'll go after him.'

The three children went and sat halfway up the stairs, watching the workmen with rapt expressions on their faces. Eve stepped aside to let two men pass carrying a gold-and-green striped sofa in the direction of the street, and turned when a voice barked out, 'Bloody hell, man, be careful! That portrait is worth a small fortune. Any damage and the buyer will refuse to take it.'

Eve strode over to the owner of the remark—a jacketless, dark, forbidding figure, his grey breeches moulding his muscular legs and thighs, his white shirt open at his tanned throat, and his hair as black as a panther's pelt. Her face was a mask of indignation.

'Do you have to swear in front of the children?' she remarked haughtily. She saw his shoulders stiffen at the sound of her voice and when he spun round and his eyes sliced over her, she could almost feel the effort he was exerting to keep his rage under control. The man had ramrod posture and an aura of exacting competence, and Eve almost collapsed when she saw his face—it was as hard and forbidding as a granite sculpture and he was looking at her as if she were a mad woman who had invaded his domain.

She also recognised him as being the man whose horse had almost trampled her to death the day before.

'I'll swear when I like in my own house...' Suddenly he froze and his eyes widened. 'Good Lord, it's you—'

'Unfortunately that is so. And do you have to shout? My hearing is perfectly sound and you're frightening the children.'

'Children? Don't be ridiculous. I'm their father.'

'Precisely, and for that reason alone you should have more control over your temper,' Eve snapped, having recovered from the shock of meeting the rude and thoroughly obnoxious gentleman for a second time.

Lord Stainton turned his dagger gaze on the terrified servants, who had ceased what they were doing and stood frozen to the spot, their eyes agape. 'Who the hell let this emotional woman into my house without consulting me first?'

'I am not an emotional woman and, as I have already told you, I am not deaf, so kindly lower your tone.' Turning on her heel, she strode to the stairs to collect Estelle.

'And what's that supposed to mean?' he thundered, striding after her irate figure with the silent sureness of a wolf, stopping in his tracks when he saw three apprehensive young faces peering down at him from the stairs instead of the usual two. Placing his fists on his hips, he glowered from the extra child to the angry young woman. 'Miss Lacy,' he shouted. When Miss Lacy failed to appear, he cursed softly and pinned Eve with his gaze. 'Where has that child come from,' he demanded, pointing a long narrow finger at the offending child, 'and what the hell is she doing in my house, today of all days?'

Eve's eyes flew to the children while still feeling concern for Sarah. After all, it was the purpose for which she had walked into the lion's den just minutes before.

'The child you are referring to is my daughter.'

'Then do you mind removing her from my house and yourself along with her? As you can see—'

'You are moving out,' Eve snapped.

'Do you always make a habit of stating the obvious, Miss…?'

'Mrs—Brody, and, yes, I do,' she said, her eyes flashing as cold fury drained her face of colour and added a steely edge to her voice.

He returned her gaze steadily, studying her as though she were some strange creature he had just uncovered in his home. He had already noted her slight American intonation; her Scottish name was another fact that intrigued a rather bemused Lord Stainton. There was a moment of silence in which he tried to calm himself.

At thirty-two years of age, six feet four inches tall and with amazingly arresting eyes he was a strikingly handsome man. Rugged strength was carved into every feature of his bronzed face, from his straight dark brows and nose, his firm and sensually moulded lips, to the square, arrogant jut of his chin. Just now he was also formidable as he glared at the young woman who stood before him on his black-and-white marble floor. Every line of his face was set with disapproval.

'Have you had an edifying look at me, Lord Stainton—I assume that is who you are?'

'You are correct in your assumption, Mrs Brody.'

'You are also the most ill-mannered, arrogant, inconsiderate man I have ever encountered,' she upbraided him coldly.

His eyes narrowed and his lips tightened. 'I dare say I am all you accuse me of. It goes with the title.'

Eve was in no mood to be mocked, and she could see by the gleam in his eyes he was doing exactly that. 'Then with you as an example, I can only hope you are the last titled Englishman I shall ever meet. Yesterday I fervently hoped and prayed I would never have the misfortune to set eyes on you again. Nothing has changed. Such an outward display of temperamental frustration is regarded as a sign of bad breeding where I come from.'

Ramming his fists into his waist, leaning forward, he stared at her in blank fury. 'Really! You really are the most infuriatingly outspoken woman I have ever met. How dare you come into my house and say these things to me—things you know nothing about.'

'Oh, I dare say a lot of things to a man who scares his children half to death and terrifies each and every one of his servants so they creep about in fear of you. The whole house vibrates with a tension that springs from you, Lord Stainton. It's a wonder you have any servants at all to order about. By the look on your face I would wager I've hit a sore spot. Please don't disappoint me by holding your temper. I would hate to see you explode with the effort.'

'Believe me, Mrs Brody, you would not want to see me explode. I have a temper, I admit it, a violent one when I am driven to it. And how I raise my children and choose to live concerns only myself.'

Eve had made her point with an icy calmness. Lord Stainton was so taken aback by her outburst and her forthright way of speaking that his superiority evaporated as he stared at the attractive young woman whose fury turned her dark blue eyes beneath gracefully winged dark brows to violet. Framed by a heavy mass of auburn hair arranged neatly beneath her bonnet, her face was striking, with creamy, glowing skin, high cheekbones, and a small round chin with a tiny, intriguing cleft in the centre. Her nose was straight, her mouth soft and generously wide. His gaze moved over her slender body with a familiarity that brought a rush of colour to her cheeks.

Mrs Brody was a young woman in her early twenties, and she moved with a natural grace and poise that evaded most of the women he knew. Despite being a married woman, she exuded a gentle innocence that he found appealing. Beneath this he sensed an adventurous spirit tinged with wilfulness and obstinacy.

Appalled that he could find the time to scrutinise a complete stranger who had entered his home uninvited and chastised him so forcefully, when all around him there was complete and utter chaos, in sheer frustration he turned from her.

'I've had enough of this charade, Mrs Brody. I have to get on. No one invited you here. There is the door. Use it.'

Eve could feel her face flaming in response to his rudeness. Her momentary shock gave way to a sudden burst of wrath. 'You're right, they didn't. I came to make sure your children's nurse arrived home safely. She was taken ill in the park and I considered it an act of human kindness to see that she made it home without mishap. Now that is done, it will be my pleasure to remove myself and my child from your house—when I have retrieved my dog from all this chaos, that is.'

He spun round to face her once more, and for

the first time Eve saw his hard façade crack. 'Dog? What dog?' he echoed blankly. There was more than irritation in his question—there was stunned amazement.

'The one that disappeared up your stairs when we came in.'

'Are you telling me that there is an animal running loose in my house?'

'That is exactly what I'm saying—but don't be alarmed,' she said, her voice dripping with sarcasm, 'it won't bite. Ah, here it is now,' she said, thankful to see Sarah coming down the stairs with Jasper in her arms. Meeting her halfway, she took the pup and got hold of Estelle's hand, impatient to get out of the house as quickly as possible.

'I see Lord Stainton is out of sorts again,' Sarah whispered softly, looking at Eve with quiet concern. 'Are you all right?' She glanced over her shoulder. 'Have a care. His lordship is not a man to listen or be reasoned with when he's in one of his infamous adverse moods.'

With her back to Lord Stainton, Eve smiled at Sarah. 'Oh, I think I can manage his lordship, Sarah.'

'Unfortunately his temper rules his head. He will soon calm down.'

'No doubt so will I—when I am out of this mad house. Now you take care of yourself, and marry that young man of yours before too long.'

Confronting Lord Stainton for the last time at the bottom of the stairs, she lifted her chin, in no way intimidated by this man. 'Seeing that you are in the middle of a self-destructive rage cycle, Lord Stainton, I'll get out from under your feet. I'm only sorry that I subjected my daughter to the rantings of a very rude lord.'

'You have caught me on a bad day, Mrs Brody.'

'Considering I have encountered you on two occasions, Lord Stainton, judging by your behaviour it would seem that you have a bad day most days.'

'Not at all, Mrs Brody. If your daughter has been in any way upset by my "rantings", then she has a small measure of my sympathy—the remainder of it must go to your long-suffering husband.'

Eve looked at him directly. 'I am a widow, Lord Stainton, and my husband's suffering was of short duration. He was killed outright by an English bullet in New Orleans. Now,' she said, grasping Estelle's hand tighter and clutching Jasper to her bosom with the other, 'I have no wish to detain you any longer. Good day to you.' She swept out of the house like a galleon in full sail, too angry to say one more word.

In a state of suspense, Lord Stainton stared at the open doorway through which Mrs Brody had just disappeared, feeling as if a hurricane had just blown itself out. He also felt bewildered and extremely angry with himself and a complete idiot, his expression holding more than a little dismay and remorse at what Mrs Brody had just divulged. From an early age he had been taught by his parents and his tutors to project a veneer of civilisation, regardless of how he was feeling, particularly when his emotions were incensed. He had just failed dismally.

'Miss Lacy,' he called, halting the nursemaid as she climbed the stairs to take Sophie and Abigail to their rooms. 'Mrs Brody? Who is she and where does she live?'

'Apart from her name I—I don't know who she is, Lord Stainton. She never said. Although she did say she lived on Berkeley Street.'

'I see.' He was about to turn away when he remembered something Mrs Brody had said. 'Miss Lacy.'

'Yes, sir.'

'Mrs Brody did mention that you weren't feeling well,' he said on a softer note. 'Do you need to see a doctor?'

'No, sir. I'm feeling much better now.' She bobbed a little curtsy. 'Thank you for asking.'

'Good.' With the skill he'd perfected when his wife had left him, he turned away and coldly dismissed Mrs Brody from his mind.

Disturbed and upset following her encounter with the insufferable Lord Stainton, and feeling a headache coming on, with a morose sigh Eve sank on to the sofa in the drawing room of the Seagroves' elegant house on Berkeley Street, unable to believe the furious altercation had happened at all. Her anger had evaporated somewhat on her walk back, but she was still shaken. The dejection that had replaced her fury was completely uncharacteristic of her.

With the children happily ensconced upstairs in the nursery and William, Beth's devoted husband, at work at the Foreign Office, glad to have some time to themselves, Beth poured them both some tea and sat back. She cast a sharp, searching look at her friend's exquisite features.

'What has you looking so grim, Eve? Tell me.'

'I met someone today.'

'Did you? Well, there's nothing so unusual about that. Is it someone I know?'

'I would think so. Lord Stainton, and I have to say he is the rudest, most conceited man I have ever met in my life.'

Beth laughed. 'Then that explains it. What happened?'

In no time at all Eve told her everything that had occurred, from the moment she had met Sarah Lacy in the park to being ordered out of Stainton House like one of the criminal fraternity. She didn't tell her about their previous encounter in the park, since Beth was always chiding her for going off by herself. When she had finished Beth looked stunned.

'Dear me! It sounds to me as if you have upset that illustrious lord.'

Eve grimaced. 'I didn't mean to—although I suppose I was somewhat rude and outspoken, and in his house, too. Do you know him, Beth?'

'My dear Eve, the whole of London knows Lord Stainton.'

'What do you know about him?'

'He's devastatingly handsome for one thing— you must admit that.'

Bringing the image of the tall, lean and superbly fit Lord Stainton to mind, Eve could not deny that despite his stern, finely chiselled mouth and the arrogant authority stamped in his firm jaw and the cynicism in his cold, light blue eyes, he was breathtakingly handsome. 'Yes, I suppose he is.'

Beth sighed almost dreamily. 'I do so like handsome men.'

'I know. That's why you married William,' Eve commented teasingly.

'Oh, no,' Beth said, chuckling softly as she took a sip of her tea. 'William is sensible, reliable and conscientious, but also sensitive, gentle and idealistic. *That* is why I married him.'

'I agree, he is all those things. William is a

paragon among men, and not a hardened cynic like Lord Stainton. What else do you know about him?'

'Well, on a physical and intellectual level there's none better. He inherited the title from his brother, who died several months ago. He lives quietly and isn't often seen in society these days, although I have seen him on occasion at the more sedate affairs. He's been the object of gossip ever since he divorced his wife Maxine about a year ago. She's the daughter of the Earl of Clevedon—Lord Irvine. At the time the divorce created a scandal that set the *ton* on fire.'

Eve stared at her in shocked amazement. 'Divorce? He divorced his wife—the mother of those two lovely children? Why on earth would he do that?'

'I don't know all the details, but what I do know is that his wife caused complications from the day he married her. Compounded in her many faults, apparently, was the fact that she was exquisitely beautiful, elegant and clever and attractive to other men. A man of Lord Stainton's character would not tolerate infidelity.'

'She had an affair?'

'Several, apparently. After the birth of her second daughter it's rumoured she indulged in one affair after another, the most intensive being with Lucas Stainton's own brother. Her behaviour really was quite scandalous. She actually walked out on Lord Stainton to live with his brother in the country.'

'She left her children?' Eve gasped, appalled that any woman could do such a thing.

'Yes, she did. Apparently the divorce turned out to be extremely expensive—it virtually ruined him. Of course Lucas's brother didn't help matters, being an inveterate gambler. The Stainton coffers were depleted long before he died.'

'Then Lord Stainton will have an unenviable task on his hands replenishing them.'

'Indeed he will.'

'Is he ostracised because of his divorce?'

'On the contrary. It all adds to his mystery and charm. The *ton* positively pander to him and no one would dare give him the cut. Of course he is free to marry again, but the aristocratic mamas on the look out for suitable husbands for their darling daughters do not consider an impoverished, divorced lord at all suitable. However, he's favoured for his looks and every hostess in the *ton* has been trying to lure him back into society, but he declines their invitations.

'I believe he's selling his London house and moving to the country.'

'Yes, I know. Laurel Court. It's close to William's parents' house in Oxfordshire and it's very beautiful, although sadly neglected. If he's selling his house in Mayfair, then hopefully it might help pay some of the debts. If not, who knows what he will do. If he wants to keep the estate, then he might even resort to marrying an heiress—and why not? He won't be the first impoverished nobleman to marry for money and he won't be the last.'

'That seems rather drastic, Beth.'

'To you, having lived almost all your life in America, I suppose it does. In English society, marrying for money is considered a perfectly acceptable undertaking. However, pride is a dominant Stainton trait and Lord Stainton will find it extremely difficult and distasteful having to resort to such extreme measures. But that said, I do believe he might honour us with his presence tonight with Lady Ellesmere being an old friend of the family and the occasion being a rather sedate affair.'

Eve's eyes snapped open as a blaze of animosity and a shock of terror erupted through her entire body. 'Lord Stainton will be there?'

Beth laughed, in no way sorry for her friend's consternation. 'Don't be alarmed, Eve. He may decide not to go.'

'On the other hand he might.'

'Try not to worry. By now perhaps he looks back on the incident with amusement.'

'If he does, then he has a warped sense of humour, Beth. He will not find the incident amusing, believe me. In fact, I might stay at home. Lord Stainton will not want to see me any more than I wish to see him. Besides, I have developed this terrible headache in the last hour. An early night suddenly seems most appealing.'

'Nonsense. You are going. With a room full of matrons and *grandes dames,* I am relying on you to talk to me. As for the headache, I'll give you a couple of my powders to alleviate it. Take one before you go and another before you go to bed.'

By the time Eve was ready to leave for Lady Ellesmere's party, her head was aching quite badly. Having taken one of Beth's powders and feeling no effect, she took the one she was supposed to take before she went to bed. After tucking Estelle in bed and kissing her goodnight, she went to join Beth and William.

Lady Ellesmere's house was a blaze of light when the carriage drew up outside. A liveried footman stepped aside as they swept into the marble-floored hall. Entering the salon, they paused and Eve's eyes swept the assembled guests dressed in their finery, the ladies beautiful in silks and satins fashionably cut.

With an eye for comfort, luxury and fashionable elegance, the walls were hung with ivory silk delicately worked with a gold-and-green design, the colours reflected in the upholstery and the heavy curtains hung at the windows. Expensive Turkish rugs covered the floor. The room was aglow with the dazzling radiance of myriad candles, the delicate crystal pendants of the chandeliers splattering the walls with prisms of light. Soft music being played by a string quartet could be heard in the background and for those guests who sought entertainment two adjoining rooms had been set aside for gaming. The French doors were set wide to catch the coolness of the night and to allow guests on to the wide lantern-lit terrace.

It was an informal affair. Lady Ellesmere, a striking middle-aged widow, was seated on a gold-coloured *chaise longue*. Like a queen, bedecked in sparkling jewels and her richly coloured silk skirts spread about her, she reigned supreme.

Taking two glasses of champagne from a silver tray, William handed them to his companions, then took one for himself and surveyed the glittering company.

'Rather splendid, isn't it?'

'As usual,' Beth answered. 'It's what you expect at Lady Ellesmere's affairs. How is your headache, Eve? Has the powder I gave you helped?'

Eve smiled. Relieved to see no one she would rather not, she began to relax. 'Yes, I believe it has—although I did take the other one just to be on the safe side.'

Beth stared at her in shock. 'You took them both? Oh, Eve, you really shouldn't have. They really are quite strong. I wouldn't drink too much champagne on top of them if I were you.'

William chuckled softly. 'Just one of Beth's powders is enough to send the sufferer off to sleep for a week, Eve. Two powders and you can guarantee being rendered unconscious for a fortnight.'

Feeling perfectly all right and in no way concerned, Eve laughed and took a sip of her champagne. 'I never drink more than two glasses anyway, so worry not, you two. In fact, I think when we've spoken to Lady Ellesmere I might partake of some refreshment,' she said, her eyes straying to the connecting salon where tables had been laid out with delicious delicacies.

Lucas saw Eve the instant he entered Lady Ellesmere's salon. Seeing her made him stop, shocked into inaction. His brows drew together in disbelief that she was here, and that the harridan who had invaded his house earlier was the glamorous red head strolling casually through the roomful of wealthy elite with William Seagrove and his wife.

Lucas was with his good friend Henry Channing, who was easy to please and the most amenable of men. Henry revelled in London life, which was a change from the backwoods of Newcastle he'd been brought up in. With his looks and his father's wealth he was well received everywhere, his trade origins being conveniently forgotten.

Henry followed his gaze, interest lighting his eyes when he saw the delightful object of his friend's attention. 'That absolutely divine creature is Mrs Eve Brody,' he provided, 'born in England and raised in America. Her father passed away recently, leaving her immensely rich, I believe.'

'Is that so,' Lucas drawled drily, staring at the champagne in his glass.

'Mrs Brody, who is a widow, has received numerous offers of marriage in America. Since coming to England, she has attracted a great deal of interest, but she discourages those suitors as soon as their intentions become apparent to her.'

Lucas turned a baleful eye on his friend. 'You seem to be extremely knowledgeable about Mrs Brody, Henry.'

'My sister is a close friend of Beth Seagrove.'

'Then that explains it. However, I am not remotely interested in Mrs Brody, Henry.' Turning his back on Eve, he smiled at Lady Ellesmere, who was beckoning him over, and began walking towards her, abandoning a bemused Henry.

* * *

Later Lucas's eyes were drawn to Eve again, standing near the refreshment room, the light from the chandelier bathing her in a golden glow. From across the room he studied her stunning figure and flawless beauty. Her heavy, fiery auburn hair had been twisted into burnished curls at the crown. Her gown was pale green with a tightly fitted bodice that forced her breasts high and exposed a daring expanse of flesh.

Having been aware of his presence for some time and feeling his razor-sharp gaze on her, Eve found the memory of their angry altercation still very much on her mind. It made her feel quite ill at the same time as pride forced her to lift her chin and rebelliously to face him across the distance that separated them, meeting his ruthless stare. For the second time within twelve short hours her dark eyes beheld another's in mutual animosity.

Lord Stainton's tall, athletic frame was resplendent in black jacket and trousers. In contrast, his shirt and neckcloth were dazzling white. He looked unbearably handsome. He also looked utterly bored.

Eve stood in resentful silence while his gaze slid boldly over her, from the top of her shining deep red curls to the toes of her satin slippers. She was accustomed to the admiring glances of gentlemen, but there was nothing gentlemanly about Lord

Stainton's insolent, lazy perusal of her body. Incensed she turned her back on him to listen to what Beth was saying to her.

'If the weather is nice tomorrow, I think we'll take a picnic to the park. Would you like that? There's to be a balloon ascent during the afternoon. The children would love that.'

'I wouldn't mind seeing it myself and it will certainly do the children good to get out of the house and let off some steam. How long will it be before your house in Camberwell is finished?' Eve enquired. There was great excitement in the Seagrove household over the large house being built for them in Camberwell, south of the river. Like many businessmen, William was moving his family out of the centre of the city, yet close enough for him to drive in to work.

'Another two months—and I cannot wait. Eve, I'm glad Estelle's settled in so well. When you arrived, I confess to being worried that she would miss New York.'

'Your brood have made it easy for her, Beth. In fact, at the moment life is one huge adventure for my darling daughter.'

Beth smiled, hiding her dismay that the same could not be said for her friend. Since Eve's arrival, she had quickly become a popular figure on the social scene. Several eligible bachelors had been plaguing her relentlessly to allow them to pay their addresses to her, but she politely shunned them all, seeming to have no interest in forming that kind of relationship with any man.

Glancing across the room at Lord Stainton, Eve watched him prowl among the guests. He seemed to radiate barely leashed strength and power. There was something primitive about him, and she felt that his elegant attire and indolence were nothing but a front meant to lull the unwary into believing he was a civilised being while disguising the fact that he was a dangerous savage.

When he began moving into their vicinity, Eve's urge to flee promptly overpowered every other instinct. 'If you will excuse me, Beth, I would like to visit the ladies' room.'

Having seen Lord Stainton arrive and the shock register on Eve's face, Beth laughed and placed a restraining hand on her arm. 'Oh, no, you don't. I think you should be properly presented to Lord Stainton and forget your earlier encounter.'

When Beth drew her forward, mentally Eve braced herself.

Unable to avoid a confrontation, Lucas stood his ground and bowed graciously to Beth. 'It's a pleasure to see you again, Mrs Seagrove. Your husband is here?'

'He is indeed, although I fear a game of faro has

caught his interest. Lord Stainton, may I present my good friend, Eve Brody.'

Eve looked at Lord Stainton's shuttered eyes. She could find no trace of gentleness or kindness anywhere in his tough, ruggedly chiselled cynical features. His slashed eyebrows were more accustomed to frowning than smiling, and he had a hard mouth with a hint of cruelty in it. It was a face that said its owner cared nothing for fools, and in the light blue of his dark lashed eyes, silver flecks stirred dangerously, like small warning lights.

'We've already met,' she stated, toying with the glass of champagne she held between her fingers.

William chose that moment to emerge from the gaming room; seeing him, Beth hastily excused herself, determined to reach him and coax him away from the game of whist that was about to start in the other room.

Lucas nodded to her and again fixed his gaze on Eve. 'That's right, Mrs Brody, we have met. I'm flattered that you remember me,' he replied, keeping a good distance between them.

Determined to appear calm and unaffected by their early encounter and not indulge in a public display of temper, Eve forced a smile to her lips. 'I've tried to forget our unpleasant encounter, Lord Stainton. It's difficult.'

'Well, here's to your future success.'

He lifted his glass in a mocking toast. Eve did the same. Unfortunately her head chose that moment to spin. Her hand shook and the champagne sloshed out of her glass and spilled down the front of her dress. Lord Stainton jumped to the wrong conclusion as to why her eyes looked glazed and, raking her with an insulting glance, his mouth curved scornfully.

'Didn't anyone tell you about the perils of drink, Mrs Brody?' he remarked contemptuously. He saw her flinch, but her gaze never faltered.

'I don't,' she bit back, resisting the urge to snatch his glass and toss its contents into his arrogant face.

'It is obvious to me that you do and that you cannot hold it,' he said imperturbably.

Desperate to appear normal, Eve was thankful when a solicitous footman was already lowering a tray of champagne to come to her aid. With a grateful smile pasted on her face, she handed him her glass and took a napkin he offered with shaky fingers. She proceeded to dab at her dress and handed it back.

'Thank you,' she said, glancing around to see if they were being observed, relieved to find the incident had gone unnoticed.

'Perhaps you would like some more champagne,' Lord Stainton said in a silky voice.

'No, thank you,' she replied tightly.

'It's a very wise person who knows when to stop.'

She glared at him. 'Go away, Lord Stainton. You really are the most provoking man alive and quite insufferable.'

Instead of being insulted or angered, he looked at her with amusement and shook his head. 'What were you expecting to find, Mrs Brody? A socially accepted gentleman? A rake or a dandified fop? I am none of these.'

Before Eve could react to his words, in a mockery of another toast, he said, 'Enjoy your evening.' And he walked away to join Henry Channing.

Chapter Two

As the evening wore on Eve was finding it more and more difficult to stay awake. What was the matter with her? All she wanted to do was go to sleep. And then it hit her. She knew what was wrong. It was those wretched headache powders she had taken. Perhaps some fresh air would help. Where was Beth? Her eyes swept around the room looking for her friend, but there was no sign of her.

Snaking her way round obstacles, she eventually came to the French windows that led out on to the terrace. Stepping out, she crossed to a low wall and placed her hands on it for support, breathing hard. The terrace was dimly lit and she did not see the tall dark-haired man, a thin cheroot he occasionally enjoyed clamped between his even white teeth, his features in shadow, quietly conversing with Henry Channing until it was too late, otherwise she would never have ventured outside.

'I say, are you all right?' Henry remarked, having watched her come outside. He was concerned when he saw her place her hand to her forehead.

Eve swayed, seeing the look of unconcealed disgust on Lord Stainton's face. Before she could reply, his icy voice said,

'I believe the lady is completely foxed, Henry. You can expect to have one hell of a hangover in the morning, Mrs Brody.'

'I would expect it had I been drinking, but I haven't, and if I had it would be none of your business. How dare you?'

'I dare say a lot of things to you, Mrs Brody, but I won't waste my breath.' Catching her by the arm as she rocked to one side, he thrust her rudely down on to the wall. 'Sit there while I summon your friends. I think they should take you home before you disgrace yourself and them with your undignified behaviour.'

Eve raised her head and stared up at him, unable to focus properly. 'You don't understand…'

'I understand all too well,' he said scathingly, his accusing eyes dropping to the damp stain on the front of her dress.

'I resent that,' she gasped, trying to get to her feet but falling back and having to close her eyes when her head began to spin in a dizzy whirl.

'She's going to swoon,' Henry predicted.

'I am not,' Eve protested, defying her pronouncement by almost toppling off the wall.

'Oh, for God's sake!' Lord Stainton thundered, casting the cigar to the ground. Grasping her about the waist, he scooped her up into his arms and headed for a bench further along the terrace. 'Find Mrs Seagrove, Henry, and ask her to come at once—and find some hartshorn or whatever it is that brings one out of a swoon. And for heaven's sake be discreet. Should anyone come outside and find me with a senseless woman in my arms, gossip will be raging through London like wildfire before breakfast.'

Henry rushed off to do his bidding while Lord Stainton carried his helpless burden along the terrace.

Coming to her senses and blisteringly aware of her close proximity to Lord Stainton's broad chest, fury and indignation shot like red-hot sparks through Eve's body. 'How dare you?' she cried, squirming against him, trying to break his hold. 'Will you put me down? No matter what you think, I do not deserve such treatment.' Her struggle only seemed to make him angrier.

'Be quiet and keep still,' he ordered, going a little further before dumping her unceremoniously on to a bench.

Eve fought the lethargy that was stealing over her and snapped her head up, intending to launch into a tirade, but looking past her tormentor she saw a figure in a pale pink gown rushing towards her.

'Beth,' she cried. Never had she been so relieved to see anyone in her life.

'What on earth has happened?' Beth bent over her friend, her face creased with concern. 'Is your headache worse, Eve?'

'No, no, it isn't, and none of this is my fault. Beth, will you please tell this puffed-up lord who has the manners of a barbarian and who is bent on assassinating my character that I am suffering nothing more serious than an overdose of your headache powders and not over-indulgence of champagne.'

'Headache powders?' Instead of looking guilty because he'd made a mistake, Lord Stainton looked infuriatingly amused. 'You are prone to headaches, Mrs Brody?'

'No, as a matter of fact I rarely suffer minor ailments, but earlier today I had the misfortune to meet you, Lord Stainton.'

'Then what can I say?'

'Sorry would be a start,' Eve bit back.

'Very well. The mistake was mine. I apologise most humbly.'

'Humble? You?' she gasped, unable to believe her ears. 'You couldn't be humble if you tried.'

'Contrary to what you obviously think of me,' he

drawled, 'I was merely coming to your rescue. Your actions, like on our previous encounter, led me to believe you were in danger of swooning.'

'And I seem to recall telling you that I never swoon—and I was not in any danger,' Eve lied coldly, avoiding Beth's questioning eyes, knowing full well that she would have to give her a full account of her encounter with Lord Stainton in the park.

Lazy mockery lit his eyes. 'And you are sure of that, are you?' he asked, as amusement seemed to drain the tension in his body.

'I most assuredly am.'

'To show you how wrong you are, Mrs Brody, I suggest that when you get up off that bench you will allow me to assist you.'

Eve opened her mouth to make some suitably scathing remark about his outrageous conceit, but his bold smile was too much for her. Swinging her legs on to the ground, she got to her feet unsteadily. When Lord Stainton reached out to take her arm, she snatched it away and glared at him.

'Don't you dare touch me. I wouldn't let you touch me to save me from drowning,' she retorted furiously.

'I understand,' Lord Stainton drawled mildly.

Placing her hand on Beth's arm, Eve completely ignored Lord Stainton. 'I would like to go home, if you don't mind, Beth. I really must go to bed before I make a total fool of myself and fall asleep in Lady Ellesmere's salon. That would never do.'

Seeing the funny side of the incident, Beth suppressed a smile. 'No, it would not. It's almost time to leave anyway. We'll find William and say goodnight to Lady Ellesmere.' She turned to Lord Stainton and Mr Channing, who was looking totally bemused and holding a bottle of hartshorn in his hand. 'Goodnight, Lord Stainton, Mr Channing, and thank you for your assistance.'

'Good Lord, Lucas,' Henry uttered after a long moment of silence, staring at his friend in disbelief. Grown men rarely dared to challenge him, yet here was this young American widow—an exquisite, extremely ravishing American widow—who had done exactly that. 'She actually accused you of having the manners of a barbarian. Mrs Brody is one angry lady,' he said, shaking his head in disbelief. 'I doubt she will forgive you in a hurry.'

Lucas glanced toward the closed doors through which the aforesaid lady had just disappeared, and in the space of an instant, Henry watched his lazy smile harden into a mask of ironic amusement.

'I'm sure she won't. But that's Mrs Brody's problem, Henry. Not mine.'

Beth insisted on picnicking away from the crowds of people who poured into Hyde Park to watch a French aviator's ascent in a huge balloon, which was the cause of much excitement among the Seagrove children and Estelle. The event had generated so much interest that it had disrupted the usual cavalcade of handsome equipages that congregated daily in the afternoon. It consisted of men mounted on fine thoroughbred horses, colourful and elaborately clad dandies and women in the best society, the carriage company some of the most celebrated beauties in London. The sun was pleasantly warm, and people were laughing and joking, all talking about the giant, hissing balloon that had taken off successfully.

Accompanying the carriage carrying Miss Lacy and his children on horseback, Lucas came upon the picnic scene by chance. It was one of complete enchantment, of a small group of people—three adults, one of them a nursemaid or governess, and three children, two boys and a girl. The adults were sitting on the grass in the shade of the giant beech trees, a white cloth spread on the ground on to which baskets of food had been unpacked. The children, in high spirits, were running about trying to catch one another, shrieking with laughter.

It was the woman, dressed in a delightful light-weight blue-sprigged dress with a wide sash of deeper blue tied in a bow at the back, on whom his attention was focused. He looked at the sunlight glinting on the flaming strands of her glorious wealth of auburn hair that tumbled on to her shoulders in a mass of curls, the sides drawn to the back of her head and secured with a blue satin ribbon. Her feet were tucked under her dress, her face upturned to the sky. She looked about sixteen, though her figure was mature. She was watching the balloon, which had just become airborne, soar up beyond the clouds, causing much excitement among the crowd.

Taking her eyes off the balloon, she turned her attention to the children, a serene smile on her face as her eyes settled on the little girl. Beth's two boys, boisterous and as audacious as a barrowload of monkeys, were a bit too much for Estelle, and she found it hard to keep up with them. But determined not to be left behind, she persevered. Suddenly Estelle stood stock still and her face broke into a bright smile at something she had seen further away, and then she was running in a fever of excitement to Eve.

'Sophie! Mama, it's Sophie and Abigail,' and before Eve could stop her she was scampering off across the grass as fast as her little legs could carry her to where a carriage had halted so the occupants could watch the balloon.

Eve scrambled to her feet and ran after her,

smiling delightedly on seeing Sarah Lacy and her young charges.

'Sarah, how lovely to see you again.' She looked at the children. 'Have you come to watch the balloon?'

'Yes,' Sophie said, her eyes shining with glee, clearly having enjoyed the spectacle. 'It was ever so exciting.'

'And it made a hissing noise like a dragon,' Abigail babbled happily, at three years old already having a good command of the English language.

'The children were so excited,' Sarah said, returning Eve's smile. 'They've never seen a balloon before.'

'Neither have I. It was quite a novel experience. Sarah, why don't you come and share our picnic? It would be lovely for Sophie and Abigail to play with Estelle—and there's ample food.'

'I don't think so, Mrs Brody. Thank you for your kind offer, but Miss Lacy and the children must be getting back.'

Eve whirled round at that familiar deep voice, and looked into the face of Lord Stainton. She knew by his expression that he was not as stunned as she was. For some inexplicable reason her heart set up a wild thumping. His face was still, but his eyes were a brilliant, quite dangerous pale blue. He lounged indolently against the back of the open carriage with the ease of a man discussing nothing more serious than the weather. The remembrance of their previous encounters, all of which had been angry and bitter experiences, touched her deeply.

He wore a plum-coloured cutaway coat and buff knee breeches tucked into highly polished black riding boots, and his neck linen was sparkling white. His gaze was sharp and penetrating and he radiated the same strong masculine appeal. Eve watched him warily, experiencing the depth to which her mind and body were oddly stirred whenever she was in his presence.

Pushing himself away from the carriage, he bowed his dark, shining head. 'I trust your headache is much improved today, Mrs Brody?'

'Yes, thank you for asking,' she replied stiffly.

'I didn't expect to meet you at such a gathering,' he remarked, his expression unreadable.

'I can't think why not. I enjoyed watching the ascending balloon enormously—almost as much as the children.' Distracted by Estelle, who was jumping up and down beside her, better to see Sophie and Abigail in the carriage, she said, 'Please let your daughters play with Estelle—just for a minute.' Lord Stainton's face became cool with the compelling arrogance she associated with him.

'I told you, we have to be getting back,' he uttered sternly.

Eve looked at his daughters. Their little shoulders were slumped in dejection and her heart went out to them. There was something rather timid about Sophie and Abigail, something cowed and contrary to the normal exuberance of children.

'Children need to run about and shout and laugh once in a while, Lord Stainton,' she said calmly, trying to speak to him without the abrasive tongue of an enemy. 'There's no harm in it.'

'Please, Papa,' Sophie whispered tentatively, 'can we play with Estelle for just a little while?'

Eve looked straight at him, waiting for him to reply to Sophie's quiet plea, hoping he was not inclined to inflict his bad temper on his children. She was relieved when she saw his expression soften.

'Very well, Sophie,' he conceded. 'Miss Lacy, please don't let them out of your sight.' Instructing the driver to wait with the carriage, he opened the carriage door and lifted his excited offspring down on to the grass, before striding back to his horse.

With Estelle and Sophie scampering on ahead, Eve took Abigail's hand and walked with her to the picnic. Lord Stainton watched them from atop his horse and he began to smile, for their laughter was infectious. His face was soft and his eyes were warm. He had a strong sense of responsibility and felt a deep affection for his daughters.

It worried him greatly that they were growing up

without the influence and love that could only come from a mother, but when his wife had walked out on him, she had also callously abandoned her children. Turning his horse away from the delightful picture of the picnicking group and feeling a knot of envy that he was not a part of that group, he trotted over to speak to an acquaintance.

Settling herself on the grass beside Sarah, Eve glanced at her with concern. Her expression was strained and apprehensive and Eve suspected things weren't well with her. 'You look pale, Sarah. Are you all right?' she enquired with quiet concern. 'It can't be easy for you working for a man as formidable as Lord Stainton.'

Sarah smiled, watching her young charges as they laughed and chattered over their jellies and buns, happy to see them fitting in well with Mrs Seagrove's two boys, Thomas and David. 'It must seem like that to you, but his bark can often be worse than his bite. I've given much thought to what I told you yesterday—about leaving my employment.'

Eve looked at her expectantly. 'And?' she prompted. 'What have you decided?'

'I'm going to marry Mark. It's what we both want—but it will break my heart to leave Sophie and Abigail.'

'Have you told Lord Stainton?'

She nodded. 'This morning. I will carry on

working for him until he leaves for the country—perhaps two or three weeks. I haven't told the children yet. I—don't know how to.'

Eve reached out and squeezed her hand comfortingly. 'I know just how difficult that will be for you, but I'm sure you'll find a way—and Lord Stainton will be sure to find someone who will care for his daughters.'

'Yes—I'm sure you're right.'

Their attention was drawn to the children who, having finished eating, with cries of delight scampered off across the grass, Sophie and Estelle hand in hand. Not intending to be left behind, Abigail shouted, 'Wait for me,' and ran awkwardly after them. Unfortunately, she was so intent on catching the two older girls that she didn't look where she was going, and the next instant she had run straight into a tree. There was a howl and Eve and Sarah turned simultaneously to see Abigail on the ground, her skirts tipped up in a froth of white lace petticoats and drawers, and a horrified Sophie running back to see what had befallen her sister.

Observing the incident from a distance, Lucas cursed beneath his breath and dismounted. As he strode towards what was quickly becoming a mêlée, an expression of immense concern clouded his face, anxious and not at all pleased.

Sophie, her eyes huge and brimming with tears,

stood looking down at Abigail, her hand still clutching that of Estelle. 'Abigail was running and bumped into the tree and banged her head,' she wailed, crying even louder when she saw the graze and the swelling bump on her sister's head, almost choking on her tears.

Eve immediately scooped the injured child up into her arms to comfort her while Sarah tried to console Sophie.

'I knew this would be a mistake,' Lord Stainton thundered, glowering accusingly at Eve. It was as if she had physically pushed the child into the tree.

For a full five minutes the picnic area was filled with the voices of crying children, the concerned voices of Beth and Sarah, and Lord Stainton's deeper, alarmed and irate voice.

Eve looked at him coldly. 'Will you please be quiet,' she said, trying to keep her voice as calm as possible. 'Shouting like that will only upset the children more than they already are and make the situation worse.'

Inconsolable, Abigail continued to sob loudly, her hand on the already swelling lump on her forehead. She was frightened and bewildered by the sharp anger of her father and she cried fiercely. Completely ignoring the glowering Lord Stainton, whose mouth had clamped shut at her firm reproach, Eve sat on a bench with her young burden and cradled her on her lap, hugging her tightly and murmuring soft, soothing words against her wet cheek.

'Does it hurt very much?' she asked the sobbing child. 'Did that nasty tree get in your way?'

She nodded. 'Yes,' she wailed, 'it did.'

'Here, let me see.' Eve wiped the hair from Abigail's wet face.

'I bumped my head,' Abigail said between sobs, 'and it hurts.'

'I know it does, sweetheart,' Eve murmured, hugging her once more, 'and when you get home I'm sure Miss Lacy will put something very special on it to make it better.'

'And will that hurt?'

'No, of course it won't. It will make the horrid bump go away in no time at all.'

Eve would have been surprised if she had looked up and seen Lord Stainton's face as he watched her cradling his daughter, her cheek resting on the child's dark curls. Looking on, he felt as though he was an intruder, a stranger, and that the two children belonged to someone else.

Mesmerised by the lovely picture the woman and child created, his expression had softened. He listened intently to her trying to sooth Abigail, which was something that came quite naturally to her. Gradually the child became quiet and ceased to cry, looking at the face of the woman with something akin to adoration and responding to the warmth in her voice.

Both the scene and the words of comfort Mrs Brody murmured bewitched him and reached out to some unknown part of him that he had not been aware he possessed. It touched and lightened a dark corner for a brief instant and then was it was gone.

Aware of Lord Stainton's presence, Eve looked at him. Abigail saw her father and was shy of him, hiding her face in Eve's neck. Standing up and carrying the child, Eve murmured, 'Come, Abigail. Let's go and find Miss Lacy, shall we? And perhaps you would like to take some of those pretty pink fairy cakes home with you that you liked so much. We shall see if we can find a fancy napkin to wrap them in. Would you like that?'

'Yes, please,' Abigail whispered, having enjoyed the warmth and the cuddle the kind lady had given her and beginning to feel better already.

As Sarah settled the children in the carriage, with Abigail clutching the fairy cakes to her chest as if they were the most precious things in the world, Eve walked back to Lord Stainton. He was about to mount his horse and paused to look down at her.

'I do not believe Abigail will suffer any adverse affects from her fall, Lord Stainton, but if you are worried unduly perhaps a doctor could take a look at her.' A slow smile curved her lips. 'In the rough and tumble of growing up, children trip up all the time.'

'I sincerely hope you are right, Mrs Brody, and Abigail suffers no ill effects. However, Sophie and Abigail are not in the habit of running about like young savages.'

'Then perhaps they should be. It's far healthier for them to be out of doors and running about. They can still be in a stable environment without being cooped up in the house all day.'

'My children have all the stability I can give them. They have had a secure upbringing and they are happy in the affection of a nursemaid.'

'Nursemaids are all very well for infants, Lord Stainton, but for growing girls—'

'They need their mother,' he interrupted in a soft, blood-chilling voice as he loomed over her, stopping her abruptly, his face taut with some emotion Eve did not recognise. 'I couldn't agree with you more, but they don't have a mother—at least not the kind of mother you are familiar with.'

'I'm sorry. If you had let me finish what I was about to say, I was going to suggest a governess.'

'If I wanted your advice, I would ask for it. My children are my responsibility and I will guide them as I see fit.'

'Then I would say that, with the attitude you've got, you will not make a very good job of it.'

'Don't you dare lecture me on how to raise my daughters, Mrs Brody. They are nothing to do with you, so I would be obliged if you would mind your own business.'

Eve stood back as he hoisted himself up into the saddle and without another word rode after the carriage. Her heart softened—she was not cruel, and she could well imagine how difficult it must be for him raising two young daughters alone. Sarah's resignation must have come as a terrible blow and she sincerely hoped he would find someone who would care for his children as much as she had.

As he followed the carriage carrying his daughters, Lucas stopped every now and then, his eyes glancing back at the young woman with the deep red hair walking back to her party. Finally he turned his head away as if she didn't exist.

The household was in bed and Eve was alone. She was tired after going with Beth and William and the children to visit their new house across the river, but she was restless and unable to sleep. Seated before the dressing table mirror, she was staring into space. She loved England and Beth's spacious elegant house in Berkeley Street was a balm to her spirits, but she felt so alone. Instead of distracting her from her grief over her father's death, being here in this alien country with a loving family was compounding the unreality and isolation she had felt since his funeral.

Her father had died suddenly just three months earlier. They had always been close and his parting had left her bereft. Lonely and lost without his support, with her daughter she retreated with her grief into her home, though it wasn't long before potential suitors, aware of the vast wealth she had inherited, began arriving at her door like a swarm of locusts.

After weeks of turning her back on each and every one of them, she had emerged from her twilight world and, when a letter arrived from her good friend Beth Seagrove inviting her to come and stay with her and her lovely family, she had set sail for England. She and Beth had been close friends since childhood. Both their families had lived in New York and Eve had been sad when Beth had married William Seagrove and had gone to live in London.

Eve envied Beth her easy relationship with this lovely, supportive man, and dearly wished things had turned out like this for her. Sadly it was not meant to be. Andrew Brody, her husband of six months, had been killed in sordid circumstances, leaving her alone and pregnant with Estelle.

With a sigh she pushed her melancholia aside and studied her reflection in the glass. Decisions had to be made about what she was going to do next. No matter how much she loved staying with Beth and William, she knew that she couldn't stay with them for ever. Besides, as yet she was unable to access her father's money; according to the solicitor she had employed here in London, his affairs could take some considerable time to sort out.

Eve was quietly concerned about this because her available funds were limited, but her lawyer had assured her that it was only a matter of time before a conclusion was reached. So for the time being, in order to be self-sufficient, she must find some kind of employment to tide her over.

One thing she was quite clear about was that she did not want to return to New York and had already decided to settle in England, but not London. The city was too big, too noisy. She had no remaining family in England, so Eve was free to settle where she chose.

Ever optimistic, the three bitter encounters with Lord Stainton two weeks ago was forgotten, but not the gentleman himself or his beautiful children, and not for the first time she wondered if he had found a replacement for Sarah Lacy. She had not heard otherwise and, if this was indeed the case, had thought of a scheme that could prove beneficial not only to her but to Lord Stainton, if he would but listen to her and consider it.

* * *

The following morning as she left her room to go down to breakfast, Eve tried to recapture the emotions she'd had last night, emotions that had made it completely appropriate and perfectly right for her to see Lord Stainton and try to persuade him to consider her as a nursemaid to his children. In the cold light of day, however, what she was planning to do seemed completely insane.

Beth was incredulous and appalled when Eve told her what she intended. Lifting a spoonful of steaming porridge to his lips, William glanced across at her. Diplomatic as always, he was prepared to listen to what their guest had planned in more detail before voicing an opinion.

'You are going to ask Lord Stainton to employ you?' Beth gasped. 'But, Eve, that's preposterous. You dislike him intensely.'

'In all honesty, I don't know what I think and it's absolutely insane I know, but I'm going to ask him just the same.'

'What? After he almost trampled you to death beneath his horse and berated you and unfairly accused you of being drunk?'

'It wasn't his fault. I suppose that's how it must have looked to him. He jumped to the wrong conclusion, that was all. He can be forgiven for that.'

'Eve, you are a very wealthy woman,' William

stated calmly. 'You have no reason to work for your living.'

'I have yet to receive my inheritance, William, as well you know, and I can't possibly go on living with you and Beth indefinitely. No, I have made up my mind to do this.' She raised her hand to silence Beth as she was about to protest. 'I have to seek temporary employment.' She smiled at the concern clouding Beth's eyes. 'You need not look so worried. Feeling as he does towards me, Lord Stainton might well show me the door.'

'Oh, dear. No good will come of this, I just know it. Have you not considered remarrying, Eve? Several gentlemen have shown considerable interest in you since your arrival in London—all eminently suitable and available.'

A darkness entered Eve's eyes and she shook her head emphatically. 'No, Beth. At this present time marriage is the last thing I want. Marriage to Andrew taught me many things—most of them unpleasant—and I am in no hurry to repeat the experience.'

Beth had always suspected that Eve's marriage had not been happy, but Eve had never spoken of it. 'But what you are doing—you, the most sensible woman I know—alarms me. Had it been anyone other than Lucas Stainton you were to approach for employment, I would not be so concerned.'

Eve laughed brightly. 'Don't be. I have made up

my mind. It is the best solution—and only temporary. It will be perfect for me and enable me to keep Estelle close at hand. I also find myself concerned for Lord Stainton's children—they are going to miss Sarah Lacy dreadfully. If their father is still in need of someone to take care of them, I hope to persuade him to consider me for the position.'

Beth frowned and carefully considered her words. 'Well, he is a very proud man and he doesn't have the inclination to make himself liked, which is something we both know. His character has many contradictions and, I suppose, if you are set on going ahead with this madcap scheme, then it's as well you know what you are letting yourself in for.'

Eve frowned. 'You speak in riddles. I don't follow you, Beth.'

'There is another side to the scandal his divorce created. You see, he is a popular figure, but there are drawing rooms where he is admitted, but not welcome—although no one would dare give him the cut direct. At the time of his separation from his wife, some people took her side, saying he was heartless and cruel to divorce the mother of his children.'

'But she left him to live with his brother. Surely he cannot be blamed for that.'

Beth lifted her brows. 'Can't he? You see, some of her friends said he drove her away, that she found it impossible to live with his black moods and that she was afraid of him. Some of the more vicious gossips even went so far as to intimate that he refused to let her see the children.'

'And was this true?'

'This piece of slander was repeated, but never credited,' William was quick to say. 'However, it has been noted that she is estranged from her children. Some regard Lucas Stainton as a cold, frightening, unapproachable individual—and you have accused him of being cold and aloof yourself, Eve. He is an exacting master who demands only the very best from those he employs—at least such was the case before he had to thin out his servants.'

Eve was thoughtful for a moment. 'He does become angry easily, but I believe there is good reason for this. He can't be happy with his situation and because of it he can be just as easily hurt as anyone else. But—did he really deny his wife access to the children?'

'I don't know the truth of it, Eve, but I do know that I shall worry about you if you go to live in his house,' Beth said, reaching out to take Eve's hand.

'You needn't, Beth. I am not afraid of him and I can take care of myself.' Eve gave Beth's quiet, fair-haired attractive husband an enquiring look. 'I believe he's in the process of selling his London house to move to Laurel Court.'

'Yes. I don't believe he has a buyer yet, although

it is a fine house and in a prime location, so I have no doubt he will soon have it off his hands.'

'And he is having to sell because of his brother's gambling debts?'

William nodded, reaching for a piece of toast. 'Sadly, Stephen Stainton exhibited a proclivity towards all manner of expensive vices. He gambled all the time—it had nothing to do with having fun, it was an addiction. He lost the astronomical sum of one hundred thousand pounds on one hand of piquet at White's and offered his estate in payment of the enormous debt. Fortunately his brother stepped in and paid it.'

'He could afford to?'

'My word, yes. At that time Lucas Stainton was a wealthy man. He's a brilliant head for business and was making enormous returns on every investment. Unfortunately it wasn't the first time he'd had to bail his brother out, but this almost ruined him.'

Eve felt a stirring of admiration for Lord Stainton. 'Clearing up his brother's mess while said brother was conducting an affair with his wife was definitely a kindness on his part, and I realise I shall have to reassess my opinion of him. He appears to be rather unapproachable and capable of giving the kind of crushing set-downs that make one cringe. Why, when he accused me of being intoxicated at Lady Ellesmere's party, so convincing was his attitude that I thought I might be until I remembered taking Beth's headache powders. It was most humiliating and embarrassing.'

'And I don't suppose you can see what women see in him either,' William teased gently.

'Yes, I can,' she responded laughingly. 'I'll do him the justice to admit he's terribly attractive. What is your opinion of him, William?'

'I like and respect him—I always have. But make no mistake. Whatever that man does, he does on his terms. There isn't a woman alive who wouldn't be impervious to him.'

'There you are, then,' Eve said, laughing lightly. 'You are one of the most sensible people I know, William, so I would believe you above all others.'

Beth smiled. 'Bless you for that, Eve, and I do agree with what you say about my husband. Lucas Stainton is one of the most attractive men on the social scene, a man who stands out among his fellow men. Wherever he goes women strive to please him, for despite his cynical attitude— although some more sensible members of the *ton* have remarked that he has good reason to be cynical where women are concerned—there is an aura of virility about him that does dangerous things to their hearts.'

'And how does Lord Stainton react to these

adoring females who simper around him? Is there not one among so many who is capable of thawing his cold heart?'

'Not to my knowledge. Oh, he is no more immune to a pretty face than the next man, but since his divorce he has conducted his affairs with absolute discretion. There are those who know him well, like my own William, who say he inspires esteem and respect because he represents a rare specimen of a nobleman *par excellence*. On the other hand, there are those who accuse him of being a brute and intolerant of others, and with his droll replies in conversation and stunned expressions, he makes people feel that they are utterly stupid.'

'Perhaps that's because they are,' Eve murmured with a half-smile. 'As you have just said, Beth, perhaps if they knew him well they would perceive that he is much nicer than he appears.'

Beth looked at her curiously. 'Eve, what is this? You aren't enamoured of him after just three encounters, surely?'

'No,' Eve replied, laughing at the very idea. 'Quite the opposite, in fact. My encounters with Lord Stainton were anything but friendly—in fact, I found the man quite insufferable—but I have seen some of the qualities you speak of and I'm willing to take a chance on him—as he might with me.'

Chapter Three

Mrs Brody had been shown into the drawing room. Lucas would have known it was her the moment he entered, even before his eyes lighted on her. It was the perfume she wore—that was the thing he remembered about her—a subtle smell, hardly noticeable at all, but nevertheless a part of her.

Dressed in open-necked shirt and light grey silk waistcoat, Lucas stood surveying her from beneath frowning dark eyebrows.

For a moment Eve stared at him blankly. He watched her in silence, fixing her with a gaze so hard that she quailed. What a strong presence this English lord had. It filled the room, momentarily distracting her from her reason for being there. His bearing was proud and he was a man of uncertain temperament. Eve wondered what dark secrets lay behind that handsome visage.

Normally she was unimpressed with exceptionally handsome men because they were either vain or after her money, but this man was neither. He was thoughtful, intelligent and thoroughly male, positively emanating masculine sensuality. All of these attributes, combined with the fact that he had two adorable motherless children, made Eve decide that he was in every respect the right man she wished to work for. His words brought her back to reality with a jolt.

'Mrs Brody! You seem to have a propensity for invading my home. What is it this time?' he asked with mock civility. 'A mislaid child or dog, or another dressing down?'

'None of those.' She could hear defiance in her own voice, which she tried to moderate. 'How is Abigail? None the worse for her encounter with the tree, I hope?' she asked in an attempt to ease the situation between them.

'Abigail is very well considering, Mrs Brody.'

'Then I'm relieved to hear it.'

'I suspect you are not here to ask about Abigail. This is a surprise.'

'And not a very pleasant one, I take it, Lord Stainton?'

'That remains to be seen, though I must admit I had not taken you for a lady who indulged in afternoon calls to gentlemen's homes. Does visiting friends not keep you busy? I imagined you to be fully occupied from morning till night on the frivolous pastimes with which you ladies fill your days.'

His tone was caustic and his gaze ironic and Eve longed to tell him to go to the devil, but with everything balanced on this interview, and not wishing to antagonise him until she'd told him the reason for her visit, with great self-control she managed to smile politely.

'As a matter of fact, I prefer to fill my time with more worthwhile pursuits, but I hardly think you would spend your time light-mindedly thinking of what I do with my time, Lord Stainton.'

'Oh, and why is that, Mrs Brody?'

'It is merely an impression you give. The picture I have of you in my mind is of a man who does not employ himself with useless thoughts of other people.'

'Really. I had no idea you had any picture of me in your mind at all, Mrs Brody. In fact, as we have only seen each other on four occasions, I fail to see how you have had time to form any opinion at all.'

'Oh, I can be charitable when I want to be, Lord Stainton—although I am certainly no saint. Far from it, in fact. My father was for ever telling me that I am not a lady, for I have this awkward habit of arguing when I should be listening and speaking my mind when I should be quiet. Our previous encounters have been unfortunate, and the one at

Lady Ellesmere's a misunderstanding. We—do seem to have got off on the wrong foot.'

'Don't we just.'

Not to be put off, she ploughed on. 'I…have given our unfortunate encounters—and your predicament—some thought, Lord Stainton.'

'Indeed!' With narrowed, shuttered eyes focused on her face, he moved closer, looming over her. 'My predicament! And you know all about that, do you?'

'I know that Miss Lacy is to leave your employment very soon and that you must be concerned for your children's future well being.'

The muscles of his face tightened and a hard gleam entered his eyes. 'Prying into my affairs is a tasteless invasion of my privacy, Mrs Brody. I am very grateful for your concern, but I can assure you I don't need it.'

Eve began to feel her spirits drop. 'I see. So you have already found a replacement.'

'No, as a matter of fact I have not—at least not yet.' Lucas was becoming extremely frustrated at the difficulty he was having trying to find a suitable nursemaid. There were plenty of available women well qualified in looking after children, but none of them seemed willing to take on the position of working for the formidable Lord Stainton. Only two had approached him. One had the hard features of a harridan he would never consider letting close to his children, and he was sure there had been the smell of drink about the other.

'Then perhaps I can be of help.'

'You? Mrs Brody, am I supposed to be impressed or flattered by your show of interest in me and my affairs? Dear me, what a persistent busybody you are.'

'I have a proposition to put to you, Lord Stainton,' she went on, ignoring his sarcastic diatribe and looking him straight in the eye, 'a proposition that may be of benefit to us both.'

Resting his hips against a rather splendid walnut desk, the only piece of furniture left in the room, he regarded her coldly. 'I am intrigued.'

Eve wasn't sure how to interpret his tone. She waited for him to ask her to go on, but instead he folded his arms and stared at her, looking oddly impatient. She'd gone over what she wanted to say to him so many times that she was afraid it was going to sound like a well-rehearsed speech, and now the moment had arrived it came out in one sentence.

'I would like to apply for the position as nursemaid to your children.'

'What?' His amazement was genuine and he looked at her incredulously. 'You?'

Eve felt a wave of desperation as she strove for control and to calm her mounting fears. 'As mad and impossible as it seems to you, yes, me.'

'Mrs Brody! Is this your idea of a joke?'

Eve stiffened and lifted her chin. 'A joke? I find nothing amusing, Lord Stainton. I have given the matter a great deal of thought and it's a solution I am sure would suit us both.'

Recovering from the shock her suggestion had caused, Lucas burst out laughing unpleasantly, his reaction telling her that her application was not only ridiculous, but laughingly so. 'You, of all people, want to look after *my* children?'

Eve flushed violently. This arrogant Englishman had a habit of crushing her with shame and anger, but she refused to retreat now she had come so far. 'There is nothing unusual in it, Sir. I like children—indeed, I have one of my own, as you know. I am eminently suitable to be a nursemaid and have the advantage of having met Sophie and Abigail. They are two beautiful girls and I get on with them well.'

'Yes, I saw that in the park,' Lucas was forced to concede, having dwelt on the charming picture that had remained in his mind of Mrs Brody comforting Abigail with soft words as she held her close. 'But—forgive me if I seem somewhat perplexed. You see, I have been led to believe that you are a wealthy woman, Mrs Brody, in which case I am bewildered as to why you should be seeking such lowly employment.'

'I do not consider looking after children to be a lowly occupation, Lord Stainton—quite the opposite, in fact. It is a worthwhile and rewarding profession. It is true that my father was a wealthy man—and as his only child that wealth will pass to me. Unfortunately, there are legal matters to be taken care of in America, and until such time as the money is made available to me, I find myself in— unfortunate circumstances. I also have a daughter to raise. It is a situation that makes it necessary for me to seek employment.'

He looked at her hard, and after a pause he snapped, 'Temporary employment by the sound of it. I am not interested in setting someone on who will see it only as a short-term post, Mrs Brody, someone who will up and leave when she no longer has the need to stay.'

Eve felt hesitant, slightly uncertain, as well she might, in the face of such cold regard. 'Yes—I suppose it would be temporary, but this might be the case with whomever you employ. I can assure you that I would not leave until you had found someone else. Of course, I realise you will need time to consider my proposition.'

He spoke through gritted teeth, his eyes hard. 'I have. It took precisely one second. The answer is no.'

Their eyes locked.

'I see. Won't you at least consider it?'

'There is no question of it.' Biting down visibly on his impatience, he brought himself to his full height. 'I have no place in my house for a woman of volatile temperament and who has no regard for her employer or his children that she would leave without a thought of how it might hurt their tender feelings. That said, the interview is concluded and I think it would be better for us both if you left.'

Eve clenched her hands tightly. When she had come here, her objective had seemed close within her reach, but now was as remote as ever. 'Really, Lord Stainton, my proposition cannot be as dreadful as all that. I would not intentionally do anything to hurt your children. I am offering to look after them, to give you the perfect answer to your dilemma, and you are reacting as though I have suggested I commit murder.'

'As I might, if you remain here a moment longer. So, before you insult me further, Mrs Brody, with any more of your outrageous proposals, I would be grateful if you would leave my house.' He saw the banked fires leaping dangerously into flames in her eyes, and he deliberately threw verbal oil at her. 'I am sure after your time in America you are ignorant of such things as etiquette, but the English place great importance on such matters. Take my advice and learn the rules before you go knocking on any more doors and offering your services. You may get more than you bargained for.'

His volatile anger was tangible, frightening and completely incomprehensible to Eve, who had never met anyone like him. Shocked into stricken paralysis, she stared at him as the insult hit home. Then her temper exploded and she silenced him with the only means available—she slapped him so hard his head jerked sideways, then she took an automatic step back from the ice-cold fury in his eyes.

'How dare you insult me when I came here with nothing but good intentions? I will not tolerate it. Contrary to what you might or might not think of me, sir, I am not a savage. Perhaps my fellow Americans are to you. If so, then that might explain how we managed to beat you in the war we fought for our independence.'

Lucas's jaw tightened and his eyes were glacial. 'Try anything like that again and I will personally throw you out on to the street while your hand is in the air,' he said, icily and evenly. 'I am a survivor, Mrs Brody, and I have an ugly temper when roused. Don't test me any further.'

His tone was implacable and left no room for argument. 'Very well. I'll go. I'm sorry to have inflicted myself on you.' Still fuming, taking a card from her reticule she held it out to him. When he made no move to take it, she slapped it down on the desk, refusing to give up on him or his children just yet. 'However, when you've had time to come to your senses, to calm down and think more rationally, you may see things differently. This is where I am staying—should you change your mind.'

With nothing more than a quick nod, with her head held high and a swish of her skirts she took her leave. As she left the house she understood that his decision was irrevocable.

'Well, what did he say?' Beth asked, having waited impatiently for Eve to get back from Upper Brook Street. 'Did he agree to your application, or did he think you were mad?'

'I'm sure he did think I was mad, Beth. He refused. Absolutely.' In frustration Eve strode past Beth into the drawing room. 'He accused me of being an ignorant American, saying that my proposition was quite outrageous—and a great deal more that I won't offend your sensibilities by repeating. The man's an overpowering, conceited beast.'

'And what did you say?'

'I slapped his face.'

Beth stared at her in shocked disbelief. 'You slapped Lord Stainton?'

'He deserved it.'

Beth watched Eve pace distractedly across the

room. 'And no doubt he was furious and asked you to leave.'

'Nothing so genteel, Beth. He didn't ask, he ordered me out.'

Perturbed, Beth sighed. Histrionics weren't in Eve's character and in all their lives she had never seen her friend so put out. After a time she ventured, 'So—that's it, then. You won't be working for Lord Stainton.'

'It doesn't look like it. I doubt he'd even consider taking on a woman who had the temerity to slap his face.'

For the next two days Lucas immersed himself in the usual duties and matters of business, firmly believing that it was the only way he could put Mrs Brody's visit from his mind, which had unsettled him more than he cared to admit. When Henry Channing arrived, he was grateful for the distraction as he tore his gaze from the letter that had just been delivered.

'Dear Lord! You call this a house, Lucas?' Henry remarked, glancing around the almost empty salon. 'This place looks like a mausoleum—all walls, pillars, statues and space.'

'What do you expect? I've sent most of the furniture and artefacts to be auctioned off.'

Never able to stand still for long, Henry helped

himself to a brandy and began to wander about the room. 'There were some rather fine pieces, as I recall. I may even buy some myself.'

'Feel free. There are plenty to choose from at Sotheby's. What brings you here today, Henry? A social call?'

'Of course. You know how I like your company, dear boy. Although,' he said, his face losing its jocular expression and becoming serious, 'I did hear some news at my club in St James's earlier that might be of interest to you—not good news, I hasten to add.' When Lucas gave him his full attention, he said, 'Those two shipping yards on the Thames have gone under, Lucas. I'm sorry.'

Genuine concern for his friend clouded Henry's eyes. They had known each other since their Cambridge days. Henry had always admired Lucas. He was so controlled, so disciplined and determined, forthright and dynamic, driven in everything he put his mind to. As a businessman he was resourceful. He invested his money wisely, buying stock in new inventions and anything he thought promising with confident expectation of future gains. They usually paid off, again and again.

Unfortunately his brother Stephen had not been so clever. Lucas had told him he could not be expected to subsidise him indefinitely, but, unable to curtail his brother's extravagance, he bailed him out every time, selling stock until his own affairs had reached the point of crisis. He went from a man of substance to being branded a bad risk, and when some of his own investments went under, losses he could normally have withstood, he accrued tremendous personal loss.

And now the news that two of the shipping yards he had invested in—practically the last thing he had to hold on to—had closed, was the final straw.

'Good grief, Lucas. You look as if I've just handed you a death sentence.'

'Perhaps you have.'

'What do you mean by that?' Henry realised that this was the worst possible time for Lucas. Suddenly alarm sprang into his eyes. 'I say, you're not—I mean, you won't—'

'What? Shoot myself?' A cynical smile curved Lucas's lips. 'Nothing so easy. I have my daughters to consider. Their mother may have deserted them, but I will not.' Looking down at the letter in his hand, he became thoughtful.

'What is it about that letter that seems to hold your interest, Lucas?'

'I'm not sure. It's just arrived from my brother's solicitor along with the deeds to some land in the north-east.'

'I didn't know you owned land in my neck of the woods.'

'I don't. Apparently it's a parcel of land Stephen won off a landowner up in Newcastle—who is now no longer with us.'

'I see. It sounds interesting. As you know, my own family have been making a profit from coal for decades in those parts. What will you do? Sell it? My father might be happy to make you an offer.'

Lucas shook his head. 'I won't sell it, not if there's coal to be got—at least not until I've made some enquiries. I'll contact a mining engineer to have it checked out.' His lips curved in an ironic smile. 'You never know, Henry, it might put me back on the road to recovery.'

'I sincerely hope so, Lucas. You always did find making money easy. I have no doubt at all that you will soon be over this present crisis and back on your feet. I wish you luck, and if you do go up there then my home is at your disposal. In the meantime, are you able to carry on?'

'Not for long—but at the moment my prime concern is finding a new nursemaid for Sophie and Abigail before I leave for Laurel Court.'

'Which is when?'

'As soon as possible. I haven't been to the old place since before Stephen died. Eventually I intend moving there permanently, but first I must go and inspect the place. Lord knows what condition it's in, although any repairs that need doing will have to wait until I'm solvent.'

'I would have thought you'd have no problem getting a nursemaid.'

'So did I, but it's proving to be more difficult than I thought it would be. I've seen several, but none that was suitable—although, perhaps there was one.'

'Then ask her to come again and see how she gets on with the children.'

'Oh, she gets on with them—and they adore her.'

'Then what's the problem? Who is she?'

'Mrs Brody.'

Henry almost choked on his brandy. Uttering a sound of disbelief, he stared at him. '*The* Mrs Brody?' he asked, astounded when Lucas nodded. 'You're jesting, Lucas. You have to be. Tell me the truth.'

'On the contrary, Henry, I am in earnest.' He went on to tell Henry about the American widow's visit.

'But—I thought the two of you were at daggers drawn?'

Lucas shook his head. 'We were, but her application could be of benefit to both of us.' He smiled wryly. 'You might say she could be the answer to all my prayers.'

'But she is an extremely wealthy woman in her

own right. Why the devil would a woman like her want to become a hired help?'

Lucas shrugged. 'She has her reasons.'

'And will you take her on?'

'I haven't decided. I confess that after giving her application a great deal of thought—and needing someone to replace Miss Lacy within the week— I am sorely tempted, if not desperate.'

Suddenly his gaze lighted on the card Mrs Brody had put down on his desk. Picking it up, he looked at it for a long hard moment. Her face came to mind. She was certainly attractive enough. Indeed, from the moment he had set eyes on her his baser instincts had been stirred. In fact, he couldn't understand why she could evoke a combustible combination of fury and the desire to know her better in him within minutes of meeting her. Slowly and methodically he began reviewing the American widow's serious proposition, making two lists in his mind—one for accepting her offer and one against. The former won.

By the time Lucas reached the Seagrove residence and was shown inside, frustration and suspense had twisted every muscle of his body into knots. His voice, demanding to see Mrs Brody, echoed through the house from the hallway, his presence like a strong wind blowing through the quiet rooms, bringing everything that was masculine and loud into the unruffled and well-ordered running of the house.

Eve came out of the drawing room to see who the visitor was, and in a flash her tranquillity was swept away. She could feel the very air move forcefully and snap with a restless intensity that Lucas Stainton seemed to discharge. Clad in an immaculately fitting dark-green coat that deepened his swarthy complexion and turned his eyes to the colour of light blue steel, he looked lethally handsome and incredibly alluring.

'Lord Stainton!'

'I would like a word with you, Mrs Brody.'

Lucas strode across the hall and walked straight past her into the drawing room, skirting the hovering servant as if she were not there. 'Leave us.'

His command was peremptory and the servant stepped back in shock. She glanced at Eve, seeking permission to leave, but Eve was not looking at her. Her eyes were fixed on her visitor. When the drawing-room door closed, shaking her head, the usually slow-moving servant slipped away at a faster pace.

'We have to talk,' Lucas said without preamble, striding into the centre of the room where he turned and looked at Eve. 'There are things we have to discuss.'

Eve raised her brows. His arrival indicated that her proposition had pricked his interest, providing her with the opportunity to chip away at his defences. Her spirits were lifted a little. 'We do?'

'Whatever I thought of your audacity to come to my house and offer yourself to look after my children, I should have had the courtesy to listen to you.'

'Yes, you should. It was most ungentlemanly of you to order me out of the house the way you did.'

A wry smile added to his hard features. 'According to your blistering tirade, I haven't done anything to give you the impression that I am a gentleman.'

Eve stared at him, her anger forgotten. 'No, you have not. Are you apologising?'

He looked puzzled for a moment, then he nodded. 'Of course.'

'Then I apologise for slapping you. It was most undignified of me and I should have known better.'

'Do you regret it?'

Eve lifted her brows, eyeing him with an impenitent smile. 'No. You deserved it.'

'You're right,' he admitted, 'but don't push your luck.'

A sudden smile dawned across his face and Eve's heart skipped a beat. Lord Stainton had a smile that could melt an iceberg—when he chose to use it.

'When you had left, I was afraid I might have been too harsh and it was unforgivable of me to ask you to leave so abruptly.'

For a moment Eve was too stunned to speak. 'And now? Are you willing to listen to me and consider seriously my application?' she managed to say in response.

'Yes, I am, but I am a cautious man and there are many aspects to consider.'

She shot a glance at him beneath her lashes, and because he seemed to be genuinely interested and approachable for the first time, she continued haltingly, 'Before…we go any further, I… would like you to know that I don't usually go around knocking on gentlemen's doors. Yours was the first and will definitely be the last.'

He grinned, his features relaxing. 'I'm relieved to hear it.'

Lucas folded his arms casually across his chest. She was standing with her back to the door, surveying him with a steady gaze. For a moment he was taken aback by the sheer magnetism of her presence. She was dressed in a riding habit of midnight blue velvet, her hair arranged in glossy twists and curls about her well-shaped head that made it look like a beacon of light, and in that room of gentle shades she was a vibrant reminder that life went on.

Hers was a dangerous kind of beauty, for she had the power to touch upon a man's vulnerability with a flash of her dark blue eyes. Holding his gaze with her challenging stare and quietly determined manner, she crossed towards him with a smooth fluid grace and he felt suddenly exposed. He was staring at her, he realised, but he couldn't help himself. He was unsure why he was so quick to anger when he was with her. Perhaps unlike so many other women—excluding Maxine—she refused to be intimidated or impressed by him. Maybe she even disliked him a little. The thought hurt.

Their eyes met, measuring each other up, thoughtfully, calculating, aware of the differences in their backgrounds, but aware, too, of a personal interaction.

'It seems I am in your debt, Mrs Brody, and I apologise for not having thanked you before now.'

'Thanked me? For what?'

'You took care of Miss Lacy when she was feeling unwell, the day you met in the park, and took the trouble to see her and the children home safely.'

Eve smiled. 'I merely did what any caring citizen would have done.'

'It was a kindness. Thank you. Now, about our last meeting—'

'You were angry and harsh,' she cut in. 'But now

you have had time to consider what I proposed, I hope you realise there was some sense in it.'

He nodded. 'What you propose does make sense— even though it would be a temporary arrangement. In that I thank you for being honest with me.'

'That is my way. I come from a proud family with background and tradition, and respectability.' She smiled slightly. 'I do not underestimate your intelligence and knew full well when I went to see you that you wouldn't agree to my proposition outright. Anything you wish to know about me you only have to ask Beth and William Seagrove.'

'I would like you to tell me why you think I should employ you, Mrs Brody, what desirable attributes you possess that makes you so certain you are capable of looking after my daughters.'

'Well, I am intelligent and sensible and I excel at whatever I put my mind to. I am well read and speak French and Latin and a little Greek—and I sew a fine seam.' She smiled, a smile that lit up her eyes. 'I am also good with children, which surely is what you are looking for in the person you employ. I would look forward to getting to know them. They are quite adorable.'

'They are?'

He seemed surprised by her remark, which Eve thought strange. 'Don't you think so?'

'Children are children, Mrs Brody.'

'Not when they are your own.'

He looked at her with narrowed eyes. 'You—know that I am divorced from their mother—that she walked out on both me and her children?'

'Yes, and for what it's worth I am sorry. It—must have been a very difficult time for you.' Her look was one of understanding. 'I am offering you a way out, Lord Stainton, and I promise that if you are willing to admit me into your household, when the time comes for me to leave it will be done in such a way as to cause Sophie and Abigail minimum distress.'

Lucas was studying her with interest. He had seen the smile flicker across her eyes and the expression had caught his full attention. For a moment they considered each other thoughtfully before Eve looked away. He was a very handsome man.

'When can you start?' Lucas asked suddenly.

'Start?'

'Your full-time employment.'

It was said diffidently, but the effect it had on Eve was quite dramatic. Her face, as she stared at her new employer, was young, full of disbelief and a shining hope, showing how much she had wanted this position. 'Why—I—I hadn't thought,' she uttered haltingly, 'but I suppose I could start right away. When is Sarah—Miss Lacy leaving?'

'Two days, so it does not give you much time. Come to the house tomorrow—we will discuss your wages and Miss Lacy will familiarise you with things you need to know. You will have full charge of Sophie and Abigail. I want to leave for my home in Oxfordshire four days hence, so there will be preparations to make. It will be a short visit—time enough for me to assess what needs to be done since I have not visited the estate for some time.'

'And the children?'

'Are to come with me. A jaunt in the country— the country air and all that—will do them good. You, of course, will accompany them.'

'And my daughter?' Eve asked tentatively, realising that she had failed to mention Estelle and that he might consider it inappropriate for the nursemaid's daughter to be in the company of his own. 'As much as I want to look after your children, Lord Stainton, I will not be parted from my daughter.'

'And I would not expect you to be. She can occupy the nursery with Sophie and Abigail. I remember they got on rather well.'

'Yes—yes, they did.'

'Good,' he said, striding to the door, where he turned and looked back at her. 'Good day, Mrs Brody. I shall expect to see you at my house in the morning at ten o'clock.'

Eve arrived at Lord Stainton's house the following morning with Estelle. They were expected and admitted by a footman, who immediately went to inform his lordship of their arrival.

The tap of decisive, familiar footsteps warned Eve of Lord Stainton's approach. Turning quickly, she watched him cross the hall towards her. He smiled, a smile that took her breath away, his pale blue eyes meeting hers.

'I hope I'm not late,' she said hurriedly, nervous now he was her employer.

'You are on time. I always make sure I am punctual for appointments, Mrs Brody, and I expect punctuality in others.' He shot a look at the footman. 'Fetch Mrs Coombs. She can show Mrs Brody what's what.'

'Mrs Coombs is your housekeeper?' Eve enquired, holding Estelle's hand tight.

He nodded. 'She is, although many years ago she was my nurse. At present I employ eight members of staff. Bennet is my butler of long standing, and Mrs Coombs is my housekeeper and cook, with Nelly the kitchen maid. There are two footmen—not forgetting Miss Lacy and my valet. There is also Herbert Shepherd, my carriage driver. He looks after the few horses I have left. When I decided to sell the house I had to let most of the servants go. There was no point in keeping them on. But here's Mrs Coombs,' he said, beckoning the elderly housekeeper who was looking at the new nursemaid with interest.

'Mrs Coombs, this is Mrs Brody, who is to replace Miss Lacy. Be so good as to show her up to the nursery. I'm sure she'd like to see the children and familiarise herself with everything before Miss Lacy leaves us.'

Mrs Brody's name was not unfamiliar to Mrs Coombs. She had heard all about the furore between this young woman and his lordship from Miss Lacy and it had caused much talk and laughter among the meagre staff. She had nothing but admiration for the young lady. There weren't many people who would dare stand up to Lord Stainton, and Mrs Brody had tested both his patience and his temper—which was volatile at the best of times—fearlessly giving as much as she got. Jolly good luck to her, she thought with a pleased little chuckle.

As she entered the nursery, Eve smiled at Sarah, who was looking at her curiously and with great interest. Eve noted again how tired she looked, her young faced strained with anxiety. 'How are you, Sarah? And how's that young man of yours?'

Sarah sighed. 'Glad that we are to be married at last. In truth, I haven't seen much of him—it's so difficult getting time off, you see. I have to arrange it so that Mrs Coombs or Nelly can look after the children, which isn't very often, them both being so busy with chores.'

'But you are to leave tomorrow and I have come to take over. I expect you are surprised to see me here.'

'I am that. Oh, Mrs Brody, I can't tell you how relieved I was when his lordship told me it was you. I feel so much better about going. Sophie and Abigail are so taken with you.'

Going over to a window seat that overlooked the garden, Eve sat down and patted the space beside her. 'You must tell me everything you think I should know, Sarah.'

'I will, although I must say there haven't been any changes in the children's lives since their mother walked out like she did.'

'That must have been a terrible time for the children—and Lord Stainton.'

'Oh, yes, it was. His wife behaved quite wickedly—leaving him for his own brother. She told everyone about her husband's abominable treatment of her as her excuse for walking out, but I never believed any of it. Lord Stainton has always treated me with kindness and I think he is a man of admirable restraint.' Realising she might have been too outspoken, she bit her lip. 'I'm sorry. It's not for me to criticise.'

'Tell me, Sarah, how is Lord Stainton with the children?'

'He—he doesn't take much interest in them, miss—which is a crime when you see how lovely they are. Oh, he comes to the nursery every day to see them and it's plain that he has great affection for them, but he doesn't give much time to his daughters. They adore him, but…'

Eve put her hand gently on Sarah's arm. 'He sees his visits as a duty rather than a pleasure. I think that is what you mean. It's all right, Sarah, I understand. All I can say is that hopefully there will be a change for the better in the future.'

'Oh, Mrs Brody, I do hope so, because him being like he is makes it so much harder for those poor motherless mites. I feel so guilty about leaving them.'

Eve rose, smiling down at Sarah's worried face, wishing she could tell her for certain that everything would be all right. 'Don't worry. I promise I shall take good care of them.'

It was a hectic time as preparations to leave London began in earnest. The children were excited to be going to the country and Eve was looking forward to seeing Laurel Court and to putting London behind her. She informed Beth of what was happening, and she also sent a letter to her solicitor, Mr Barstow, informing him where she could be contacted.

Everyone was relieved when the following day dawned fine and warm. Having completed the packing the night before, Eve had the children fed and dressed and ready for the long journey by nine o'clock prompt. The servants were assembled in the hall and were to follow on in one of the large travelling coaches stacked high with baggage.

Lucas appeared at the specified time. He was to travel on horseback for much of the journey. Eve had seen little of him since taking up her position.

She was glad when they left London behind and the beautiful English countryside slid past the windows. The journey passed relatively calmly. She kept the children occupied by reading them stories and playing games, but after a while the lolling of the coach sent Estelle and Sophie to sleep. The same could not be said for Abigail, who became fractious and tearful, complaining of being hot. No amount of cajoling could pacify her and her crying began to unsettle her sister.

In desperation, Eve called to the driver to stop the coach and climbed out.

'Come on, darling, out you get,' she said, lifting a red-faced Abigail down into the road. 'Good girl.'

'Is something wrong?' A concerned Lucas rode towards her.

Faced with her father's dark countenance peering down at her, Abigail burst into fresh tears. 'I don't want to go back in the coach,' she wailed. 'I—it's too hot and I feel horribly sick.'

'Just take some gulps of fresh air, Abigail, and then you must get back inside,' Eve told her.

'But I don't want to,' she cried, gulping on her tears.

Eve looked up at Lucas. 'It's most unlike her to be difficult. Perhaps you could take her in front of you for a little way.'

Abigail immediately caught on to the suggestion and her little face became alight with hope. Looking up at her father, she raised her arms. 'Papa—can I ride on your horse?'

Eve thought this to be the best solution, but one look at Lucas looking down at Abigail with the suave indifference with which he generally treated his children, and she thought he was about to refuse. However, she was pleasantly surprised when his expression softened and he reached down and hauled the delighted child up on to his horse and settled her in the saddle in front of him. The transformation in Abigail was immediate. A wide, happy smile stretched her pink lips and she giggled happily, her little legs dangling on either side of the horse.

Lucas cocked a dark brow at Eve. 'How I wish I could pacify all the women in my life as easily as I can my youngest daughter.'

Eve responded with a wry smile. 'Perhaps if you didn't go around with a face as black as a thundercloud and barking at everyone like a bear with a sore head all the time, you wouldn't find it such a problem,' she dared to say, amused when she turned away and heard him chuckle softly.

Climbing back inside the coach, she watched him canter on ahead with his precious bundle sandwiched between his arms. They trundled along country lanes, winding onwards at a steady pace, passing charming, sleepy villages and fields where uninterested cattle and sheep grazed.

It was late afternoon and the clouds were gilded with sunshine as they approached their destination after stopping several times to take refreshment and stretch their legs,

Huge wrought-iron gates bearing a family insignia stood half-open and Eve's eyes lighted on a beautiful house at the end of a long curving drive lined with giant elms. She leaned forward to see it better. A park spread out in front of the property and a stream at the base of a gently falling hill was flanked by weeping willows. Lilacs and other flowering shrubs bloomed unhampered and untamed beside giant trees, their soft colours blending together in natural splendour. Beyond was a panoramic view of fields and forests and the gently rolling Chiltern Hills. The whole place had an air of sorry neglect, but this did not detract from its beauty—in fact, in a strange way it enhanced it.

It really was quite the most beautiful place Eve had ever seen. A brief shiver passed along her spine and she experienced a surge of joy when the coach passed through the wide gates and swept along the gently arched driveway to the house. The coaches stopped at the front, the tired horses wearily hanging their heads.

Eve stepped down and stood looking at the house. The breath caught in her throat with a gasp as she stared up at the magnificent edifice with its diamond-paned leaded windows glinting in the sunlight and the soaring roof.

'It really is quite beautiful,' she breathed, oblivious to the way Lucas had paused to look at her and the children's cries of delight on escaping the confines of the chaise.

In that first encounter with Laurel Court, Eve was irrevocably touched by the timeless splendour of the house. She felt helpless in the grip of something she could not name, or escape. As if spellbound, she turned and looked at the lush green acres spread out before her, impressive and heartbreakingly beautiful in its neglect. There was a fresh breeze in her face, warm and soaked with the fragrance of the countryside. She smiled with a feeling of content. It was like nothing she had experienced before and she felt herself ensnared by this lovely old house that seemed to be closing itself around her and claiming her for its own.

She was unaware that Lord Stainton had come to stand beside her until he spoke, his voice soft and warm to her ears.

'The house never changes,' he murmured. 'It smiles, it beckons, it invites and welcomes. I have loved it since I was a child. There is nowhere quite like it.'

'I know what you mean,' Eve answered without turning to look at him. 'I am a stranger here, yet I feel it too. Who could resist it?'

'Who indeed!'

At that moment she had no doubt at all that Laurel Court was part of her destiny, that she belonged here, that she could be happy here. Coming back to awareness, she shook herself, telling herself that these were fanciful thoughts and such things were not possible, that things did not happen like that, but then when a woman was as wealthy as she was, perhaps it was possible to make such things happen.

Chapter Four

From inside the house sounds of bolts being drawn could be heard and then the door swung open and Mr Evans, the caretaker, emerged.

Lucas took him aside and had a word with him and then turned to Eve.

'You will be relieved to know the house has been kept in a state of readiness. Take the children up to the day nursery to settle in.' He glanced at the second coach, which was already being divested of baggage. 'I'm sure Mrs Coombs will know what to do. If there is anything you need, ask Evans.'

Everyone piled into the house. Some of the servants had worked at Laurel Court when the previous Lord Stainton had lived there, and were glad to be back in familiar surroundings.

Eve looked about her in awe. Doing a quick sweep of the cavernous hall, which was filled with warmth and sunlight, she glanced through open doors, seeing the luxury of the rooms beyond. Taking a deep breath, she absorbed the atmosphere of the great house. It seemed alive but dormant, quietly waiting for the return of a family to fill its rooms with the voices and laughter of children, to make it a home again.

The nursery, which had housed generations of Staintons with its connecting bedrooms, was a lovely room; large, light and warm since it faced south. The children immediately began to explore. They were thrilled with the toys they dragged out of boxes and Abigail claimed the rather splendid rocking horse for her own.

Everything was chaotic as fires were lit and baggage unpacked and Mrs Coombs became more and more frustrated as she set about familiarising herself with the layout of the kitchen. Eve was to occupy a room that adjoined the nursery. It was of reasonable size, simply and elegantly furnished, the walls hung with cream silk, patterned with peach and pale green coloured flowers. Eventually things quietened down and the children were fed and all in their beds but too excited to sleep. Eve doubted they would drop off in a hurry.

'Will you tell us a story, Mama?' a bright-eyed Estelle asked, pushing back the covers and kneeling on the bed.

Sophie sat up in her bed and Abigail, not to be left out, copied the other two.

'Get back into bed, Estelle,' Eve ordered gently. 'I think you've had enough excitement for one day.'

'Oh, please, please,' Sophie pleaded. 'Estelle says you tell her a story about a princess who rides on an elephant covered in jewels—and another one about a dragon. Please tell it to us.'

Eve looked at the three expectant faces and relented. 'Very well, but you must promise to go to sleep when I have finished.'

Sitting beside Estelle, she patted the bed and immediately Sophie and Abigail scrambled out of their own and climbed into Estelle's. Eve put her feet up and, resting her back against the bed head, she gathered the children around her. The story had the children enthralled.

This was how Lucas found them when he pushed open the door. The unfamiliar scene in the dimly lit, warm room made him stop short and catch his breath. He had never seen anything more delightful or touching than Mrs Brody's closeness to his daughters, who clearly thought Eve was the best thing to come into their young lives. She had kicked off her shoes and her hair was unbound and rested on her shoulders. Abigail had fallen asleep, but Sophie and Estelle were cuddled up close and listening avidly, their faces flushed and rapt with wonder.

All three were in the circle of Eve's arms as she finished telling them a story about dragons and castles and a knight on a snow white charger rescuing a beautiful damsel. It was a beautiful tableau, one of homeliness and content and something deep and profound stirred within Lucas.

At the end of the story Sophie spoke importantly. 'I like the story about the princess best. I want to be a princess when I grow up and Papa will find me a prince to marry—a handsome prince who is very, very rich with lots of jewels.'

'And an elephant?' Eve asked, her expression as grave as Sophie's pronouncement.

Sophie thought about it for a moment, then said, 'No. He doesn't have to have an elephant. I think it would look silly in London and I don't really want to live in India.'

'Then I think a fine horse would do just as well, don't you—like the snow white charger in the last story?'

She nodded. 'But I still want to be a princess.'

Eve would have laughed, except that she could see that Sophie was deadly serious. 'You can be anything you want to be, Sophie,' she said, lightly kissing her brow, 'and I am sure when the time comes for you to marry, your father will find you the perfect prince.'

Sensing Lord Stainton's presence, she looked up.

With his shoulder propped against the door, he was a towering, masculine presence in the children's bedroom. He had shed his neckcloth, but otherwise was dressed in the same clothes he had worn for the journey. He was watching her intently. 'Lord Stainton?' Her voice was quiet.

'I came to say goodnight to the children and to make sure you have settled in.'

'Yes, thank you.'

Sophie and Estelle immediately went to their beds. Gently disentangling a sleeping Abigail's arms from her waist, Eve tried to sit up.

'Here, allow me to put her to bed.' Lucas quickly crossed the room and tenderly lifted the child into his arms.

'Of course. She is your little girl, after all.'

Momentarily their eyes met and then he looked away and carried Abigail to the vacant bed. Pulling the covers over her, he gazed down at the fragile features of his daughter, and for the first time in months he placed a kiss on her soft cheek, inhaling the sweet innocence of her. Sophie, not to be outdone, held out her arms. He went to her and, after tucking her in, kissed her nose.

Sophie gazed up at him adoringly. 'Will you really find me a prince to marry when I grow up,' she whispered, 'just like the one in the story?'

His face had a satisfied look about it and he smiled

into the upturned face of his child. 'If I can find one who is handsome and rich and will love you with his whole heart, then I promise, sweetheart.'

Sophie sighed and, closing her eyes, snuggled beneath the covers, clutching her favourite, a rather battered stuffed cat. 'Thank you,' she murmured sleepily. 'You are the best papa in the whole world.'

Lucas smiled. He loved his children and felt a profound need to protect them both. He was about to turn away when Sophie whispered, 'Don't forget to kiss Estelle goodnight too, will you, Papa?' Without looking at Estelle's mother, Lucas went to her. The little girl was looking up at him shyly, much in awe of the dark, forbidding man. Ruffling her hair, he smiled and gently kissed her brow. 'Goodnight, Estelle. Sleep tight.'

Eve watched him, her throat tight with emotion. She could see that his daughters' need of him as the father they had never really had, the man in their lives to protect them against bad things, was a role he would relish. There were times when she thought he didn't even know his children existed, but now, struck by the various emotions playing over his features, the love reflected in his eyes could not be concealed.

'They are quite exhausted, poor lambs,' she whispered when he came to stand beside her, 'as I am.'

'Then you must go to bed.'

'Yes, but first I must speak to Mrs Coombs about the children's breakfast.'

She accompanied him out on to the landing where, seemingly reluctant to leave her, he fell into step beside her.

'I can see why you love this house,' she said by way of conversation, already feeling very much at home herself.

'I always have. Laurel Court means a great deal to me and it feels good to be back. I have been absent too long.'

Looking at his handsome face, curiosity stirred inside Eve. She didn't want to pry into information Lord Stainton didn't want to offer, but she would like to get him to open up and tell her something about himself.

On the assumption that if she offered personal information about herself, he might be inclined to follow suit, she said, 'Have you ever been to New York?'

'No—never. Have you always lived there?'

'Yes, until my father died. He wasn't ill, he—he just collapsed and died. The doctor said it was his heart. It came as a terrible shock and I felt his loss deeply. Nothing was the same any more. Suddenly the house seemed too quiet and too big—too empty. That was when I decided to come to England.'

'You have no other family?'

'I was an only child. My mother died when I was ten.'

'And you were close to your father?'

'There was no one like him. He was always there for me. He took care of me—and Estelle. When he wasn't working we went everywhere together, and when he wasn't there any more I became uncertain about a lot of things.'

Lucas looked at her with interest. 'I am surprised to hear that. You always come across as being a level-headed, confident young woman who knows her own mind.'

'I do have a soft side, but I am no weak-willed female to be shunted around by fate and circumstance.'

'That is something I found out about you the moment we met,' he said softly, amused by the memory of how he had almost run her down in the park and how angry she had been. 'Tell me about your father. How did he come by his wealth?'

'He was a speculator and financier. He invested money in ideas of other people who had a talent for running businesses.'

'And how did he decide which people he should invest in?'

She shrugged. 'Instinct, I suppose. Whatever it was, he was successful.'

'And your husband? I recall you saying he was killed.'

She wanted to be evasive, but that wasn't possible with his rapier ice-blue gaze pinning her. 'Yes—in New Orleans. We had been married just six months. Later I found I was with child,' she confided, forgetful that she had intended to draw Lucas out and not the reverse.

'I'm sorry. It must have been a difficult time for you, to find yourself a widow at such a young age,' Lucas said, so gently that Eve could hardly believe it was he speaking.

Strangely comforted by the deep resonance in his voice, she studied his hard, sculpted features. With her normal reserve greatly diminished by her memories of Andrew, tipping her head to one side she said softly, 'I was just eighteen when he was killed. You must have lost someone you were close to.'

Before her disappointed gaze, his expression became aloof and she deeply regretted asking the question.

'I was too young to remember my mother. My father was as unapproachable as I am, and my brother didn't give a damn.' He turned to face her and inclined his head slightly. 'I hope you have a comfortable night, Mrs Brody. I'll see you in the morning. Goodnight.'

* * *

Over the days that followed their arrival, Eve fell in love with Laurel Court. She saw little of Lord Stainton during those early days. He came to the nursery each afternoon and night, but mostly he was busy riding about the estate seeing what needed to be done after so many years of neglect. As he went about his affairs he smiled little. Clearly his worries were many.

She often drove into the village with the children and sometimes Lord Stainton accompanied them on horseback. She observed how relaxed he had become and that he cut an exceptional figure. He knew most of the local people, calling them by name, and he was the very soul of kindness and consideration. Comments passed reinforced her opinion that Lord Stainton was well liked by all.

It would surprise Eve if she knew how often Lucas's thoughts turned to her. He found as he went about his work on the estate that he antici-pated seeing her when he returned to the house. Then it crossed his mind that he was looking for her, looking forward to seeing her. He found himself wondering about her husband, what sort of man would appeal to her.

Good Lord! What was he thinking of?

In spite of his initial reservations about employ-ing her to look after his children, he found himself increasingly drawn to her as the days passed and he got to know her a little better. There were a number of reasons for this. One was that she displayed no hint of disapproval in respect of his own divorced state. In Eve Brody he thought he recognised a kindred spirit, albeit one whose non-conformity had taken a different direction from his. He was also relieved by the fact that she genuinely cared for his children, and in that alone he was thankful.

One day brought an unexpected and unwelcome visitor to Laurel Court. When Lucas walked into the drawing room, the woman who had been his wife and was the mother of his children turned to look at him, the arrogance in her demeanour by no means diminished by the eighteen months they had been apart. Lucas stopped dead, looking at her with the cold, speculating expression of a long-standing opponent.

Beautiful, seductive—Maxine was both these things, but as Lucas eyed her coldly, he wondered not for the first time why he had ever felt attracted to this woman with her pale hair and eyes and her vicious temper. He could still feel the anger and every second of his helpless fury when she had turned her back on him and their children and gone to live with his brother at Laurel Court.

Her voice sounded exactly as he remembered

it—forceful and cool. Her gaze slid warily over his tall frame and in her well-remembered deep, throaty voice, with a tight smile on her lips, she said, 'It's been a long time, Lucas.'

'Not long enough,' he snapped. He tore the freezing blast of his gaze from her face and passed a contemptuous glance over her, his face tightening with distaste as he looked at the glittering necklace spread across her swelling breasts above the daring bodice of her ruby-red gown. 'Say what it is you came to say and then get the hell out of my life and stay out.'

Maxine was doing her best to remain steady in the face of what she knew would be a battle. She could see it on Lucas's face and in his eyes, which were as hard as iron. Resentment of her former husband wasn't an unusual emotion for her these days. After putting her through the bitter humiliation of a divorce, she hated him. Slowly she moved towards him, a sneer on her lips. 'Still the same old Lucas, I see—like some black bear waiting to pounce on a poor defenceless creature.'

'Defenceless? You? What do you want, Maxine? If you are here to gloat, then you can get out.'

She didn't flinch. 'Gloat? Nothing could be further from my mind. Since you failed to answer my letters, I realised the only thing left to me was to confront you. I intended going to see you in

London, but when I learned you had come here I thought I'd come and take a look at the house in which, it might surprise you to know, I was happy for just a short time. I find myself somewhat financially embarrassed. I've come to ask you for some money, Lucas.'

He smiled thinly. 'Now why doesn't that surprise me,' he sneered. 'You always were greedy, Maxine, the greediest woman I have ever met. For one mad moment I thought you might have come to see our children—although you have probably forgotten you have two daughters.'

'Children,' she scoffed wrathfully. 'Are they still all you care about?' Anger flared in her eyes. 'I have not come here to discuss the children, Lucas, and I will not pretend anything different. I'm sure they are in good health and being well taken care of.'

'The children were never real to you, were they, Maxine? Just burdens you were forced to carry around for nine months, fetters that kept you chained to the house, stopping you doing what you enjoyed doing most—pleasure seeking. May God help them when they are older and discover why their mother walked out on them, that she is a woman without character or decency who thought money and flaunting herself in society was all that counted. Stephen was stupid and short-sighted and you reeled him in just like all the others before him. If he'd had any sense, he'd have kicked you out.'

For a moment Lucas thought he saw hurt or some other emotion flicker across Maxine's enigmatic face, but it vanished almost as soon as it had appeared. 'The grass was greener—initially. Stephen was fun to be with. His death was—unfortunate.'

'Wasn't it?' he bit back. 'Leaving me with one unholy mess to clear up.'

'For what it's worth, Lucas, I am sorry. I never meant things to turn out like they have.'

'Sorry? I do not settle for apologies for what is unforgivable, Maxine. Try saying you are sorry to our daughters—if you can. I allow you into my house because you are their mother and for no other reason. Isn't it time you moved on with your present lover—Sir Alfred Hutton, I believe—who is not only old enough to be your father, but also penniless, I hear? Perhaps you should go home to your parents. Would they want you back there? Are you not still their precious daughter?'

Her eyes narrowed. 'You know I was never that. My sisters, yes, but not me. Father will not allow me back.'

Lucas raised an eyebrow. 'And can you blame him? The damage your scandalous behaviour brought to the respected Irvine name almost drove him to his grave. You were an adulteress, and when I caught and sought to dispose of you, you decided to hound me to extort money out of me at every turn.'

'Oh, for God's sake, don't drag all that up again. I am the mother of your children. Your treatment of me was harsh, to say the least.'

'You lied, deceived and cheated on me—with my own brother. What did you expect? Forgiveness?'

Maxine scowled at him. 'No, never that, but no one treats me like you did and gets away with it. Forcing me to go through a humiliating divorce, having my friends laugh at me—it is beyond tolerable!'

'You pushed my tolerance beyond all bearing with your faithlessness and your duplicity. You'll get nothing more from me, Maxine.'

Maxine stood white faced, watching him as he turned on his heel and walked away from her. Refusing to be thwarted, she hurried after him into his study.

'You will pay for what you did to me,' she said in desperation to his retreating back. 'Do not think that a divorce will release you from your debt to me.'

He spun round. 'Debt?'

'Oh, yes. You would not have your precious children were it not for me. I mean it, Lucas. You have to give me some money. I am in daily danger of being arrested for debts. It is this dire state of poverty which brings me here. I need it.'

Lucas gave a short hard laugh. 'You are not alone, Maxine. Had you come to see me in London, you would have seen an empty house—and all thanks to that worthless brother of mine, who drank heavily, gambled even more heavily so there was no money left, and seduced my slut of a wife. Why do you think I should give you anything, had I anything left to give, after that?'

Maxine moved ever nearer and thrust her face close to his, her eyes glittering and mean, her words vicious. 'I'll tell you why, Lucas,' she hissed, her voice shaking with suppressed rage. 'So that your brother's bastard won't be raised in poverty. That is why.'

Rendered silent, Lucas looked at her with blind incredulity. 'A child? Stephen fathered a child—with you? For the love of God tell me you are lying,' he demanded, grinding the words between clenched teeth.

'No, I am not lying. The child—a girl—is thriving. I have placed her with a woman who will look after her. Give me some money and I'll leave you alone. You'll never hear from me again.'

'And the child?'

She shrugged. 'I told you. It's being looked after by a good woman. I don't wish the child any harm. I just wish it had never been born. I thought you might like to keep it in the family.' She smirked.

'Your nursery is big enough. One more won't make any difference.'

'You callous, heartless bitch,' he ground out, his eyes alive with some dreadful emotion he was unable to conceal—Maxine felt the need to recoil from the expression she saw in them. 'I am disgusted by your behaviour. You have come here to try to extort money from me and compel me to raise your bastard child as a Stainton. Good God, Maxine, it beggars belief.'

'It is Stephen's child. I swear it.'

'Do you seriously believe that after what you have done I will give you anything? You could have come back to see the children at any time, but you chose not to. And now you come tricked up like a whore hoping to fleece me of money. Well, Maxine, you can go to hell—to the hell in which I have been confined these past two years.'

Maxine backed away from him. 'I can see there's no talking to you when you're in this mood, Lucas.'

'You're damned right there isn't,' he said, his face hard with contempt. 'Now get out, Maxine. And don't come back.'

Her expression was vicious. 'Oh, I shall leave now, but I will come back, Lucas. You see, I know you, Lucas, and you will not rest easy knowing there is a child out there that has Stainton blood in its veins. If you want to know where the child is to be located, then you will find me at Sir Alfred Hutton's house in London. But remember, Lucas, it will cost you. As far as I am concerned, divorce alters nothing between us. I didn't ask for it and I didn't want it. I'm the mother of your children and for that reason I demand recompense.'

Lucas's eyes narrowed dangerously. 'I will not be blackmailed, Maxine. If there is a child, then I shall find it—with or without your help. Now get out.'

When the door had closed behind her, Lucas raked his fingers through his hair. Dear Lord! What a mess. Just when he thought matters couldn't get much worse. And now there was the added burden of another child that Maxine had abandoned as callously as the first two. If the child was Stephen's, then he could not in all decency turn his back on it. But with two children to raise already, his situation was even more dire than it had been before Maxine had arrived at the house. He couldn't raise them on fresh air.

After putting the children to bed, Eve rested in the gathering darkness, listening to the night sounds beyond the open window. Too restless to sleep, fully clothed, she lay on her bed willing her body to relax as she waited for Lord Stainton to return.

She knew his former wife had visited Laurel Court earlier—indeed, the whole house did and could talk of nothing else. When Eve had been mounting the stairs she had heard voices raised in anger coming from the drawing room, and when Maxine had left the house some perverse instinct had drawn her to the window of the nursery, where Sophie and Abigail were happily engrossed in playing with their dolls, blissfully unaware of their mother's visit.

As Eve had watched her carriage disappear along the drive at speed, she felt that in the brief time she had been there, the ugly reality of Lord Stainton's marriage to Maxine had invaded the cosy atmosphere of Laurel Court. A short time later a horse and rider galloped across the park as if he had the devil riding on his tail.

As yet he had not returned and Eve could not rest until he did. It was some time after dark when she heard the weary clop of a horse's hooves on the gravel below. Relieved that Lord Stainton had returned home safely she drifted into a light sleep, to be woken when she heard a loud crash, the sound coming from somewhere downstairs.

Driven by a compulsion to know that her employer was all right and blind to everything but her intention, she left her room and moved silently along the landing and down the stairs. On the bottom step she paused and listened. No one else had been disturbed by the noise. A light shone from beneath the drawing door that was slightly ajar. Trembling with her own apprehension, she moved towards it and, pushing the door open, took a few cautions steps inside.

In the dim light of the room she saw Lord Stainton. He had his back to her. The light fell on his strong, strikingly beautiful hands braced against the mantelpiece. He had discarded his coat, waistcoat and neckcloth and above his biscuit-coloured breeches and top boots, his fine white linen shirt was stretched taut across his powerful shoulders. His head was bowed, his hair tousled, a heavy lock falling over his brow.

Eve might have stood there for a long time without moving if some animal instinct of Lord Stainton's had not made him sense someone's presence.

'Leave,' he snapped harshly.

Eve paused and summoning all her courage, said, 'Lord Stainton?'

At the sound of her voice he turned his head slightly and she saw the stern pride stamped on that lean profile, his jaw as rigid as granite. In agonised silence he looked at her for several seconds, his face preoccupied and stony—he looked like a man in the grip of a nightmare.

'I'm sorry,' she murmured softly, turning away from him. 'I—heard a crash and thought we might have an intruder… I'll leave you. I did not mean to disturb you.'

His head came up and he peered at her. Clothed in a dove grey gown, her hair bound with a ribbon in a single heavy fall down her back, she was like a pale ghost haunting the night.

'Wait,' he said, striding towards her as she turned away. 'Please—don't go. I apologise if I sounded harsh. It's been a long day.'

'And a long ride. I saw you leave,' she explained when he lifted a questioning brow. 'You were a long time coming back.'

His lips twisted in a tight smile. 'Don't tell me you were worried about me, Mrs Brody.'

'I—yes, I suppose I was,' she murmured, an embarrassed flush springing to her cheeks at what Lucas thought to be a touching confession. 'She—your wife must have upset you.'

'Maxine is no longer my wife,' he retorted curtly.

'Yes, I know. I'm sorry if you would rather not talk about this for some reason,' she said, sensitive to his changing mood. 'There's no need to do it.' It was not her place to pry into the personal affairs of this tall, powerful man looming in front of her.

'If I don't talk about it, it's because I find it very unpleasant,' he retorted, rubbing the muscles at the back of his neck. 'Much as I would like to forget that Maxine came here today, unfortunately she has presented me with a situation that has to be dealt with right away, and I have no choice but for us to return to London sooner than I intended.'

Disappointment overwhelmed Eve. She loved being at Laurel Court and had no desire to leave for London just yet, if at all. 'But—is it necessary for the children to leave? We would be perfectly all right here.'

'It is a delicate matter—and I may require the assistance of a woman. In short, you, Mrs Brody. It is a situation that is entirely too vexing and I should not trouble you with it, but suddenly things have become—complicated.'

'Oh?'

'Another child—a two-month-old baby to be precise.'

Eve looked at him closely, noting the worried frown that creased his brow. 'You seem overly concerned about the child. Is it kin to you?'

'It's a girl, and, yes. I believe she is my niece,' he replied tightly. 'If what Maxine told me turns out to be true, the child is Stephen's—my brother's child. She is also a half-sister to my daughters and Maxine has abandoned it in the same callous manner as she did Sophie and Abigail.'

'I see.' Suddenly Eve glimpsed in his eyes the pain of a man deeply wounded by what he saw as his brother's betrayal of his trust. She tried to conceal the shock she felt, unable to understand how a woman could abandon her child, but without success. 'I am not unaware of what went wrong between you and your wife, Lord Stainton. However, it is not my concern. My concern is for the children, and to my mind a two-month-old baby should still be with its mother.'

Lucas's lips curled scornfully. 'Normally that would be the case, but nothing Maxine ever did was normal.'

'No, I'm beginning to realise that. Does she not realise that what she is doing is sheer wickedness?' Eve burst out, unable to conceal her anger at the woman.

'Maxine is aware of that. She simply does not care. I can't fathom what goes on inside that head of hers, what makes her like she is. She was never satisfied. Perhaps it was the frustration of being married to me,' he murmured with a resigned shrug, 'or maybe it's some unknown flaw inherited from her family that has made her like she is. It is a question I have asked myself many times.'

All of a sudden he looked vulnerable—vulnerable and hurt. He was a decent man, Eve knew that now. It was always the decent ones who agonised this way, always the decent ones that suffered.

'It wasn't your fault. Your wife caused a great deal of trouble that beset you and your children. It must have been difficult for you. I can see that. I can also see why you don't have a very high opinion of women.'

'That's not quite true and I apologise if I have given you that impression. It's only Maxine I have an aversion to. God knows where she has placed the child—probably on some lice-infested slag heap in Covent Garden or the like. Heaven knows what diseases it might be exposed to. I cannot leave it there. I have to find the child before it's too late.'

Eve frowned up at him. 'Too late? But—you don't think anything awful could happen to her? She's only a baby.'

'It makes no difference. There are some cruel people out there, Mrs Brody, people who would think nothing to using children for their own disgusting ends.'

She looked at his proud, lean face and she felt as if her heart would break. The more she saw of him and got to know about him, the more she understood why he was like he was, that the bitter experience of being married to a woman who had callously left him and their children had yielded up this bitter, unpredictable man, with his hard opinion of people and the world at large. His life with his wife and his brother's betrayal had not been a happy one, yet he had got on with it because he had tremendous strength of mind and will. He felt things deeply, but he rarely showed it.

'Then I can understand the need for haste. I would be happy to be of help—if that is what you want.'

Lucas looked down at her. Her face was rosy and lovely and her eyes glowed into his. He was known for a hard man, a stubborn, iron-willed man, but he stood before Eve Brody—his children's nurse—immensely shaken by what Maxine had divulged, and Mrs Brody was making him feel more than he should feel.

'You have helped me already.' He looked down at her for a moment and Eve fancied there was a strange expression on his face she had not seen before, but it was fleeting and soon gone. 'I swear Sophie and Abigail have never been so happy and it is all down to you. Now go to bed. I have inconvenienced you enough by knocking over the table and waking you. Could anything be more disconcerting? We have much to do before we leave in the morning.'

'Yes, yes, I will. Goodnight.'

The following morning, with a small brood of disappointed children who were only placated with promises of an early return to Laurel Court, they went back to London.

Lucas became a man with a mission. He mobilised himself into finding his brother's child and he was awe inspiring to see in action. From the side lines, Eve watched him at his desk writing letters to anyone who had known his former wife. He would leave the house for hours at a time and arrive back exhausted.

Knowing he needed to keep a cool head for what lay ahead, Lucas did his best to stay calm and in control. It was not like him to get worked up, but the thought that somewhere Stephen's daughter might be at the mercy of some evil woman was almost more than he could bear.

He had to think where Maxine might have taken her, where the most likely place could be. She was devious, black-hearted and clever. He must put his brain to working out how he could find out—the trouble was his mind had been snarled up of late, barely able to function as he had sought a solution to the crisis in his life brought about by his lack of finances, let alone deal with this.

The answer to his dilemma came from the maid who had attended Maxine before she had left Laurel Court. At first the maid was reluctant to speak to him, but, convinced that she was concealing something, he persisted, his questioning becoming more of an interrogation, and by the time he had finished with her, she had told him everything he wanted to know.

She recalled that when Stephen had died Maxine had made enquiries about women who looked after babies when their mothers were indisposed—in other words, unwanted. The woman she had sent her daughter to was in St Giles.

Lucas felt a familiar quickening in his veins when Mrs Brody joined him in the hall. Her pelisse and the dress beneath were charcoal grey and deceptively simple, and a black bonnet covered her hair. A shawl was draped over her arm. He searched her features as she walked towards him and he saw nothing but a deep concern.

'You've found the child?' Eve asked quietly.

'Her name is Alice. Are you quite sure you are willing to come with me?'

'That is why I'm here.'

'I do know that I shouldn't be burdening you with all this.'

'I want to help, and if I am to look after the child then I'd like to start from the beginning.'

Narrowing his eyes, he locked them on hers. 'I must warn you that where we are going will not be pleasant.'

'I can take it. The important thing is the child.'

'I would rather people didn't know anything about this, that my useless first wife is capable of doing anything so vile as to farm her daughter out to a woman who goes by the name of Mrs Unwin. I shudder to think of the conditions she is living in, but I am compelled to do something to remove her from that.'

'And—you are certain it is your brother's child?'

'As certain as I can be. I managed to locate Stephen's valet and one of the maids that attended Maxine when she resided at Laurel Court. Both of them knew of her condition—Stephen, also. Apparently he was looking forward to the birth, but he died six months before Alice was born.'

'That is so very sad. I'm sorry. I—suggest we leave now.'

'I agree. Come.'

In no time at all they were leaving the well-structured world of the gentry in Lucas's carriage for the less wholesome district adjoining Soho and Covent Garden—St Giles. Everyone knew it was an area that was home to some of the most brutal and depraved people in London.

They left the carriage at the entrance to a narrow street, Lucas telling his driver to wait until they returned. Eve's heart was thumping with trepidation as they made their way through the rabbit warren of narrow, stinking alleys, hampered by an assortment of laden handcarts, people and animals.

Lucas had told her that what she would see would not be pleasant—indeed, she knew St Giles was a dreadful, hideous place—but even so she hadn't imagined anything as bad as what she now saw. With the accumulated dirt of years, it was grim. She was disgusted by the filth, appalled by the number of men and women slouched in the sagging doorways, and barefoot, malnourished children with empty eyes playing in the gutters. It was the smell that almost overwhelmed her. It was the smell of poverty, the foul, unacceptable smell of humanity at its lowest level.

Even though she was dressed in her oldest clothes she still felt conspicuous, and Lucas, also dressed in his plainest clothes, attracted as much attention as if he had worn a crown and ermine cloak. A group of women gathered in a doorway gossiping turned to look at him with sharp, suspicious eyes, and the same kind of interest the sight of him always kindled in the eyes of the more well to do.

He stopped to ask directions from a passer-by, who pointed to an alley ahead of them. Hurrying on, they entered the alley, which sloped slightly towards the centre to make a central drain, in which festering rubbish and things unrecognisable lay stagnant. Having the presence of mind to lift her skirts out of the filth, Eve's heart sank lower with each step she took. They seemed to be penetrating into a noisome slum, but when at last they reached the end it opened out into a space with better houses on three sides and they both gave a sigh of relief.

Seeming to know which house to approach, Lucas rapped loudly on the door, stepping forward when it was flung open by a woman dressed noticeably better than those they had seen so far.

'Well?' she asked, crossing her arms over her sagging bosom as she surveyed them, recognising them immediately as gentry but not intimidated by them.

'Mrs Unwin?' Lucas asked curtly.

'Who wants to know?'

Lucas's eyes narrowed and his jaw tightened. 'I am looking for a child and I have reason to believe she is here,' he said, ignoring her question

Mrs Unwin peered at him. There was about him a handsome, eye-catching arrogance and authority that kindled alarm in her and she stepped back. 'I look after a lot of children. Does this child you're looking for have a name?'

'Alice Stainton. I have been sent by the child's mother.'

Mrs Unwin looked at him doubtfully. 'And how am I supposed to know that?'

'You don't.' Raising his cold, glittering eyes to the woman, he said in an ominous voice, 'If you value your living, you will hand the child over to me—the right child, for I have ways of discovering the truth you won't like,' he warned softly.

Hearing the cold voice of authority and looking

into eyes that were alight with the brilliance of a demon, Mrs Unwin instinctively knew better than to argue. Before she could say anything else, Lucas pushed her aside and stepped inside. Incensed that he thought he had the right to come barging into her home, uttering angry words of protest she followed after him.

After her came Eve, her nervousness increasing as she emerged from a passage into a dimly lit room. She stopped, rooted to the spot. The room was barely warm, the small fire having difficulty in maintaining the feeble flames. Several pans were hung on nails on the wall at the side of the fireplace, and an unappetising smell leaked from one that was balanced on the bed of embers.

The walls and ceiling were damp, and the floor was beaten earth. A dresser stood against the wall and a battered old armchair was set at an angle beside the fire. In the centre of the room was an old table on which the remnants of a meal on chipped and greasy plates stood. Around it was an assortment of wooden boxes to seat what appeared to be a multitude of children who stood about the room, their faces white and thin. Eyeing the newcomers warily, they moved together to form a protective, anxious circle, and from a box in the corner came a thin wail.

Lucas studied the squalid room from the threshold. His face showed no expression as his gaze swept over the children, while inside him a storm of such proportions raged he felt he might explode with the fierceness of it. 'Where's the child?' he demanded.

'Over there,' Mrs Unwin grudgingly replied, already seeing the weekly money the child's mother sent running out. 'I've taken good care of her, like I told the lady I would. Said she was in difficulties—that she would come and get her or send someone else when more permanent arrangements could be made.'

'I'm sure she did,' Lucas ground out. He could not bear to think of the fate that awaited this child if he did not remove it from this house. Many unwanted babies were left out in the streets to die. Those that survived were put out to parish nurses, most of them gin drinkers, who were known to maim or disfigure them before turning them out to beg by exciting pity. Others by the age of eleven or twelve, already eaten up with disease, were forced into prostitution, which would perhaps be the fate of many of these that were looking at him with hunger and fear in their eyes.

Looking past Lord Stainton, Eve's gaze did a quick sweep of the room. It fell on a box on the floor in a corner. Brushing past him, hesitantly she went towards it and, leaning over, she peered inside the makeshift cradle. The child was a small scrap of a thing. She knew instinctively that this was the child of Lord Stainton's first wife, but whatever its relationship to Lord Stainton, they could not abandon it to the miserable life it would be consigned to here.

'This is the child we are looking for, isn't it?' Eve asked of the woman, thinking there might be other babies in the house and wanting to be quite sure they had the right one.

'That's Alice,' Mrs Unwin replied, nodding.

Reaching into the cradle, Eve picked up what looked like a bundle of rags. As she wrapped it in the shawl she'd had the presence of mind to bring with her, she had no doubt that the child was alive with lice—already she could feel the itching begin on her flesh.

'I've done me best with the bairn,' Mrs Unwin said. 'Although it's not easy with so many mouths to feed under one roof, as you can see. Mothers come and dump their offspring, leaving a bit of money to pay for their keep and promising to come back with more, but that's the last I see of 'em.'

'Then how do you manage to feed them all?' Eve asked, deeply moved by the pathetic faces of the children. 'And why do you agree to take them in? Would the parish not take them?'

Mrs Unwin smiled scornfully at Eve's naïvety. 'The children beg on the streets—some pick pockets, some do better than others and what they get helps feed those that don't. As for the parish—children are a burden. The children you see here may not have enough food in their bellies, but they're not knocked about like some.'

'What will happen to these children, Mrs Unwin?' Eve asked, suspecting that nearly all of them would turn to crime in desperation as they struggled against poverty and the misfortunes of the world.

She shrugged. 'They'll leave, I suppose—like all the rest.'

Eve turned and looked beseechingly at Lucas's stoic features. Reading what she was thinking, he reluctantly delved into his pocket and brought out some loose coins—not a large sum, but more than Mrs Unwin had seen in a year.

'See that they get something to eat,' he said.

Without another word Lucas took Eve's elbow and led her outside.

When they emerged into the light Eve saw that his face was ashen and she thought he was trembling. He was a strong man, but what he had just been through had burdened him and his shoulders were slumped.

'Come,' he said to Eve. 'Let's get out of here. Are you all right carrying the child?'

She nodded, clutching the tiny bundle within her arms, as eager as he was to leave this place behind.

With Lucas close by Eve's side, they hurried back the way they had come, and not until they were in the carriage and it lurched forwards did they both breathe a sigh of relief.

Chapter Five

Settling the bundle on her knee and holding it in the crook of her arm, Eve turned back the corner of the shawl and peered inside. What she saw brought a stabbing pain to her heart and tears sprang to her eyes, for the baby was awake, her gaze solemn and steady as she looked straight at her with pale blue eyes surrounded by sweeping black lashes. She was a dear little thing who seemed to sense that she had had a poor beginning and seemed not to know how to raise her voice in protest.

Her eyes held a shadow as though some anticipation of the future, unknown and mysterious, held her fast. Her little face was thin, her skin never having been into contact with water, and her hair, laying in a swirl of flat curls about her skull, was as black as coal. Remembering her own Estelle when she was this age—a bonny, spirited, healthy baby with bright eyes and rounded cheeks and plump limbs of the well fed—a lump came to her throat and her heart turned over with pity.

Leaning back into the corner of the carriage, Lucas studied Mrs Brody's face as she looked down at the child, noting that her high cheek bones were tinted pink, her expression one of melting softness. The longer he looked at her he reluctantly faced the fact that Eve Brody was a far cry from being an ordinary woman. In reality she was intelligent, spontaneous, courageous and naturally sensual. As the sun had penetrated the overhanging roofs of St Giles and he had looked down at her upturned face, he had been astounded to see how beautiful she looked surrounded by all the rot and filth—like a rose on a dung heap. He had been wrong to think of her as a bad-tempered, interfering woman. She was proving to be more unexpected than that.

Raising her head, Eve looked across at Lord Stainton, her eyes shining with unshed tears, surprised to see him staring intently at her. She was prompted to ask him why, but instead she said, 'Who could treat a baby in this way—to discard it as though it were nothing at all? How could anyone be so heartless or so cruel?'

'Maxine. She is a selfish wretch. I never knew how much until today. Is the child all right?'

Eve nodded, smiling down at the beautiful,

solemn little person she hardly knew. 'She is malnourished and in desperate need of a bath, but she's beautiful. It's easy to see she's a Stainton.'

'It is?'

'She takes after her Uncle Lucas, with her black hair and light blue eyes. Poor little thing. She's had an awful time of it.'

'God knows what harm it's done her.'

'Possibly not much. They're very resilient, children. All a baby needs is food and warmth— and love, if it's available.' Eve took the baby's small hand in her own. She grabbed at her finger and held on, making a small baby noise that sounded like a gurgle. 'She's going to be strong. Look how she's holding on to my finger.'

Lucas looked, but said nothing.

'Do you intend to keep her with you?'

'What else can I do? There is no decision at all to make. This is Stephen's child, and my own niece—my daughters' sister. I intend to keep all the girls together.'

'What if Alice's mother decides she does want her? What will you do then?'

'After abandoning her other children and now this one, without a trace of compassion or remorse, there isn't a court in the land that would grant her custody. But what of you? The Stainton nursery seems to be increasing at an alarming rate.'

She smiled. 'And you know how much I love children.'

Eve held the little girl up for Lucas to see. She began sucking noisily on her fist. Fixing his gaze on the huge enquiring eyes staring at him out of a pathetically thin little face, a wave of sickness overwhelmed him, not only at the sight of the pathetic child, but because its mother, the woman he had married, had inflicted this on her own flesh and blood, a small defenceless child.

He looked at Eve but said nothing. What could he say? Dear God, he had never been a violent man, but now he felt violent. He hadn't believed in retribution, but now he did. At the first opportunity he would pay Maxine a call, but to begin with he must ask Eve for her silence.

'There is something I must ask of you.'

'What is it?' she asked, making the child comfortable in the crook of her arm.

'Do you think you can keep this to yourself, that you will never mention what happened today?'

'Yes, of course.'

'Not even to Beth Seagrove.'

'No, of course not. I am not given to gossip. I leave that to others.'

'Thank you. I ask you as a great favour to me.'

'But what will you say to the servants when we

arrive back at the house? Look at the state the child's in. Questions are bound to be asked.'

'I'll deal with them in turn. I'll also deal with the one who took her to that—that hell hole.'

'It's the child's good fortune you found out where she was. Why did her mother not tell you?'

'Because she thought to blackmail me. She wants money—and a lot of it.' But more than anything else, Maxine had done this for revenge, Lucas thought bitterly.

On reaching the house, Lucas helped Eve out of the carriage, then ran up the steps to the front door, holding it open for her and the child.

'Mrs Coombs,' he called, and from the nether regions of the house the small woman emerged. She was dressed in black except for a snow-white starched frilly lace cap and apron tied about her stout waist.

Mrs Coombs waited. She asked no questions and showed no surprise. It was as though his lordship turned up every day with the nursemaid holding what she assumed was a baby. However, as she took one disapproving look at the soiled hem of Mrs Brody's dress and their boots caked with something quite unmentionable, her expression stiffened with distaste.

Aware of what the housekeeper must be thinking, Eve stepped forward with the child. 'Mrs Coombs,

I'm sorry about this. Lord Stainton, please hold the child for a moment.'

Before he could protest, to both Lucas's and Mrs Coombs's amazement, with complete unconcern for the damage the soiled bundle might do to his lordship's jacket, Eve had thrust the child into his arms. A look of consternation flickered across his face and, standing awkwardly, he wrinkled his nose at the stench that rose from the soiled rags, while Eve sat on a chair, and, to Lucas's and Mrs Coombs's astonishment, removed her boots and placed them beside the door. Standing straight in her stocking feet, she looked at Lucas.

'In respect to whoever it is that scrubs the floors, Lord Stainton, I think you should show some consideration and do as I have done. I'll take the little one.' Eve turned to Mrs Coombs and smiled as Lucas sat on the chair Eve had just vacated to remove his boots. 'Will you please heat some water, Mrs Coombs. I am sure you will agree this poor little mite desperately needs a bath and some clean clothes—perhaps some of Miss Abigail's have been put away somewhere.'

Mrs Coombs looked from Eve to Lord Stainton bemusedly.

'Do as Mrs Brody says, Mrs Coombs.'

Mrs Coombs smiled at Eve. 'There's plenty of hot water and I'm sure some of Miss Abigail's baby clothes can be found. I'll go and take a look, shall I?'

'Thank you, but we must hurry. The baby is hungry and I'm afraid I have no idea when she was last fed.'

'I'll see to it. Some fine oatmeal soaked in warm milk should do the trick. Shall we go up to the nursery?'

'If you don't mind, Mrs Coombs, I don't want the baby to come into contact with the other children until after she has had her bath.' She cast the house-keeper a conspiratorial look, which Mrs Coombs understood perfectly.

'There is a room next to the kitchen we can use. It's warm so the child won't be chilled.'

'Mrs Brody.'

As she was about to follow Mrs Coombs, Eve turned to Lord Stainton, unable to suppress a smile when she saw him scratching the back of his head.

'Is there anything else you might need?'

'I think we can manage perfectly well with what we have.'

'If you say so. Meanwhile I'll arrange to have the crib that was used for the children brought down from the attic.'

'Thank you, and after that I would instruct your valet to prepare you a bath. You may find some of Alice's small associates have hopped on to you.'

Amusement touching her gaze, she watched as he slowly absorbed what she said, and when the realisation hit him, his expression was so comical that she laughed.

Eve followed Mrs Coombs through the kitchen and into a laundry room. The housekeeper was a good-natured, middle-aged, bustling sort of a woman. Taking to the baby instantly, she fussed over it like a mother hen, stripping the poor mite and discarding what could only be described as infested rags into a bin to be burned.

'My goodness, what a thin little thing she is!' Mrs Coombs exclaimed, horrified on seeing the thin little body, chafed raw in places.

'She is, isn't she, but I have every faith that in no time at all she will begin to put on weight. Apart from being undernourished, she looks healthy enough.'

'She's staying, then?' Mrs Coombs asked bluntly.

'Yes, I believe so.'

'Then she's going to need a wet nurse.'

Eve looked at her hopefully. 'Do you know where we could find one at such short notice, Mrs Coombs?'

She nodded. 'Leave it with me. Lady Carstairs along the street had to employ a wet nurse, a Mrs Price, since she had no milk to feed her last baby. As far as I know the child is almost weaned, so I might be able to persuade her to come here.'

'It would be a relief if you could.'

Eve carefully lowered the baby into a large bowl

of warm water. Her thin little body and cap of ebony
curls were soaped and sluiced and Alice seemed to
enjoy rather than object to this new experience.
Without so much as a whimper she gazed at these
two people and about the room, and, as she kicked
and flapped her arms, she gurgled and grinned.
Afterwards, she was smoothed all over with rose
powder and wrapped in a large fluffy towel.

Leaving Mrs Coombs to tidy up, Eve carried Alice
up to the nursery where Nelly, the kitchenmaid, had
been looking after the three girls in her absence.

The children were mesmerised by the new
addition to the nursery and watched wide-eyed as
Eve dressed her in some of Abigail's small baby
clothes. Mrs Coombs brought some fine oatmeal
soaked in warm milk, and the children moved close
to watch as Eve slowly spooned it into the baby's
mouth. She was hungry and slurped it all up. Then,
after being put over Eve's shoulder to be winded,
unable to keep her eyes open, sticking her thumb
into her rosebud-shaped mouth Alice fell asleep,
the curve of her long dark lashes casting faint
shadows over her cheeks.

Standing up, Eve hugged the little body close,
before placing it in the crib and pulling the covers
over her. She stood back and sighed. As yet neither
Mrs Coombs—who had disappeared to the
kitchen—nor Nelly had asked anything about the

child, and Eve had offered no explanation. It was for Lord Stainton to tell them. The three girls were leaning over the crib, unable to take their eyes off the baby. Kneeling between them, Eve smiled warmly and put an arm around each of them.

'She's a lovely baby, isn't she?'

They nodded in unison, causing their curls to bounce about their faces. Their eyes were dreamy, soft and glowing, and Sophie whispered so as not to disturb this wonderful little creature who been thrust into their lives, 'Is she going to stay with us?'

'Would you like her to stay, Sophie?'

'Oh, yes, we all would. She's so pretty.'

'What do they call her?' Abigail asked.

'Alice.'

Sophie smiled. 'That's a pretty name.'

'So it is. And will you and Abigail and Estelle help me to look after her?'

'Oh, yes,' they said in unison.

'Good.' She looked at Nelly, who was tidying the room. 'Stay with them, will you, Nelly. I have to go and speak to Lord Stainton—and then I must take a bath.'

Eve found her employer in his study—a solitary brooding man standing with his shoulder propped against the window, staring out into the street, but seeing nothing. Compassion swelled in her heart as she realised that although he appeared cold and unemotional in front of her, he had come in here to worry in lonely privacy. His very presence dominated the room. Having had a bath and a change of clothes, damp curls clung to his nape and around his face.

Suppressing the urge to go to him, she quietly said, 'Lord Stainton?' He turned and looked at her, his face impassive. He looked tired and Eve could just make out the fine lines beginning to form at the corners of his eyes. She didn't know his exact age but thought him to be thirty or thirty-one, although on the occasions when he smiled he did look younger.

'How is the child?' he asked, pushing himself upright and strolling towards her.

'She's settled and is sleeping soundly. I think that young lady will end up being thoroughly spoiled. Already Sophie and Abigail are her devoted slaves—not to mention Mrs Coombs and Nelly.'

Mrs Coombs chose that moment to bring them some tea. Neither Lucas nor Eve had asked for it—she placed the tray of wafer-thin bone china on the desk.

'Here you are. You'll need a cup of tea, I don't wonder, now the infant's been taken care of—bless her heart. Pretty little thing, too.'

'Thank you, Mrs Coombs,' Lucas said bluntly.

Ignoring the dismissal, Mrs Coombs turned an appraising look on Mrs Brody. 'I should think you'll be wanting a bath and a change of clothes yourself, Mrs Brody.'

'Most certainly, Mrs Coombs. I'll just have a cup of the tea you've so kindly brought and then I'll do just that.'

'Will there be anything else?'

'No, thank you, Mrs Coombs.' Lucas had raised his voice, but his expression was tolerant.

Unperturbed, Mrs Coombs turned her back on him and smiled at Eve. 'He's a proper gentleman is Lord Stainton,' she told her, 'for all his blusterings. He was born yelling as lusty as the best of them and never stopped—and I should know because I delivered him.' On that note, casting Lucas a fond look, she left them alone.

Lucas had looked on with some amusement while he watched Mrs Brody's expression throughout Mrs Coombs's appraisal of him. Having removed her bonnet, her hair seemed to glow with every different shade of red and gold in the sun's rays shining directly on her through the window. He watched her with fascinated interest, amazed by the gracious ease with which she conducted herself and the way she fitted into his household and effortlessly charmed Mrs Coombs.

There was a natural sophistication about her that

came from an active mind and a genuine interest in others. He smiled to himself, remembering her courageous penetration into St Giles to assist him in his search for Maxine's child. He had known a few men with true courage in his lifetime, but he had never met a courageous woman until now. She was full of surprises, full of promise, he thought studying her surreptitiously, with beauty moulded into every line of her face.

'Mrs Coombs has obviously taken to you. You should feel honoured. She doesn't take to people easily. No doubt you find her overwhelming,' he said with a short laugh.

Eve liked to hear him laugh, which gave his stern features a tranquil benevolence she had once not thought possible. 'I think she's very nice and she has gone out of her way to make things easy for me—and it is clear she is extremely fond of you.'

'Mrs Coombs says and does as she pleases. She's been here for more years than I care to remember and has the idea that I won't dismiss her because I cannot do without her. And she's right—although she can be quite unmanageable at times.'

Eve poured the tea, placing a cup and saucer on the desk for Lucas, who accepted it with a brisk 'thank you'. Sitting in one of the two padded leather chairs on either side of the desk, the hot tea helped to soothe her.

'Will you be able to manage in the nursery?' Lucas asked, his tone expressing some concern.

'With a baby to take care of I shall need some help. Nelly is all very well, but Mrs Coombs needs her in the kitchen. Would you object if I looked for someone suitable—a girl, perhaps, and a wet nurse for the baby? Mrs Coombs says she knows a woman who might be glad of the position. It would only be for a short time and of very little expense.'

'Since it is you who will have to deal with them, I have no objections. All I require is that they are honest, trustworthy, reliable and hard working.'

'I understand.' On a sigh, with some dismay Eve glanced down at her soiled dress. 'I think I should go,' she said quietly. 'I desperately need to bathe and change my clothes.'

The following morning Eve received a letter from Mr Barstow informing her that she could expect to have access to her inheritance very soon and that he was only awaiting a letter finalising this from her father's solicitor in New York. This forced her to consider seriously what she must do next.

One thing she was sure of, she did not want to abandon her care of Sophie and Abigail and now Alice, but how could she remain working as a hired help when she was an heiress in her own right? Suddenly she had the stirrings of an idea, a faint hope that began to rise. The idea was perhaps ridiculous, and if she had any sense at all she would cast the notion aside without giving it a moment's consideration, but all her feelings were heightened.

The more she thought about it, the more it seemed the only plausible solution. Lord Stainton and his children had been a consistent part in her life for some considerable time. Sophie and Abigail seemed always to have been there. She now wanted them to be there always in the future, too. She only had to think a minute and she could see Laurel Court laid out like a picture, and Lord Stainton's presence there, strong and vital.

Feeling more relaxed and in control of her feelings, she had made her decision and would throw every caution to the wind. She wanted to live at Laurel Court. She wanted to raise Estelle at Laurel Court with Sophie and Abigail and Alice, and now she only needed Lord Stainton to agree. The thought suddenly invigorated her beyond all reason.

Knowing Lord Stainton to be in his study working at his desk, knocking on the door, Eve went in without waiting to be told to. When she looked at his head bent over some papers, a wave of apprehension swept over her. There was a tightness around her throat, a hollow in the pit of her stomach.

'Yes, what is it?' he asked without looking up.

'Lord Stainton, would you spare me a moment? I—there is something I wish to discuss with you.'

Lucas raised his head and wary eyes looked back at her. He pursed his mouth, a dimple playing about his cheek. Noting her lovely eyes, richly lashed under excellently marked eyebrows, and the way in which she looked at him, she suddenly looked so young and defenceless. She seemed uneasy. Clearly something of a serious nature was on her mind.

'Oh? Is it important?'

'Yes—very.'

His eyes brightened a merest fraction as he motioned her to a seat across from him. 'Then you'd better sit down.'

'No,' she said quickly, twisting her hands nervously in front of her. 'I would rather stand, if you don't mind.'

Lucas pushed back his chair and standing up, walked slowly round the desk to stand in front of her. 'As you wish. What is it, Mrs Brody? Is there something wrong with the children?'

'No,' she was quick to assure him. 'It's nothing like that.'

Folding his arms across his chest, he rested his hips against the desk and tilted his head to one side, looking at her intently. 'Then don't you think you'd better get to the point?'

Eve turned her back to him and walked to the window. Looking out, she knew her next words could be the turning point in her life—that it could be for the better or she was about to make a complete fool of herself.

Lucas found himself wondering if she had forgotten he was there. Then at last she turned and looked at him and smiled as if she knew an amusing secret. She had kept him waiting long enough to intrigue him. He had grown tense.

'I have a proposition to put to you, Lord Stainton, a proposition that may be of benefit to us both.'

'Mrs Brody, the last time you had a proposition to put to me it was to apply for the position of nursemaid to my children. What is it this time?'

'Well—I—I would like to ask you, in all humility, to marry me?'

'What?' He was incredulous. The startling pale blue eyes swept over her face. 'Mrs Brody, I think you must have taken leave of your senses.'

'I assure you, Lord Stainton, I have never been saner.'

'Then it's the strangest marriage proposal I've ever heard. You! Asking me to marry you in all humility? You could not be humble, Mrs Brody, if you tried. You are without a doubt, a most unprincipled, impulsive creature—the most impulsive creature I have ever met.'

Eve straightened up and walked towards him. 'Please have the good sense to take me seriously.'

'I do,' he ground out, angry now and insulted, 'and the answer is no.' It was an instant response. Unconsidered. Automatic. His wife's infidelity and the costly divorce had strengthened him, and the bitterness had left him mistrustful. He had iron in his soul now, something this American woman would know nothing about.

'Whatever you expected to find when you came in here, I am not a charity case, nor am I a beggar or some broken-hearted, jilted husband who is so impoverished that I will grab the offer of a proposal of marriage from a woman in my employ and sink to my knees with gratitude. Why, if it weren't so serious it would be laughable.'

Eve stiffened. 'Laughable? I find nothing amusing to laugh at, Lord Stainton. I have given the matter a great deal of thought and I have decided that it is a solution that would suit us both,' she went on hurriedly before her courage and confidence deserted her. 'I have a lot of money coming to me very soon—money that doesn't risk being lost as a result of a poor harvest. My father had good, sound business sense and affairs that will go on increasing.'

Recovering from the shock her proposal had caused, Lucas burst out laughing unpleasantly.

'Have you any idea how ridiculous this sounds? I? Marry an American?'

Eve flushed violently and stiffened with indignation. She refused to retreat now she had come so far. 'I was born in England and come from good stock and I am proud of who I am. One might think I am suggesting mingling common stock with blood royal. My blood is as pure as yours, sir, and just as ancient, for my family on my mother's side descends from the English nobility.'

'Really,' he drawled coldly. 'And what happened to this noble line, pray?'

'The title was entailed to the male line and when there were no more males it passed out of the family. If you were to marry me, you will have a secure family environment for your children—which is the most important thing of all—and all the money you want. Come now, you won't be the first Englishman who finds himself down on his luck and required to marry an heiress. I am not ignorant of the fact that in the upper classes large sums of money and extensive estates are involved in such marriages.'

Eve met his eyes. This man was sharp, intelligent and observant. Her thoughts had been guarded as she had spoken so matter of factly, but it occurred to her suddenly now that he understood her far better than she had realised. The thought was not reassuring.

Lucas gazed at her unblinkingly—a sudden interest seemed to appear in his eyes, and then it was gone. 'So, in exchange for my illustrious family name and title, you will bring with you a nice fat dowry.'

'Yes.'

'It cannot be. There are too many differences between us.'

'I don't care about differences. They don't matter. Circumstances have changed all that. Can't you see? I know how you worry about your children's future. I shall take good care of their well being—it will be as if they were my own.'

'But you do that already—and admirably so, so nothing will change there.'

'It will when my inheritance is made available to me, very soon—and then I must leave. I am reluctant to do so, having become extremely fond of Sophie and Abigail. Alice, too, so recently come, will have a place in my heart. When I applied for the position of nursemaid to your children, I told you then that when the time came for me to leave I would do it in such a way as to cause them the minimum distress. If we were to marry, they would suffer no distress. They would be delighted.'

Lucas studied her gravely for a moment and then his mobile mouth curved in a smile. 'I can see you have it all worked out—and you are an extremely attractive woman, Mrs Brody, I grant you that. You also have money and money gives you power. If one has those, one can do anything.'

'It may seem that way, but it is not true. I may have the means to do whatever I please, but, being a woman in a man's world with a child to raise, I do not have the opportunity.'

'So why me? If it is a husband you require, then surely London is full of gentlemen who would prove to be far less trouble than me—although in exchange for your wealth you will obtain a title if I agree to the marriage.'

'Titles are meaningless to me, and the men who come hoping to court me have no opinion whatsoever about my looks. It is my father's money that attracts them to me and nothing else—I know this.'

'Then I am no different from them—an impoverished lord who would be marrying you for your money.'

'That's where you are wrong, Lord Stainton. You see, *I* chose you,' she said, with a little smile in an attempt to lighten the tension. 'That is the difference. I see marriage to you and being able to reside at Laurel Court a good way of investing in my own and Estelle's future happiness. Besides,' she murmured with a little quirk to her lips, 'I would rather face a firing squad than marry any one of the gentlemen who came to offer their suit to me in

New York. I am also a good judge of character and I see you as the most needy.'

'Thank you,' he quipped drily. 'Now that remark really does make me feel like the worst kind of charity case.'

'I didn't mean it to sound that way. You should know that I have no intention of returning to America. I wish to settle in England, and I have quite fallen in love with Laurel Court,' she told him with a softening of her features and a glow to her eyes. 'It is very beautiful. The perfect place to raise a family, and Sophie, Abigail and Alice would be stepsisters to my own Estelle.'

'And I would acquire a stepdaughter.'

'Yes, you will, and your children's future will be secure in a settled family environment. I am not naïve regarding my worth, Lord Stainton. Is it not an accepted fact that in England society is full of marriages of convenience and political and financial alliances?'

'It is common—although I am surprised you can be so matter of fact about an issue that is supposed to be the most important event in a woman's life. My world is so very different from yours. We may not be compatible.'

'I'm not overly concerned with compatibility. I have been married once—and so have you.' His expression chilled the moment she referred to his marriage, but, undeterred, she went on. 'I must tell you that I am not used to being idle, so I have no intention of being a full-time lady of leisure. If you do marry me, I shall look forward to playing my part in the restoration of Laurel Court.' She tilted her head and gazed at him enquiringly. 'Do you still intend to sell this house?'

'That is my intention. Unfortunately, Laurel Court, as you will have seen for yourself, has become sadly neglected. It will need some money injected into it right away if it isn't to fall into ruin.'

Already Lucas could feel his pride and self-respect being stripped away bit by agonising bit. When Maxine had left him for Stephen there had been no deliverance from his seared vanity and the wound continued to fester. His peers, who seemed to thrive on scandal and others' misfortunes, had watched with amusement his fall from grace. Meeting their sneers with his head held high, he had projected an artificial image so no one would see his helpless fury, his deep-rooted resentment and sorrow and his immense fears as he had watched Stephen and Maxine squander the Stainton assets until there was nothing left but insurmountable debts.

'Then it would seem my offer is timely. I have received a letter from my solicitor here in London telling me that my inheritance should be made available to me any day now. A bank draft will be handed over to you on the day we marry to enable you to begin restoring the house to its former grandeur right away. If you wish to retrieve any articles of furniture and paintings you sent to the auction, then you can have them returned.'

Turning sharply, Lucas strode away from her, loathing himself for prostituting himself like this, selling himself to this American woman so he could restore his estate and secure his children's future, but their well being and Laurel Court were important to him and he would strive to keep hold of them with his dying breath.

Eve stared at his rigid stance and smiled and said with understanding, 'I do understand how difficult this is for you, Lord Stainton.'

Spinning round, struggling to keep the irritation out of his voice, he said, 'Believe me, Mrs Brody, no part of this dilemma is remotely easy for me. Wealth gives you an advantage over me I don't like, but I know I will have to accept—for the time being at least.'

She tilted her chin up ever so slightly, meeting his eyes squarely. 'Yes, I suppose you will, just like I will have to accept that you want neither my respect nor my kind regard, only to ensure that your children have continued security in their lives—and, of course, my money. However, there will be three conditions you must agree to if you decide to accept my proposal.'

A gleam appeared in Lucas's narrowed eyes. 'Conditions?' he said, deliberately mocking the very idea.

'First you must promise to treat my daughter with kindness and take as much care of her as you do your own children and Alice. She is the most important thing in the world to me and I do not want a union between us to cause her any unhappiness.'

Lucas nodded. 'You have nothing to fear. Estelle is a delightful child. I would not do anything to harm you daughter, Mrs Brody. And the second condition I must adhere to?'

'My daughter must never know of this arrangement between us. I—would be embarrassed if I had to explain how I proposed marriage to you and I doubt she would understand.'

Lucas gave a brusque nod. 'I see no problem with that. And the third condition?' He waited rigidly, not feeling particularly complimented by her insistence that he should promise not to harm her daughter—as if she saw him as some kind of monster. He was even less flattered when she continued.

'You will accept on the grounds the marriage is considered a business arrangement. You need someone to look after your children and financing. I need a home for myself and Estelle and respectability. It will be a marriage in name only—an affair of convenience.'

'I see,' Lucas replied caustically, feeling more humiliated and degraded than he cared to admit. Having listened as she told him of the conditions he would have to agree on, he was fascinated by the rules of conduct that she'd recited with such absolute certainty. 'You appear to have thought of everything.'

'I told you, I've given it a great deal of thought.'

When Lucas next spoke his expression was resolute. 'Then before we go any further, I want to be sure you don't have any illusions about me. I'm telling you this because, if I agree to your proposition, I never want you to look back on our marriage with any kind of regret.'

'Go on,' Eve urged when he paused to let the words sink in.

'By your own admission you are a wealthy woman—and a very capable and attractive one. I am destitute—which is a fact that you already know. I am also arrogant, which you have accused me of being, and I am given to moods, temperamental and difficult to live with.'

Eve tilted her head on one side. 'Are you trying to discourage me, Lord Stainton?'

'Not at all. I am merely pointing out the flaws in my character and trying to establish some ground rules of my own.'

He stepped closer, and Eve almost retreated from those suddenly fierce eyes. But she steeled herself and held her ground before his glare.

'As long as we are totally honest with each other in advance,' he went on, straightening his spine and squaring his broad shoulders, his eyes holding hers in bondage, 'and make sure we have no false illusions or unrealistic expectations, it should not be a problem. However, if we marry on your terms our life will be a whole series of charades and false fronts. Do you really think you will be strong enough to keep it up when we are sharing the same house, living together, being watched day in and day out by all and sundry, including the children?'

'I—would hope so.'

'I'm sure you would—having given it a great deal of thought,' he said, quoting her own words and noting the slight doubtful hesitancy in her reply. 'However,' he said on a softer, more provocative note, 'it would be interesting to see if the arrangement would outlast the testing of the flesh.'

Feeling that he had turned the tables on her, restlessly Eve moved away from his searching eyes. She was becoming less and less sure of her reasons for wanting to marry him. The way it looked, if the marriage did go ahead, the two of them were unlikely to lead a docile life. 'I can see you are a man proud beyond measure, Lord Stainton…'

'Lucas.'

'What?'

'My name is Lucas. Lord Stainton is far too formal in the circumstances.'

'Very well. Lucas. I suppose if it were to be any kind of proper marriage I don't see how I could keep myself apart from it, but ours would not be a bond of marriage, but an arrangement, and I hope you would not bend local ears with matters personal to us.'

'It will not be a temporary arrangement, Mrs Brody…'

'My name is Eve.'

He nodded ever so slightly. 'As I was saying, it would be a permanent arrangement. One divorce is enough for any man, and I have no intention of living the life of a monk. Would you expect me to remain faithful to you?'

'I—I—yes, I would.'

He smiled thinly. 'Then you had better rethink our arrangement, otherwise I may insist on a few conditions of my own.' He turned and strode to the door where he stood and held it open for her, indicating that the interview was over. 'I shall give it serious thought and give you my answer tomorrow.'

'Thank you.'

Making time to consider Eve's proposition, suddenly Lucas remembered how it had been when he had married Maxine. Successful in his business life, he had turned to finding a wife, wanting a beautiful woman by his side, to grace and light up his home, a woman to warm his bed, to fill his arms, a woman to give him children—a son. He had succeeded in all those things except two—the woman he had married and her failure to bear him a son and heir. When he had divorced Maxine he had known that one day, if he was not going to die without an heir, he needed to marry again. The prospect was distasteful, but perhaps it was time that he considered it.

Like a caged tiger he prowled the length of the room, cursing fate and himself. Heiresses were few and far between and the idea of placing himself in the hands of the American widow was anathema to him. But if he agreed to Mrs Brody's proposition, he wouldn't come out of it too badly. It could be the answer to a problem he could see no other way of solving—a means to an end.

Besides, Maxine's visit to Laurel Court and her attempt to blackmail him had left him with a deep feeling of unease. To ensure his children could never be taken from him by his greedy, selfish wife, marrying Mrs Brody would be an excellent way of making sure that they remained with him in a secure and loving family environment.

But for now he was furious at not having the

upper hand. He was considering trading his aristocratic lineage for the sake of his children's future security and Mrs Brody's money—a commonly accepted practice, but it made him feel less of a man for doing so.

Chapter Six

The following morning Eve was summoned to the drawing room. With a rustle of skirts and more than a little trepidation, she went in. Lucas spun round from where he was standing by the window and fixed her with his hard gaze.

'You asked to see me,' she said, amazed that she could speak without her voice shaking with nerves. Moving towards him she managed to smile. 'Have you considered my proposition?' she asked without preamble.

'I have.'

She waited for him to continue, the silence scraping against her raw nerves as he stared rigidly at her, his profile harsh, forbidding. She knew he must have thought hard for some way out of marrying her, and she also knew that beneath that tautly controlled façade of his there was a deep anger that he had failed to do so. But she also knew that he must see the sense of what she had proposed, and that it would be beneficial for them both.

'And?' she prompted. 'Have you decided against marrying me?'

'On the contrary,' he said, each word laced with bitter regret as he felt the noose of matrimony once again tightening inexorably around his neck. 'You will be doing me a great service. I agree to the marriage. The main reason being to secure my children's future security and happiness—the other reason is to ease my present circumstances. I should tell you that my financial embarrassment is only a temporary affair and I anticipate acquiring wealth in the future. I promise in time I shall rectify my circumstances and pay you back every penny borrowed with interest.'

'It is not a loan, Lucas. I am not ignorant of the fact that everything a woman possesses at the time of her marriage belongs to her husband as a matter of common law. I know you will use it wisely.'

'Nevertheless, that is how it will be—a business arrangement. I still have several irons in the fire, so to speak, and in time I foresee them making me financially solvent once more. Unfortunately, the returns will come too late to see me over this present crisis.'

'Then I sincerely hope you acquire some profit from your investments, Lucas, and I am glad I am able to help just now.' Eve's lips curved in a little smile and she did not pursue the matter, for, no matter how hard she argued, Lucas Stainton was a fiercely proud man and would refuse to allow a woman to take on his debt unconditionally.

'Why do you smile?'

'Because I knew when I chose you that I was not mistaken in your character. You are a man of honour, Lucas, and pride, and I admire that. I also trust you. Loan or otherwise, I am well satisfied with the arrangement.'

As he turned and slowly walked away from her, with a slight nod of his head, his eyes became shuttered, his expression thoughtful, inscrutable.

'Is there something wrong?' Eve asked, feeling a small *frisson* of alarm.

'No, nothing is wrong—although you might not see it like that when I tell you that the "arrangement" is not as cut and dried as you would like to think. I too have certain expectations of this marriage. I have a condition of my own that I would insist upon—one that may not meet with your approval. It may even make you consider changing your mind about becoming my wife.'

Feeling suddenly nervous and unsure of herself, Eve swallowed. 'What is that?' she asked, peering at his well-chiselled profile, trying to fathom his mood. 'Tell me.'

Turning to face her, he looked at her long and hard before saying, 'I want an heir, a son to carry on the Stainton name and preside over Laurel Court when I am gone.' His eyes locked on to hers.

Stubbornly Eve shook her head, rejecting his statement. She felt the heat rise to her cheeks with embarrassment at having to repeat one of her own conditions she had put to him on their previous encounter. 'But—I said…'

'I know what you said, that ours would be a marriage in name only, but that is not acceptable to me. Should your feelings toward me border on anything that resembles love, then forget them. Love is a silly, romantic notion that has no place in my life. I don't want to be loved and I have no love to give. I don't need you. I don't need any woman. Give me a son and afterwards you can do whatever you want—within reason, of course. Should you become homesick for America, then you can return there—on an extended visit, if you so wish. You can even set up house on your own here in London. But whatever happens, you will remain married to me—and one thing I will make clear is that I will not tolerate you taking a lover.'

Dumbfounded, Eve stared at him in appalled disbelief. 'Return to America? And if I were to do so, would you permit *our son* to go with me?'

'No. I would expect him to remain with me.'

'And if I decide to set up house on my own?'

'The same would apply.'

Speechless with dismay and horror at that heretofore unthought-of idea that he would come up with something like this, that he had considered everything with the cold and calculating brain of a man who was used to making his own decisions and doing everything his way, Eve simply stared at him, her cheeks flushed, as he casually paced the carpet in front of her.

'I'm sure you understand that it would have to be that way.'

'And what sort of mother do you think that would make me if I agreed to such a preposterous, cruel and completely heartless suggestion? Why, I would be no better than your first wife. A child is a commitment. It needs its mother from the day it is born until it comes of age.'

'I agree absolutely and I would be happy for you to remain with me permanently, but that will be entirely up to you. Who knows? I will endeavour to make myself agreeable to you, in which case you might find being married to me is what you want and have no wish to leave.' He ceased pacing and moved to stand close to her, his penetrating gaze locked on hers once more.

'Moreover,' he continued, 'I shall expect you to grant your favours to me in bed without resentment. In other words,' he finished lightly, 'you will co-operate willingly until you conceive.'

'And if the child is female, what then?'

'We shall continue sharing a bed until I have a son.'

'But—that could take years—or I may never give you a son.'

His eyes narrowed and gleamed with a look that was positively wicked. 'In which case, think of the pleasure we will have—trying.'

Having given little thought to the intimacies of marriage Lucas would be entitled to, Eve's mouth dropped open in disbelief at what she was hearing. 'Have you any idea how cold and heartless your proposition makes you sound?'

Lucas's brows snapped together over ominous light blue eyes. 'Quoting your own words, Eve,' he said, his voice dropping to a low, icy whisper, 'you said that ours would not be a bond of marriage, but an arrangement, and as such that is how I am treating it. It also suits me perfectly.'

What he said was true, and Eve was beginning to regret ever saying those words. He really was discussing the terms of their marriage as he would a business arrangement—cold and without emotion.

'Will you not reconsider that particular condition?' Lucas continued. 'It is ridiculous to expect us to go through married life without carnal knowledge of one another.'

Eve remained silent, not with acquiescence, but she was determined not to let her emotions get entangled with being his wife. She was becoming less and less sure of her reasons for asking him to marry her. The way it looked, the peace and contentment she craved would be beyond her grasp with Lucas as her husband.

'Does the idea of sharing a bed with me strike you as distasteful?' he asked harshly.

'It's what might happen in the bed that worries me,' she replied quietly. Somewhere deep inside she could feel an uneasy stirring of something that had lain dormant for the five years she had been a widow. She often thought about Andrew, whether she realised it or not, and the memories of their union were not pleasant.

She had hoped her union with Lord Stainton would be a union of convenience and that their relationship would be conducted outside the bedroom. The humiliating details of those nights with Andrew came back in painful clarity and she cringed. He had used her as if she were a dumb animal, without feeling or emotion, unworthy of tenderness. It had been an ugly and humiliating thing, and she never wanted to experience anything like it again.

There was always the possibility that because of her memories, she would experience some understandable revulsion when she was again faced with the intimacy shared between man and wife, and if she did react to those intimacies with fright, was the experience Lucas had gained with women enough to be able to handle any problems of that sort? Feeling as vulnerable as a child, she lowered her gaze beneath his close scrutiny that was making her feel uncomfortable.

Lucas's jaw tensed. 'You play the reluctant virgin to the hilt, when both of us know you have no cause. You have been married once—you have a child, so you know what to expect—unless,' he said as a sudden thought struck him, thinking he might have found a chink in her armour-plated skin, 'you found marriage to your first husband so repugnant that you have no wish to repeat the experience.'

The colour in Eve's cheeks deepened. 'No—I—of course not,' she said, flustered, trying her best to avoid his penetrating gaze. 'It's just that I—I thought you would prefer it if we didn't...'

'What? Make love?' A smile touched the corners of his sensual lips and a gleam entered his eyes. Ever since he had met Eve Brody she had stood up to him courageously, defying him to his face. Recalling how harshly he had berated Eve when she had proposed marriage, how she had defiantly set her chin against him and angry pride had blazed in her eyes, now, her lovely face mirroring her confusion, she looked vulnerable and much younger and she had the innocent appeal of a bewildered child.

'What will you do if I say no to your terms?' she asked quietly.

'Turn you down,' he replied bluntly.

'Even though you are quite desperate?'

'Even so.' As he shoved his hands into the pockets of his snug-fitting trousers, one dark brow lifted, knowing what he was about to ask her would challenge her. 'The question is, Eve, how desperate are *you*? Just how desperate are you to marry me?'

Impaled on his gaze, Eve stared at him. Perilously close to losing her composure but unable to shake his, she sighed and moved away from him, turning her back as she considered the matter. She had already decided there was more to Lucas Stainton than she had realised. Beneath the hard veneer there was an aloof strength and a powerful charisma that had nothing to do with his good looks or that mocking smile of his that was locked away behind an unbreachable wall. That was his appeal—the challenge. Despite their volatile beginning, Lucas made her want—and probably every woman of his acquaintance—to penetrate that wall, to find the boy he had been.

'Would you consider a compromise?' she murmured at length.

Interest kindled in his narrowed eyes. 'A compromise? I might. Go on. I'm listening.'

'I will agree to your condition, but I ask you to give me time, not to make demands on me immediately.'

Lucas thought about it for a moment. 'How long? One week—two—a month?'

'When—when I am ready,' she said hesitantly. 'When I think the time is right.'

He looked at her hard for a moment and then he nodded. 'Very well—as long as you realise you will eventually become my wife in every sense— and no longer than six months.' His eyes softened. 'You won't find me a cruel husband, Eve, I promise you that.'

With her pride somewhat soothed by that, Eve hesitated and then nodded slightly, noncommittally. 'It's a highly irregular proposition…'

'But not an unreasonable one,' he pointed out.

'No, I don't suppose it is, but all of a sudden I feel that the risk is all one-sided.'

A gleam of amusement lit his eyes. 'Not all. Consider the risk I am taking. I might lose my head completely and become enslaved by you. Then where would I be?'

Eve stared at this cold, dispassionate man before her. He looked so unemotional, so completely self-assured. It seemed impossible that he would want her, or anyone.

A slow smile curved her lips. 'If such a thing were to happen, where would either of us be?'

'Indeed. So what is your answer? Have we reached an agreement that is satisfactory to both of us?'

She nodded. 'Very well, but I will not be manipulated by you, Lucas, for you to dictate what is to become of me and my lovely Estelle.' Tilting her head to one side, she smiled at him softly.

'Then I shall strive not to be a dictatorial husband.'

'Of course you will have to take on more staff,' she said. 'And what will you do about this house? You might like to keep it now.'

'I could take it off the market, I suppose—but not until after we are married.'

Eve raised a brow, meeting his penetrating gaze. 'Just in case something goes wrong to prevent it— that I might withdraw my offer, perhaps?'

'Exactly.'

'I won't,' she told him firmly. 'We have both agreed to the arrangement and I shall not renege on it.'

'I may prove to be a purchase you will regret.'

'Whatever your failings, I doubt they will be different to any other man I may marry, and what good is wealth if one cannot use it to one's advantage?'

'When would you like the ceremony to take place?'

'Whenever you wish? When it is convenient.'

'There is just one more thing we have to discuss. It is usual for two people who are to be married to become engaged first.'

'Oh! I hadn't thought…I suppose you're right. What do you suggest?'

'I have been invited to Lord Gradwell's ball in Piccadilly next week. We will go together.'

'Would you care very much what people might think if we just went ahead and got married without becoming betrothed first?'

'You're mistaken if you think I give a damn about what other people think, but after being married to a woman who didn't have any principles whatsoever, one thing I have come to realise in the short time we have known each other is that they are important to you. It's only right that we do everything that is proper and that we are seen together in public. To make it official I shall see to it that our betrothal is announced in the papers on the day of the ball so that everyone will be prepared.'

'How will they react, do you think, when they learn you are to marry your children's nurse?' she asked with a teasing smile. 'Do you think there will be a storm of protest from your friends and the rest of society who will think you are marrying beneath you?'

'If they don't already know that you are an American heiress, then they soon will.'

'They must have been terribly confused when I came to work for you. It's not exactly how things are done, is it? It must be a matter of fierce conjecture. I…don't want any fuss, Lucas—about the wedding, I mean.'

'There won't be any. After the ball when everyone has had an edifying look at us together, we will set a date for the ceremony and shortly after that we will leave for Laurel Court with the children. Do you have any objections?'

She smiled. 'Not to the last part.'

He grinned at the enthusiasm that always lit her eyes when Laurel Court was mentioned. 'I knew you wouldn't. So you have no objections to me proceeding with the arrangements without delay?'

'No—none whatsoever, although for propriety's sake I think Estelle and I should go and live with Beth and William until the wedding.' She frowned, suddenly thoughtful. 'Providing I can sort something out for someone to look after the children.'

'Do you have anyone in mind?'

'Yes, Sarah Lacy.'

'Sarah? Is she not settled in a new position?'

'I don't think so. She wrote and told Mrs Coombs of her marriage, but as yet I don't believe she has taken up any employment. Perhaps she could be persuaded to return.'

'And her husband?'

'Well, that depends. You see, he is head groom on a large estate in Surrey. It is a good position, but I recall Sarah telling me he isn't happy working there. However, he would not want to leave unless it was for a position of equal status and pay.'

'The man would be a fool to do that.'

'Exactly.'

Lucas fixed his penetrating gaze on her face. 'What do you suggest?'

'That—you offer her husband a position here.'

'Make him my head groom, you mean.'

'Well, you don't have one.'

'Because I had to shrink my stable when my circumstances took a turn for the worse, I do not have the need for a head groom—and nor can I afford one.'

'That won't be a problem when we are married.' Eve's expression became earnest. 'Lucas, think how delighted Sophie and Abigail would be to have her back. I've seen Sarah with your children. She loves and understands them and she is a good worker. For your children's sake, please allow me to write to her.'

He nodded. 'Very well. Although you must be prepared for her to refuse. She might not want to come back.'

Eve's smile was one of immense relief. 'Oh, I think she might.' It was going to be overwhelming living with this man and she felt a nervousness at the new responsibilities she would have to take on as his wife. But as she looked into his pale blue eyes, she made a pact with herself to never show him her fears and to encourage his children to love and trust her. 'In the meantime it would be nice if we were to get to know each other a little better before we marry, Lucas. After all, I know very little about you or your family.'

Abruptly Lucas moved to the window. Eve followed him and impulsively laid her hand on his arm.

'Lucas,' she began. He turned his head and looked down at her, his gaze narrowing on her long fingers resting on his arm. 'I sense you don't like talking about your family—or any matters that are of a personal nature, but if we are to marry, then I would like you to feel that you can confide in me.'

Lucas looked down at her expectant face and a small rock tore loose from the wall of indifference he'd erected and maintained against beautiful women since his divorce. His conscience suddenly developed a voice after years of silence on the subject of sexual ethics, and it was disturbed over the true picture he'd just formed of Eve.

At Laurel Court she had told him about her family and her closeness to her father, and he had noted the softness that crept into her voice and the glow that lit her eyes when she spoke of her daughter. As she spoke it had been obvious even to him, who had little knowledge of loving family relations, that Eve had loved her father deeply and was still grieving over his death.

'Why are you staring at me?' she asked.

Lucas was staring at her because she had the deepest blue eyes, the smoothest skin, and the softest, most beautiful mouth of any woman he'd ever known. And if the tender way she had spoken about her daughter was any indication, she also had the softest heart.

'I'm having an attack of conscience,' he said with disgust, 'and I'm trying to deal with it.'

She smiled. 'Is this an unfamiliar occurrence for you?'

'In these circumstances, it's unprecedented,' he said bluntly. 'I realise that you instigated the situation, and I despise myself for taking advantage of your offer.'

'You needn't feel that way,' Eve replied, confused and uneasy and becoming more so by the moment.

'I do, but Maxine's visit and her blackmail attempt has hastened my decision to remarry. It would be a sensible thing to do at this present time.' He suddenly smiled, surprising her. 'I was also thinking that you are really quite charming.'

The unexpected compliment filled Eve with

pleasure. 'I hope you continue to think so, but it does concern me that now you have agreed to my proposition—and I to yours,' she said, her cheeks colouring a soft pink, 'you will resent what marriage to me has gained you.'

'Don't. If my children are secure, there will be no resentment.'

'Very well. And now I think I'd best be getting back to the children, otherwise Mrs Coombs will scold me for keeping Nelly from her duties in the kitchen.' She went to the door where she paused and glanced back at him. 'Earlier you said you didn't need anyone. You were wrong about that. Everyone needs someone. They may not know it, but they do.'

'You know, if you'd asked me to name the last man on earth I would have expected you to marry, it would have been Lucas Stainton,' Beth said, having been told by Eve a week ago and still finding it hard to believe .

Eve and Estelle had returned to live with them at the house on Berkeley Street until her wedding. A delighted Sarah had returned to look after Lord Stainton's children, and Mark, her husband, had been made head groom now circumstances had taken a turn for the better.

'I have to confess that in the beginning I felt exactly

the same,' Eve replied as they strolled arm in arm in the garden. 'When I took up the position to care for his children and I went to Laurel Court, everything changed, Beth. Be happy for me, won't you?'

'I am, Eve, and so is William, but I just hope Lord Stainton will make you a good husband. Even though he seems very civilised on the surface, there's a ruthlessness about him, a forcefulness. In business he has developed a reputation—that he stops at nothing when he wants something. At this moment he wants your money, but I can't help worrying about what he will do when he has it.'

'Lucas is convinced that his financial embarrassment is only temporary, Beth, and if he really does have the golden touch in selecting the right ventures to invest his money in, then I am sure he is right.'

'I just hope you know what you're doing is right. You really do wish to marry him, don't you, Eve?'

Seeing Beth's concern for her—which she always gave to others, and was a quirk in her nature that made her the most loyal of friends—Eve was quick to reassure her.

'I would never have suggested it if I didn't. Please don't worry about me, Beth. It is what I wish to do.'

Beth gave a sigh of relief and her countenance brightened. 'I'm so glad. Have you decided how soon you will be married?'

'Not yet, but it won't be long—and nor will it be a grand affair. I want as little fuss as possible and afterwards to disappear to the country.' Seeing an excited, calculating gleam enter Beth's eyes, Eve laughed and hugged her to her. 'I'm perfectly serious, so don't make any plans without my say so.'

Lucas cast an amused glance at Henry and handed him a brandy. 'I assume you have heard the news and are here to take me to task on the subject of my choice of bride, Henry.'

'As a matter of fact, you could have knocked me down with a feather when I heard the rumour that you are to marry your children's American nurse-maid, a woman you know practically nothing about—apart from the fact that she is an heiress.'

'As a matter of fact, Eve was born in England and raised in America. So you see, Henry, I do know something about her—and she likes children.'

'After your disastrous marriage to Maxine, I suppose that's a relief. But doesn't it bother you that you will be marrying out of your class? After all, she has been your hired help. The gossips will have a field day and the scandal will be enormous.'

'Personally I don't give a damn what people say, in particular those members of society who believed I was to blame for my divorce from Maxine. What does concern me is if the scandal hurts Eve, but she is strong and I believe will weather the storm, so to speak.'

A thoughtful frown suddenly creased Henry's brow. 'Lucas, I have long passed the point where anything you do surprises me,' he said, but his irritated tone completely denied his philosophical words. 'I have been a detached observer of your marriage to Maxine and your affairs before and after, and because I've always avoided marriage you might think I am inexperienced in dealing with the female mind.'

'What are you getting at, Henry?'

'I have gathered that you are going to marry the delectable Mrs Brody for her money. I find it strange that with half the males in London, rich and poor alike, available to her, she chose you. You are not in love with her nor she with you. So, what is in it for her? What is it that she wants?'

'Security for her and her daughter. She has also become particularly fond of Sophie and Abigail, and I can't tell you what that means to me. She has also fallen in love with Laurel Court.'

'She said that?'

Lucas grinned. 'She didn't have to. You should have seen her face when she saw it for the first time. She was smitten.'

'It's a fine place, there's no denying that.' Henry's

eyes narrowed as he regarded his friend. 'You really are going to marry her aren't you, Lucas?'

He nodded and a soft smile curved his lips as he perched his hips on the edge of his desk in a relaxed pose. 'Actually she's quite beautiful and seems very young to have a five-year-old daughter. Like I said, she adores children, which I find quite endearing. I want a son, Henry, an heir to my estate,' he said, making no attempt to conceal the yearning in his voice. 'I intend to work damned hard rebuilding it and I want to see it passed on to the next generation.'

From the moment Henry had heard the rumour that Lucas was to marry Eve Brody, he had been both shocked and surprised—not unpleasantly so, since he considered marriage might be just what Lucas needed at this time. Ever since his divorce from Maxine, Henry had tried from time to time to broach the subject of remarriage, but Lucas was not a man to listen or be reasoned with when in one of his infamous adverse moods—which was most of the time.

'I believe you. You've got yourself a treasure in Mrs Brody—a pile of money and a bride and a mother for your children into the bargain.'

It was the evening of the ball when Lucas and Eve would appear for the first time in public as a betrothed couple. The announcement in the papers had appeared that morning, causing great excitement in the house. Eve had explained to Estelle as best she could that she was going to be married, but the excited little girl was more interested in knowing Sophie and Abigail were to be her stepsisters than in her mother's impending marriage to the formidable Lord Stainton.

Undecided about what to wear, Eve searched through her wardrobe, surveying her fashionable gowns she'd had made on her arrival in London with Beth.

Beth considered them with an experienced, appreciative eye. 'I have to say you have exquisite taste, Eve. You haven't worn any of these, have you?'

'Until now I've had no occasion to wear them.'

'Well, now you have. Let me see,' Beth murmured thoughtfully, completely absorbed in her task of selecting Eve a suitable dress to wear for what Beth considered to be the most important occasion in her friend's life. She was twenty-three, so it had to be something mature yet simple so as not to detract from her youth and her fair skin, and her hair was of such vibrancy that she needed a colour that would throw it into prominence.

They both agreed to discard the creams and pastel shades, finally deciding on a peacock-blue gown that matched the lustre of Eve's eyes and clung to every curve of her slender body. With only an hour to go before Lucas was due to arrive, Beth and Cassie, the maid who had taken care of all Eve's personal needs since she had come to live in the Seagrove residence, began making Eve look presentable.

The high-waisted dress of shot silk had a scooped bodice and the hem was delicately embroidered in a deeper shade of blue and gold thread. When Cassie produced a petticoat, Beth shook her head, determined not to spoil the shape of Eve's figure and the outline of her long slender legs.

Eve considered this to be rather daring, feeling only half-dressed, but Beth obviously knew what she was about so she made no comment.

Reading her thoughts and sensing her unease, Beth smiled. 'There's no shame in showing your beauty, Eve,' she said, standing back and admiring her handiwork. With Cassie's assistance she had managed to transform a beautiful young woman into a magnificent goddess. Her appearance could not be faulted. The dress complimented her lustrous hair, which was caught up at the crown in a mass of thick, glossy curls. A small and elegant gold-feathered headdress, satin slippers and elbow-length gloves which matched her dress completed the effect.

'There, are you not pleased with the way you look, Eve?' Beth asked, standing her before the cheval mirror.

Checking her reflection, Eve's lips parted in pleasure and disbelief. She was unable to believe the transformation. 'You've performed miracles, Beth—you, too, Cassie. I can't believe it's me.'

'Nonsense, you were beautiful to start with, now you look spectacular. You will eclipse every other woman present,' Beth teased gently. 'When you arrive at the ball on Lord Stainton's arm, all heads will turn and conversation cease—and you will be the envy of every female who has ever coveted your betrothed.'

But it wasn't the other women Beth was concerned about. It was Lord Stainton, and she hoped to see if Eve, in all her finery, would have any noticeable effect on the way he looked at her.

From the window in the hall, Beth watched Lord Stainton's shiny black carriage draw up in front of the house. Immediately she went to inform Eve and was surprised to see her coming down the stairs.

'Lord Stainton is here,' Beth announced, her cheeks flushed with excitement.

'I know. I saw him from my bedroom window.' Eve took a deep, fortifying breath, taking the fan

Beth handed to her. 'Wish me luck. I'm going to need it to get through tonight. There will be those members of society who will think Lucas is marrying beneath him. But I refuse to let it get to me. It doesn't matter what people think. What matters is that Lucas and I will be married and the children will be in a stable and loving environment.'

'Of course they will and you will be just fine. How I wish we had been invited to watch you make your entrance. The whole of London will be humming with talk of your engagement by now and dying to set eyes on the woman who has managed to snare Lord Stainton.'

'Snare being the appropriate word, Beth, because that's precisely what I have done. As for the gossip—it will be short lived when something else occurs to pique their interest.'

Beth's delighted enthusiasm, which had been increasing all day, was so contagious that Eve couldn't help smiling as she walked towards the door, nor could she suppress the unexplainable joy that surged through her when Lucas was admitted. His flowing crimson-lined evening cloak rested lightly on his shoulders, and his black evening clothes beneath matched his hair and contrasted sharply with his snowy frilled shirt and accentuated the long, lean lines of his body.

Eve noticed again how incredibly piercing his eyes

were. It was impossible not to respond to this man—his masculine magnetism dominated the scene.

Lucas looked automatically in Eve's direction, and what he saw caught his breath. The exotic creature in a peacock silk gown and shining hair and high, delicately moulded cheekbones, generous lips and a perfect nose and a warm glow in her deep blue eyes, looked provocative and sensual and he could not take his eyes off her. He could well imagine the *ton*'s reaction when she appeared at Lord Gradwell's ball and he introduced her as his betrothed.

From where she stood, Beth felt a surge of relief and gladness as she observed Lord Stainton's expression. His face was soft as he gazed at Eve, the softness melting away the defiance, the stubbornness and the headstrong, overbearing determination to do and to shape everything to Lucas Stainton's liking. Despite the businesslike arrangement of their marriage, these two had much in common. Hopefully it would work out well for them both.

Without taking his eyes off her face, Lucas took her gloved hands in his own, his eyes gently appraising. 'You look beautiful, Eve,' he said, his voice low.

Eve favoured him with an eye-teasing, twinkling appraisal of her own. 'You look rather splendid yourself, my lord.'

Turning to Beth, Lucas inclined his head and

held out his hand to William, who emerged from his study to greet him. They exchanged pleasantries, William and Beth offering their congratulations on their betrothal.

Lucas turned to Eve, placing her gold satin cape that Beth had handed to him over her shoulders. 'Are you ready to leave?'

Eve nodded, then, with solicitous care, he ushered her out to the waiting coach. Caught in the spell of his compelling light blue eyes as he handed her inside, Eve yielded to the temptation to let herself enjoy the evening, which had the promise of enchantment.

When the door had closed, Beth gave a wistful sigh. William placed an arm around her shoulders and drew her close, affectionately placing a light kiss on her cheek.

'Stop worrying about her. She knows what she's doing, and I am confident that she's in good hands.'

'I know you're right, William. I'm just worried that she might lose her heart to Lord Stainton and that she will be deeply hurt in the process.'

'Whatever happens, Beth, it's for them to sort out. Eve is a grown woman who knows her own mind. It is not for us to interfere.'

Eve sat back and relaxed as the carriage lurched into motion. The setting sun trailed its golden hues across the roofs and trees and gave off a warm glow, softly illuminating Lucas's handsome face and making her aware of his casual gaze.

'How is Alice?' she asked. 'Has she settled into the nursery?'

He nodded. 'Without any difficulty—and thriving. Sophie and Abigail adore her.'

'Does she resemble her mother in any way?' Eve dared to ask.

He shook his head, his expression hardening. 'She's more like Stephen.'

'I—do so look forward to seeing the children again. I have made enquiries for a young woman to help Miss Lacy in the nursery. One of Beth's chambermaids has a sister who would like to be considered for the position. Her name is Miriam Clegg. She has worked as a nursemaid, so she is no stranger to children.'

'Then I shall leave it to you. If you think she is suitable, then you can employ her.'

Content to be in his company, Eve hardly noticed when he left his seat to sit beside her. When she turned her head and looked at him, he caught her brief, anxious glance and smiled.

'I have something for you. I would like you to have it before we reach Gradwell House.'

In his hand he held a black velvet box. Opening the clasp, he withdrew a diamond necklace, with one large single-drop diamond in the centre. It was the most beautiful necklace Eve had ever seen. Dangling it through his fingers, he held it up so that it caught the light.

'Do you like this?'

'It is very beautiful.'

'Turn around.'

'What?'

'I said turn around and I will put it on. This necklace is my engagement present to my future wife—to seal our bargain.' Noting how her features stiffened, he smiled apologetically. 'Our betrothal,' he corrected. 'Now turn around.'

Wordlessly Eve turned her back to him and pulled down the neck of her cape. His long fingers on her nape sent tiny tremors down her spine as he fastened the diamond clasp. The single diamond settled just above the creamy flesh swelling invitingly above the low bodice of her gown, feeling cool against her skin. Turning back to him, she fingered the jewel and smiled awkwardly.

'Thank you, Lucas. I've never seen a necklace quite as beautiful.'

'It is a family heirloom,' he explained. 'The necklace was my mother's and my grandmother's before that.'

Eve stared at him, uneasy about receiving a gift that must have sentimental and family value. 'Then you should not have given it to me. I cannot accept it. It should be given to—'

'My wife.'

'I was about to say your eldest daughter, Sophie, when she is of age.'

'Do not deprive me of the pleasure of giving you gifts, Eve. There are other heirlooms to be handed down to both Sophie and Abigail—and it is you they have to thank that they haven't had to be sold to pay my brother's creditors. I want you to have this particular necklace,' he said, lowering his eyes to the single-drop diamond, and Eve was deeply touched that he thought her worthy of such a priceless gift on so short an acquaintance.

'Then what can I say?'

Lucas smiled lazily, having the perfect answer, for with her beautiful face turned towards him, the sweet scent of her and the sensation of her alluring body next to his acted on him like a powerful aphrodisiac. Later, on reflection, he was uncertain what happened next. All he knew was that he desperately wanted to hold her, to feel her lips on his. It never occurred to him to ask himself if this was prudent.

'You—could thank me with a kiss,' he suggested softly.

Her eyebrows rose a fraction and her lips twitched with nervous humour. 'A kiss? Lucas, it seems I must remind you of our arrangement, which we both agreed to and which I hoped you would properly observe, and yet here you are trying to use your subsequent gift to seduce me.'

The expression in his eyes changed for a heartbeat, then darkened again. 'You are to be my wife.' His voice was soft, though his smile was knowingly chiding. Reaching out, he touched her cheek in a careless, intimate gesture, unaware of the inner turmoil his sudden request had brought. 'It is not so unusual for two people who have just become betrothed to seal their pact with a kiss—especially when the groom to be has just presented his bride-to-be with a beautiful diamond necklace.'

Only for a moment did Eve hesitate, a moment in which she recalled the brutal kisses Andrew had forced on her, but for some strange reason she didn't feel any revulsion at all with Lucas. 'Very well, a kiss in exchange for a necklace.'

As she leaned towards him, her eyes focused on his mouth, on his sensuous and slightly parted lips. A curious sharp thrill ran through her as the force to her senses seemed to ignite. He was watching her, silently challenging, his eyes alert above the faintly smiling mouth, and she promptly forgot her reasons for marrying him.

She shook herself, willing herself not to give in so easily to the pull of his seduction and lean, hard body. Self-consciously she pressed a kiss on his smooth, freshly shaven cheek, the smell of his cologne sharp and pleasant. Sitting back, she looked at his scowling countenance.

Tilting her head to one side, coquettishly teasing, she asked, 'What's wrong? Wasn't that what you're used to?'

'Your kiss was pathetic, Mrs Brody,' he reproached, his gaze on her mouth. 'I'm sure you can do better than that.' He ran his thumb along her lips, the touch warm and soft, and Eve stopped breathing in anticipation and fear of the kiss she knew he would give her.

'What are you doing?' she whispered, seeing something primitive and dangerous flare in his eyes. Her voice was unsteady and she wondered if he could hear her heart beating with trepidation.

'I'm going to kiss you as you should be kissed,' he answered, placing his hands on either side of her face. 'And, please, no protests,' he murmured as he felt her try to draw away from him.

Before Eve knew what was happening he had pulled her close and taken her lips with sudden, demanding insistence in a hot, hard kiss that stunned her into frightened immobility. She tried to break free, but his strong hands held her fast, and before she knew what was happening, heat ran down her spine, warming her in delicious places she was certain she could not tell him about.

It was a hot, deep, plundering kiss and he kissed her with a sure expertise, his lips moving on hers with hungry ardour. Eve was powerless to resist and she found herself wondering whether other women felt so intoxicated, so overwhelmed by his attentions. Dear Lord, let them reach their destination soon, otherwise she didn't care to think what liberties he might take with her on the carriage seat.

It was one thing to be attracted to the man she had proposed to and insist on a temporary arrangement of abstinence—to admit she was attracted to him would be as good as announcing that the arrangement they had made was null and void and allow him free rein to do just as he pleased, which was unthinkable to her. A kiss was one thing, but anything of a more intimate nature she could only think of with abhorrence at this present time.

After what seemed like an eternity, Lucas relinquished her lips. Drawing a long, audible breath, he sat back against the upholstery. Soft and flushed and with shining eyes, Eve stared at him.

'I apologise,' he murmured. 'I should not have done that. It was a mistake.'

'One you regret?'

'Not in the slightest. And you?'

She shook her head. 'No, but our arrangement still stands. The kiss was in payment for this beautiful necklace,' she said, gently fingering the shining jewels, 'and nothing more. Besides, I was in no danger of being seduced,' she said assuredly.

Lazy mockery lit his eyes. 'And you are sure about that, are you?'

Eve wasn't at all sure and she tried desperately to control her raging emotions and match his casual mood. 'Absolutely.'

'Then I suggest you remove that appealing look from your eyes and move away from me before I am tempted to show you how wrong you are.'

Eve slid farther away from him and glanced out of the window. She smiled, seeing they were approaching Piccadilly. 'I'm afraid not. We're almost there.'

His mouth curved in a wicked smile. 'I could instruct Shepherd to drive on by.'

'I don't think so. Think how disappointed the *ton* would be if we failed to appear.'

'At least it would give them something to gossip about.'

He sighed and relaxed into the corner of the carriage. His eyes moved over her with unhidden masculine appreciation. Pride and ownership were evident in his possessive gaze and Eve's stomach clenched. He had never looked at her like this before—as if she were some tasty tit-bit he was planning to devour at his leisure.

'You know, Eve, you have the most disconcerting ability to look and act like a termagant one moment and an incredibly alluring and vulnerable young woman the next.'

'Thank you,' she said uncertainly. 'At least I think so. Was that meant to be a compliment?'

'It was,' he assured her. 'But perhaps it did not come out as I intended. I shall be more careful the next time.'

Eve was touched by his indication that he intended to try to change to please her, but she doubted his decision to do so would outlast the night.

In no time at all their equipage joined a steady stream of dignified carriages disposing only the cream of London society at the splendid portals of Lord Gradwell's mansion. The evening light was suffused evenly with gold and peach and pale blue, the trees dark splashes of colour. Eve sat forward in the seat, immediately tense and nervous. Lucas caught her brief, anxious glance and reached out to take hold of her hand.

'Don't be nervous. You'll likely set them all agog,' he said softly.

A smile wavered on her lips. 'I sincerely hope not. I'm not one for parading myself. I hope to remain as inconspicuous as possible—preferably in a corner and behind curtains.' He laughed softly and she watched as he brought her fingers to his lips to kiss their tips slowly. Even though she was wearing gloves the gentleness of his gesture did strange things to her heart and stirred a bittersweet yearning which she instantly quenched. His gaze softly caressed the delicate visage.

'That will never do. I think we'd better go in before I really do decide to forgo the ball and instruct Shepherd to drive on by.'

Eve waited as he stepped lightly to the ground, then he turned back, offering up a hand. Though any contact with him sent the blood racing through her veins, she accepted his assistance to the door of the mansion. Within the large and impressive hall, he removed his cloak and drew the cape from her shoulders, handing them to a footman. Taking her hand, Lucas led her in the direction of the ballroom. Long French windows were thrown open to the evening air and spacious gardens, where small lights had been hung and twinkled in the trees.

In the entrance the major-domo stepped ahead of them and decorously announced them. Two hundred men and women dressed in silks and satins and with jewels glittering in the light of the chandeliers turned to look. There had been much talk of Lord Stainton's betrothal and speculation about his intended. Quizzing glasses were raised by guests anxious to appease their curiosity about this woman who had been in his employ and managed to capture the cool, cynical and unapproachable Lord Stainton, and curiosity was matched by envy from the women and open admiration from the men.

Eve saw a sea of faces. She wondered if it was her imagination or did the babble of conversation from the guests already assembled in the huge white-and-gold ballroom really go quiet as she appeared on Lucas's arm? Lucas allowed himself a look of approval at her, his eyes lingering on the auburn curls and lovely features. All the other women paled into insipidness beside her vivid beauty and vitality.

Keeping her proudly and protectively by his side, Lucas strolled nonchalantly into their midst. Eve noted with amusement the number of women that were following his every move, and she couldn't blame them. With his thick black hair, piercing light blue eyes, and tall, athletic physique, Lucas Stainton was magnificent.

Aware of the tension in Eve's body, Lucas bowed his head to her. 'They are all dying of curiosity. Word of our betrothal has spread, as I knew it would. The first rule of social survival at these events is to always present a calm and united front, so smile,' he murmured, 'and enjoy yourself.'

'That's easier said than done,' Eve murmured, but in keeping with that rule, she smiled at him as if there were nothing in the least extraordinary about her arriving conspicuously on the arm of the elusive, devilishly handsome Lucas Stainton, a man who treated her with the possessive familiarity of his betrothed. 'Between us we should be able to put on a show for them.'

Chapter Seven

Every neck in the ballroom craned to see Eve, tall, proud and very lovely, walk beside Lucas. The folds of her gown clung to her slender body, down to her exquisite slippered feet, and her necklace gleamed with prisms of sparkling light.

Impressed and amused by Lucas's supreme indifference to the excited curiosity their appearance was generating, Eve watched as he bowed to acknowledge friends and acquaintances, introducing her to what seemed like hundreds of people. An admiring coterie of young bucks gathered round her, and half-heartedly she wrote their names on her dance card, recognising those who had left their calling card at Berkeley Street when she had come to England in the hope that she would accept their suit.

Lord Gradwell, a widower who seemed in no haste to remarry, was a middle-aged, imposing man with a relaxed congeniality that came from leading a privileged lifestyle and being descended from an illustrious blood line. His parties and balls were always popular and informal, with people clamouring to be invited.

Taking two glasses of sparkling champagne from the tray of a hovering footman, Lucas handed one to Eve, clinking his glass to hers in a toast.

'To the future, Eve.'

For the benefit of their audience she gave him a dazzling smile. 'To the future,' she murmured, taking a hasty swallow, aware that her hand was shaking slightly. As she met his gaze she thought back to the kiss he had given her. She should never have let that happen. What a foolish, uncharacteristic, impulsive thing for her to do. But it had been such a wonderful kiss—awkward for her as she came into close contact with another man after five years. His mouth had covered hers with casual expertise and increasing demand, and when he had raised his head, ending the kiss, he had stared into her eyes with an unspoken promise of seduction.

Eve's cheeks reddened with embarrassed heat and without warning she knew a moment of blind panic. Somewhere in her mind a voice cried out that she was making a dreadful mistake and that what she was doing was madness, committing herself for the rest of her life to a man she did not love, a man who had told her in no uncertain terms that he didn't want to be loved, that he had no love to give, that he didn't need her and never would.

This was the beginning, and after they had said their vows, there would be no turning back. Lucas said something to her and she looked at him, meeting his gaze, and she wondered if he felt as she did, a sense of being caught up in an implacable destiny, that whatever the future held, they had to endure it together for the rest of their lives.

'I'm sorry, Lucas, I wasn't listening. What did you say?'

'That you look exquisite and are by far the most beautiful woman here tonight.' His eyes flicked about the room, taking note of the men who were eyeing her. He guessed their thoughts were not so different from his own. Decorously he presented his arm. 'Come, people are staring, and I would have this dance before I find you swept away by some overzealous swain.'

He led her forward on his arm and the guests parted to let them through as the musicians struck up a waltz.

Caught up in his arms, that was the moment the chill in Eve's heart and her doubts disappeared and the dance passed in a euphoric dream. She glanced up at Lucas's disciplined, classical face, her features soft and warm with gratitude, and the light blue eyes regarding her from beneath half-lowered lids seemed preoccupied and thoughtful.

'Has anyone ever told you that you are rather gallant and kind hearted?' she said, feeling quite reckless after her fortifying glass of champagne.

'Certainly not,' he replied, pretending offence. 'The general consensus is that I am cold, heartless and ruthless—in fact, I do recall on one occasion a certain lady taking me to task in my own home and accusing me of being an arrogant, inconsiderate, puffed-up lord—oh, and that I have the manners of a barbarian.'

Eve's reply was an irrepressible giggle, knowing full well that she was the lady he was referring to, but pretending ignorance. 'Why, I am aghast at the injustice of that. It is clear to me that you must be the most maligned, misjudged and misunderstood gentleman alive.' The deep blue eyes flashed with puckish humour, and the barest hint of a smile curved her lips to mock him. 'How could anyone accuse you of being anything other than kind, considerate and—sweet?'

He looked stung while trying to bite back a smile. 'Sweet? Sweet is one thing I am not. Ruthless and arrogant, not forgetting the barbarian bit, I can live with—but sweet? Never in a thousand years,' he said, sweeping her across the room in a swirling rhythm that dazzled her and made other couples seem clumsy in comparison.

One only had to look at them to see that they were in accord. In fact, it gave rise to considerable amusement when the cream of fashionable society beheld the formerly aloof, austere Lucas Stainton smiling almost affectionately at his betrothed as he waltzed her around the room.

Aware of the attention they were attracting, Lucas smiled down at Eve's face upturned to his. 'You do realise that the announcement of our betrothal will bring forth invitations from all and sundry, don't you, Eve?'

'It will?'

'Absolutely, so prepare yourself to be invaded. Tomorrow morning the Seagrove household and my own will be awash with calling cards and invitations to this and that.'

Eve wrinkled her nose. 'One of the most dispiriting aspects of my introduction to London society was that I found it an ordeal. The Season that excites so many people, to me resembles an obstacle race of so many events that, to respect the custom, they must be got through and must be dreadfully arduous to the participants. Personally I have found some of the events excruciating and a dreadful bore.'

'New York isn't so much different in the upper echelons of society. Your father must have moved in such circles.'

'Yes, he did and I accompanied him on occasion, but on the whole we lived quietly. Before I came to England I must confess that I tried to familiarise myself with everything English by immersing myself in a study of your newspapers in order that I might talk about current affairs and British politics—with William being attached to the Foreign Office I thought it inevitable that I would meet politicians, you see.'

'And have you? Met many politicians, I mean.'

'Some, and all they seem to want to talk about is America. I even spent hours poring over whatever I could find about the English peerage in an attempt to familiarise myself with the aristocracy, but I found it so complicated and confusing that in the end I gave up.'

Transfixed, Lucas stared down at her sagely, strangely moved as he listened to her confession of how she had tried to learn about everything English before leaving America. 'That was a very wise thing to do, since the English aristocracy is confusing to even the best people—even to the aristocracy.'

'Even you?' she asked, gazing into his unfathomable light blue eyes, seeing the cynicism lurking in their depths.

'Even me.'

'Thank goodness. Then we shall make a pact never to discuss that particular topic when we are wed.'

His eyes gleamed with amusement. 'I promise I shall make a note of it,' he said laughingly, 'and the subject will never pass my lips.'

They spent the rest of the dance talking about anything and everything, and for his part Lucas confirmed what he already suspected about Eve—she was extremely well read, intelligent and witty, and yet there was a naïvety about her that he found appealing.

The waltz ended all too soon and Lucas was about to take her on to the floor for the next dance when an elaborately attired young dandy by the name of Sir John Forsyth appeared and bowed before her.

'Excuse me, Lord Stainton, but this is my dance, I believe,' and before Lucas could object Eve had been whisked away from him.

Momentarily thwarted, leaning his shoulder against a pillar, Lucas was content to watch her swirling about the floor in a lively country dance. Beside him Henry Channing observed him with amusement.

'Your future bride is proving to be a popular distraction, Lucas. Congratulations, by the way. I read it in the *Times* in case you're wondering.'

'Nothing like making it official, Henry,' Lucas replied drily, without taking his eyes off Eve.

'And you have come to Lord Gradwell's ball to celebrate.'

Lucas smiled sardonically. 'Marriage is not high on

my list of reasons to celebrate. You should know that.' He frowned with disapproval when the dance ended and Eve remained on the dance floor to partner the same young man in another country dance. 'I'll be damned if she isn't going to dance with Forsyth again. Clearly she is ignorant of the impropriety of dancing with the same gentleman twice.'

'And you are beginning to sound like a jealous beau,' Henry remarked, slanting him an amused look.

Lucas ignored him.

When Eve finally left the dance floor, seeking sanctuary to catch her breath, she fled to the designated ladies' room and closed the door. After freshening up and checking her appearance in the mirror, satisfied that she looked poised and relaxed, she was about to leave when she heard two women in the room adjacent.

'Who would have thought Lord Stainton would be here tonight,' one voice remarked, 'and just as handsome as ever, don't you agree?'

Eve paused. She hated eavesdropping, but she felt compelled to wait to hear what would come next.

'He certainly is. Pity he's penniless though. I haven't seen anything cause quite a stir as his betrothal since his scandalous divorce from Maxine. No one thought Lord Stainton would ever marry again and I was positively shocked when

Mama read it out of the *Times* this morning—and to an American of all people, who has been nursemaid to his children. Of course Mama has always said he never got over Maxine.'

'Then he shouldn't have divorced her. Poor Maxine. He made her look an utter fool. The humiliation she suffered was quite dreadful. She never thought he would go through with the divorce.'

'What could he do? Continue turning a blind eye to her affairs? I have no sympathy for her—despite what your mama says. Lord Stainton's too proud to be branded a cuckold.'

'Nevertheless, the divorce was granted pretty quickly—often it can take years.'

'That's because Maxine's adultery was proven without any difficulty and he refused to bring charges against his own brother. He was the innocent party and there is no reason why he can't remarry.'

'I suppose not, and the American woman is stunning, don't you think, despite her unfashionable red hair?'

'Perhaps next week red hair will be all the rage. Fashions come and go. She's very rich, too, by all accounts—although what she was doing caring for his children is a mystery, but I'd wager her money is what attracted him to her.'

'I'm sure you're right, although there was no mistaking the gleam in his eye when he looked at her—and the look he gave Sir John Forsyth when she stayed on the floor to dance another dance with him was hot enough to reduce him to a cinder. I think Maxine has yet to meet her. It will be interesting to see what happens when she arrives with Sir Alfred. Fireworks, I shouldn't wonder.'

'They are invited?'

'Of course, but you know what Maxine's like—always one to make a grand entrance. It wouldn't surprise me in the slightest if she tries to get her husband back.'

Having heard quite enough, with burning cheeks Eve quietly opened the door and went out, her spirits slightly dampened by what she'd heard. Lucas was standing on the edge of the dance floor close to the open doors leading on to the terrace. Crossing towards him, she was waylaid by Henry Channing, whom she remembered from Lady Ellesmere's party. Hearing her name, she spun round.

'Have you decided to conquer the *ton* as you have my temperamental friend, Mrs Brody?'

Eve laughed into his boyishly handsome face. 'Hardly that. I think it's virtually impossible for anyone to conquer Lucas. I'm happy to meet you again, sir—in more favourable circumstances, I hasten to add. Have you just arrived?'

He nodded. 'A little while ago. However, I have just heard that a particular lady Lucas will be far from pleased to see has just this moment arrived.' He chuckled softly. 'I think Lord Gradwell only invited them both to cause mischief.'

'Oh? What lady?' Recalling the conversation she had just overheard, Eve paled. 'His wife?'

'His former wife, and, yes, I'm afraid so, and I have a feeling that she's going to be difficult to deal with as usual.'

Together they turned and faced the door.

Maxine made her late and daring entrance. A small, confident woman, she glided into the room, her arm possessively looped through that of the lacklustre Sir Alfred Hutton. All eyes automatically turned in her direction. A gown of the sheerest emerald green silk enveloped her voluptuous body, flowing about her and revealing more than a hint of her cleavage. She sailed forth, very much aware of the stir she had created and obviously enjoying it. Eve glanced at Lucas. If he was at all embarrassed by her arrival, he gave no sign of it.

Maxine's eyes latched on to her former husband immediately and her eyes narrowed. Like everyone else in London she had read about his betrothal to an American heiress and her anger towards him had seethed to great heights. That Lucas would marry again was not what she had expected. Not at all. She moved towards him, swaying slightly, with an uneasy-looking Sir Alfred trailing in her wake.

'Well, well, Lucas. Here we are.'

Lucas stiffened and looked at her, an ironic twist to his finely chiselled lips in an otherwise cold face. 'Maxine.' His eyes passed over her contemptuously. 'You've been drinking.' Turning his back on her, he stepped out on to the terrace, away from prying, inquisitive eyes and scandal-mongering tongues.

Maxine smiled thinly and followed him. 'So I have, and I intend to drink some more before I leave.'

Eve watched, seeing a woman whose eyes were turned up to Lucas. She was an incredibly beautiful blonde, with diamonds twined in and out of her shining curls. That woman had been his wife, had known him intimately and borne him two children. Her heart sank.

'So, that is Maxine.'

'I'm afraid so,' Henry confirmed.

'They make a striking couple.'

'Once, perhaps, but that's in the past.'

'Is it?' Eve murmured, her eyes clouding over as she recalled one of the women in the retiring room saying that Maxine might try to get him back. She felt a stab of painful jealousy as she watched them together. But, she reminded herself, Lucas had divorced Maxine and he was going to marry her. 'There is no denying that she is very beautiful.'

Henry's eyebrows rose in amused mockery. 'In Maxine's case, beauty really is only skin deep. If you don't mind, I think I'd best intervene and try to alleviate a situation that could become embarrassing to all concerned.'

Curious to meet the woman whose children would very soon become her stepchildren, Eve followed him. As she approached she was subjected to a searching scrutiny by Lucas's former wife, her cold eyes set hard and uncompromising. She stood beside Lucas. He was a proud man whose marriage had been full of acrimony. She knew how angry he felt towards Maxine, and she could see how he restrained himself with great difficulty from losing his temper completely.

'And you must be Mrs Brody,' Maxine remarked without bothering to wait for Lucas to introduce them. Her pale eyes did an insolent sweep of her rival, and she said, as if Eve didn't exist, 'Why, Lucas, the lady looks positively divine—and I expect money increases her desirability. She's extremely wealthy by all accounts. Her father left her a large fortune—is that correct, Mrs Brody?'

Maxine's eyes took on a new gleam. Eve was well acquainted with people, men and women, whose only pretence of friendship was the lure of her wealth and she recognised the cold avaricious greed in Maxine's eyes. 'He might have,' she replied, equally as cold as the woman she was addressing. 'That's for me to know and everyone else to speculate on.' She smiled. 'Although I do manage a few creature comforts.'

Maxine's eyes narrowed and her lips curled. 'You're sharp, Mrs Brody, but would you be sharp enough, I wonder, to hold a man like Lucas without your money.'

'That's enough,' Lucas snapped, his fists clenched tight as he took a step towards her.

Eve placed a restraining hand on his arm. 'No, Lucas. Let her have her say.' She took a deep breath, but her eyes did not flinch as they held Lady Irvine's. 'Let me assure you, Lady Maxine, that I do have other assets that are attractive. It is Lady Maxine, isn't it? I believe you reverted to your maiden name on your divorce.'

Maxine made no attempt to hide the cool smirk in her smile. 'Naturally.' Her gaze shifted to Lucas. 'One Lady Lucas Stainton is enough for anyone. I'm really surprised, Lucas. Who would have thought that you would tie yourself to an American?'

He looked at her, his eyes hard as his face moved from grimness to intense anger. 'You are making a spectacle of yourself, Maxine, as well as being most indiscreet and immature and extremely rude to Mrs Brody. Leave before any fresh scandal blows up. I had hoped we'd done with all that.'

Maxine glared at him from two stormy eyes. 'I might remind you, Lucas, that you do not order me to do anything any more—not now, not ever. You know what it is I want from you and I will give you no respite until I get it.'

Eve's glance shifted to Lucas and she saw that his expression had become positively savage. 'Go to hell, Maxine.'

'Then I shall continue pestering you. Don't think I won't. I told you on our divorce that I would not go quietly.'

'I made adequate restitution to you in the divorce settlement. If you have squandered it, then that is your misfortune. I am no longer under any legal obligation to hold myself responsible for what you do.'

'Legally, maybe not, but what of your moral duty? That is another matter entirely.'

'Because of the children? They are nothing but bargaining tools to you Maxine—all three of them.'

Maxine was thrown off guard and she looked in surprise, somewhat uneasy. 'Three? You speak as though you are already familiar with Stephen's daughter, Lucas.'

'She is in the nursery with Sophie and Abigail. I rescued her from a filthy hovel in St Giles.' He glared at her with absolute contempt. 'You might just as well have thrown her on the dung heap.'

'So you did your snooping, Lucas, and came up trumps. I should have known you wouldn't rest until you found her.'

'It wasn't difficult.'

'I saw your daughter,' Eve said. 'I was with Lucas when we found her—malnourished and riddled with lice. You are her mother. Don't you care?'

Maxine gave her a hard stare. 'No, Mrs Brody, quite frankly I don't. I didn't have the coin to keep her—and don't embarrass yourself by telling me you would have been more than happy to bear the expense, Lucas. You're penniless—remember. You haven't two halfpennies to rub together.' She turned her sneering face on Eve. 'So what do you do? You marry an American heiress—who, for some curious reason, has been looking after our children. How degrading for her and yet how sensible of you to marry her. Be wary, Mrs Brody. He divorced me. Once he gets his hands on your money, he might dispose of you in the same way.'

Eve hastened to allay the possibility. 'I shall, of course, release Lucas to whatever decision he might make. There is time for him to reconsider. But when we are married, he will never divorce me. I promise you that.'

'I know how difficult this is for you both,' Henry said, 'but you would do well to remember that you are Lord Gradwell's guests and people are watching. Besides, we are not here to indulge in the rights and wrongs of your first marriage, but to celebrate the imminence of your second, Lucas.'

Eve was impressed by Henry's intensity, by his knowledge of the situation, which proved to her how well he knew them both, and led her to wonder how many times he'd had to calm the situation between Lucas and his former wife in the past.

Maxine drew herself up and looked at Henry. 'You always were the peacekeeper, Henry.'

Looking apologetic, extremely uncomfortable and ill at ease beneath the glare of the superior Lord Stainton, Sir Alfred took her arm none too gently. 'Come away and let us take some refreshment, Maxine. Lord Stainton is quite right. You are making a spectacle of yourself,' he chided crossly. 'Nothing can be gained from this.'

She shook his hand off in frustration and glowered at him. 'How would you know, Alfred?'

Glaring from Eve to Lucas, Maxine tossed her head flippantly. 'I have plenty more to say, but for now I will wish you luck, Lucas. It will be interesting to see how you deal with being a kept man, totally dependent on your wife. It will be a whole new experience for you—and not a pleasant one.' Hooking her arm through that of her escort, she sauntered away through the crowd.

The musicians struck up another waltz, at which Lucas, his face dark and tense, turned to Eve and Henry. 'Henry, I would be grateful if you would partner Eve in this dance. I think I'll take a turn about the garden.'

Eve looked at him in alarm. 'But—would you like me to stay, Lucas?'

'No, thank you,' he answered tersely, avoiding her eyes, his body ramrod straight. 'I would appreciate some time by myself.'

'Very well. If you're sure.' She smiled at Henry. 'Come along, Mr Channing. Show me how well you waltz.'

He glanced at Lucas concernedly and then, thinking some time to himself was what he needed, he offered Eve his arm, smiling broadly. 'It will be my pleasure. I'm sorry about that unpleasant scene, Eve—I may call you Eve?'

'Of course you may. I'd like you to.'

'And you must call me Henry.'

They danced in silence for a while before Henry spoke again. 'What do you think of him, Eve? He's not the easiest man to get close to.'

Her smile became nervous. 'He's—better for knowing, I think,' she began with caution, 'and guarded about what he thinks and does.'

'And do you find him handsome?'

Eve gave an astonished laugh. 'He is extremely attractive. From the looks I've seen cast his way tonight, I'm not the only woman who thinks so.'

'It's always been the same. Wherever he goes,

without opening his mouth he draws attention to himself. You know, Eve, Lucas is a fine man—one of the finest. Before this he was a man most envied—always one to take risks—a gambler if you like—something I would never dare do. But it was his own money he gambled with on investments—some might say they were unsound, but he was always lucky.'

'Some would say far-seeing,' Eve said, a flash of pride in the man she was to marry putting a gleam in her eyes.

'This business with Maxine set him back considerably, but he'll get to where he was. I'm certain of that. He isn't the sort to stay down. He'll put the bad times behind him and get on with it. I admire him for that.'

'He has a good friend in you, Henry.'

'We have been friends for a long time, Lucas and I. He has tremendous strength of mind and will. I cannot match him in that, and he rarely meets with opposition from anyone.'

'Only Maxine,' Eve murmured quietly.

'Yes, only Maxine,' he agreed. 'She hurt him cruelly when she walked out without a word, leaving Lucas alone with the children. She made no attempt to hide the fact that she did not love her children. They were unwanted and a trial to her since the day they were born. Sometimes it's the case that when a woman leaves her husband she has no place in society, no future—Maxine is determined she will not be ousted. Lucas still finds that hideous affair between Stephen and Maxine difficult and painful, and it turned him irrevocably against marriage—which is why I was so surprised when I found out he was to marry you.'

Her curiosity won over her desire not to pry. 'What was he like, his brother?'

'Oddly enough, I liked Stephen—but Lucas must be the one to tell you about that. It was a nasty business and it's not for me to divulge matters of a personal nature Lucas might not want to resurrect.' A smile flickered across his face. 'But I believe he will tell you some day. He told me of the circumstances that brought you together, Eve. I hope you don't mind.'

'No, of course not. I hope you don't disapprove, Henry.'

A smile drew Henry's firm lips apart as he expertly danced her away from a knot of couples to a less crowded part of the floor. 'If my humble approval can be of any comfort to you, Eve, I give it to you gladly.'

It was Eve's turn to smile. She knew she would see much of Henry in the future and she was glad. She would always come to an understanding with him. 'Thank you. It means a lot to me—and gives me courage to face an uncertain future knowing that in you I have a friend.'

'Whatever the reasons that brought you and Lucas together, I sincerely hope the two of you will be happy. Lucas deserves to be. He needs to be taught how to love again, and trust, and I think you are beautiful and sensible enough to stand a chance of winning both.'

Unconvinced of this, Eve gave a little ironic smile and said, 'Lucas and I are not marrying for love, Henry. I might even go so far as to say it is a forced marriage on his part, and that the feelings I inspire in him, far from resembling love, rather approach the feeling of anger and even resentment.'

'I think you are beginning to know Lucas and to read his moods. For the time being your position is strong, his is weak, and that is where his resentment lies. But it will not always be like that. I know Lucas. He will rise above it, I promise you.'

'I hope you're right, Henry, otherwise we are going to be horribly unhappy.'

'You must be optimistic. I think your marrying him is a good thing. Now it's a question of your union being a success. Your marriage is convenient to you both, but that does not necessarily mean that affection, tolerance and even love itself will fail to blossom once the deal is done. I would like to offer you some advice.'

'Oh? And what might that be?'

'After the ceremony, get him to return to Laurel Court. He loves that place. He's been working himself into the ground sixteen hours a day for months now, trying to get himself back on top— and he will eventually, I have every faith in that. But some time away from London will do him good.'

'I will bear that in mind, Henry, and thank you for being so open with me.'

'My pleasure.' On a lighter note he grinned down at her upturned face. 'You dance divinely by the way, Mrs Brody,' he said, swirling her round. 'In fact, you dance so well that I shall insist on partnering you in one more dance before we leave.'

When the dance ended Eve returned to Lucas on the terrace, a smile on her face that faded slightly as she beheld the hardness of his taut jaw and the cold glitter in his eyes. Her heart filled with compassion and understanding.

'Lucas? Is something wrong?'

At her soft use of his name, the muscles of his face clenched so tightly a nerve in his cheek began to pulse. 'Wrong?' he repeated cynically. 'The only thing that is wrong is me. Maxine was right.'

'What? Lucas, was it what she said about you

being a kept man, because, if so, please ignore what she said.'

'I can't, Eve,' he ground out. 'That's the trouble.'

Startled, Eve's eyes flew to his, and took new meaning from the steely quality of his dark expression. Her mouth went dry and her heart began to beat in a heavy, terrifying dread as she sensed Lucas had withdrawn from her, as if the closeness they had shared so far tonight had never existed. Of course he was struggling to survive and was lashing out like a cornered animal.

'Are you telling me you won't marry me, because, if so, I do understand.'

'Our reasons for marrying are hardly the reasons on which to build the strong foundations of marriage.'

Eve took a deep breath, not knowing what to say, but she felt the bite of cruel truth in his words.

'God knows I don't want to marry you,' he went on. 'I don't want to marry anyone, but at this time I have no choice.'

'And you hate yourself for it, don't you, Lucas?'

When he looked at her, Eve stepped back in alarm from the unexplained violence glittering in his eyes.

'Yes, I do.'

The dark frown that accompanied his angry reply surprised Eve. She stood back to see his face. Without warning the dark side of his mood had returned, and she was already mourning the parting of the frivolous, capricious Lucas Stainton she had briefly glimpsed.

'Maybe you acted in haste when you agreed to my proposal.'

'No, Eve. I acted in greed.'

'Arguing over semantics will not gain you anything. Do you have to be so proud? This needn't be a disaster. Accept that you need my money. Of course, I could always withdraw my offer,' she said irately and hating herself for saying it.

The betrothal had been made official. The ridicule that would ensue should they retract it would be horrendous; besides, Eve could not forget there were children involved, his children, who had a father, and a mother who didn't want them.

'That is entirely up to you,' he retorted coldly. 'As far as I am concerned the arrangement still stands and I intend to make the best of it. Come. We will not talk of this now. It's neither the time nor place. Let us return to the dancing and try to get through the rest of the evening as best we can.'

Eve allowed him to escort her back inside and on to the floor of swirling couples. Suddenly she felt as though he'd erected a solid wall of rock between them. When she'd proposed marriage, she'd had it all worked out in her mind as to what kind of arrangement their marriage would be, naïvely believing Lucas would be so relieved that he would fall in with her plans, but somewhere between her proposal and their first kiss, she'd discovered she liked being with him, and she had an inbred urge to knock down that wall of rock and delve beneath the rubble and discover the man beneath.

When it was time to leave, Eve was coming out of the retiring room only to find herself confronted by Maxine. Eve was painfully aware of the other woman's close proximity as she stood her ground, determined that Eve would not pass. Eve looked into her face. She was a beautiful woman and carried a certain elegance and charm, but there was a coarseness in her manner and her eyes betrayed the truth of her nature. They were small and calculating, deep and dangerous and ever watchful.

'I see you are leaving, Mrs Brody? I hope it isn't because of something I have said.'

'Not at all, Lady Maxine. Please step out of my way. I don't think we have anything further to say to each other.'

'Of course. Don't let me detain you. Have you decided when the happy event is to take place?'

'Not yet.'

Maxine gave her a long measuring look and then she smiled, a calculating gleam lighting her eyes.

'You know,' she said, tapping Eve's arm with her fan, 'your marriage might just prove to be advantageous.'

'To you?'

'Who else? Lucas treated me very badly.'

Eve looked at her incredulously. 'Whatever happened between you and Lucas has nothing to do with me, but I am of the opinion that he was not to blame. You left him. You humiliated him, and I believe you almost ruined him. He has not done this to you. You have done it to yourself.'

Maxine looked at her. The American woman was too bold to be either threatened or cowed. Maxine's poise wavered before those merciless, bright young eyes.

'You are arrogant, Mrs Brody,' she hissed, beginning to sound erratic and breathing heavily, feeling the effects of the wine she had consumed throughout the evening taking hold of her. 'Don't think that marrying Lucas will be a bed of roses. It will be anything but. Remember that I am speaking from experience—and you must also remember that since you are to be step-mother to my children, I have no intention of letting you forget it.'

Eve's eyes met Maxine's, a silent challenge flared between them. This woman is not going to go away, Eve thought. She will cause trouble if she can. For what seemed like an age Maxine made no move. Instead her smile grew colder, more devious, and then she stepped aside to let Eve pass. Eve walked away, feeling inside the disturbance of something she didn't fully understand, and in the silence that followed, the unpleasant incident lived on in Eve's mind, filling her with the restlessness of many questions.

It was a different journey returning to Berkeley Street to the one coming. Lucas's face was turned away from her, his profile a hard, chiselled mask. His confrontation with Maxine had created a breach between them that might never heal. He was furious and Maxine's cutting remark about him being a kept man had been humiliating and had dented his pride, adding more tension to his already overburdened emotions, and he had turned his resentment on Eve.

It was the early hours when his coachman pulled the spirited bays up before the house. Neither Lucas nor Eve had spoken a word since leaving the ball. Lucas leapt out of the coach and held his hand out to her. She took it and climbed out and stood looking up into his face.

'Thank you for a lovely evening, Lucas. I'll wait until you contact me.'

'Goodnight, Eve. I apologise for that unpleasantness with Maxine.'

She shrugged. 'It wasn't your fault. You weren't

to know she would be there.' Unable to bear the atmosphere between them another moment, she said goodnight and went inside.

Lucas watched her go up the steps and disappear into the house before getting back into the carriage.

Chapter Eight

Six weeks to the day that the arrangement had been struck between Eve and Lucas, they were married. When they had been told of the betrothal—that his lordship was to marry the new nursemaid—the staff at the house in Upper Brook Street were astounded, but, as the shock wore off, highly delighted. Mrs Coombs broke into her much guarded bottle of sherry and insisted everyone raise their glasses in a toast to the couple, declaring that after his lordship's last disastrous marriage, never did she think she would see the happy day when he would marry again.

The morning dawned sunny and warm—a good omen? Eve sincerely hoped so. In the Seagrove house grooming and preparations had taken most of the morning, the ceremony just ten minutes, which was performed before noon at St George's Church in Hanover Square. Both Lucas and Eve had agreed that it was to be a quiet affair without fuss, with just a handful of Lucas's friends and the Seagrove family. Anything more elaborate would be inappropriate under the circumstances.

Despite Eve's efforts to ignore it, her wedding had a distinct aura of unreality and tension. On the brink of a new life, she couldn't understand why her feelings seemed to seesaw between excitement and gloom.

Standing in the open doorway to the church before the ceremony, William smiled at her in an attempt to dispel her serious expression. 'Headache bothering you again, Eve?' he murmured. 'If so, mention it to Beth. She's wonderful with things like that.' He winked teasingly. 'She might even give you one of her powders.'

Knowing William was trying to get her to relax, Eve was grateful. Her mood lightened and she laughed softly. 'Absolutely not. I mean to remain awake and upright when I speak my vows.'

With her hand hooked through the crook of William's arm, Eve walked slowly down the aisle to where Lucas stood before the cleric. Estelle, Sophie and Abigail—all three of them bridesmaids in their lavender dresses and with matching ribbons in their hair and carrying posies of summer flowers, identical to her own—were enthralled by the proceedings and the changes it would bring to their own lives.

Henry was among the guests, waiting to witness this strange union between the American heiress and Lord Stainton—a man she barely knew yet to whom she was still willing to entrust her life and all she possessed. Sarah Lacy, holding a babbling Alice, was dewy eyed with emotion, content in the knowledge that her new mistress would be as happy as she was with her beloved Mark.

Eve noted all this in the last moment as she moved closer to Lucas, looking magnificent in a splendid suit of midnight blue velvet and white neck linen. His tall body and broad shoulders threw a shadow across her path. There was an undeniable aura of forcefulness, of power about him.

He half-turned to look at her so that he might watch her progress towards him. His face was serious and it looked as if it had been sculpted from granite. Eve wasn't to know how he was fighting to control the strong rush of emotion that engulfed him at the sight of her, for, from the top of her shining hair to the hem of her gleaming ivory satin gown embroidered with ivory silk thread, she looked radiant.

However, he felt a certain amount of unease when he met her unwavering speculative gaze. It was as if she were studying the man she had bought and was wondering if she was getting value for money. The thought put a stiffener into his spine and he lifted his head to a lofty angle and squared his shoulders.

And then, incredibly, he found she was smiling at him and his heart and soul felt as though they were being lifted by that smile of astounding beauty. The unease of a moment before melted away. Never had he met a woman like Eve Brody, a woman who was about to give herself and all she possessed to a man she scarcely knew. A man she did not love—a man who did not love her and never would—at least not in the romantic sense.

Taking her place beside Lucas and handing her posy to Estelle, who was trying to look very grown up, for a moment Eve was transported back through time to her marriage to Andrew, when her father had placed her hand into that of the young man who was to disappear so quickly and so tragically from her life. Taking a deep breath, she thrust the memory aside and tried to bring back the smile Lucas had found so incredible, but couldn't. This was a different wedding, a wedding of her instigation. In a few minutes from now she would become Lady Lucas Stainton and there would be no going back.

The cleric was a quiet man and confused by the attitudes of the bride and groom towards each other. He was used to conducting marriage ceremonies, but this was the first he had conducted between a widow and a divorced man, a man who had already promised to love one woman until death and was now about to do the same to another. This marriage was not illegal, but it did not conform to what he as a servant of God approved of.

The cleric faced them, seeming to look through them, but not at them. In sepulchral tones he began reading the words of the marriage ceremony, words that would bind Eve to Lucas for ever and she heard Lucas repeat them in his deep rich voice. He spoke sincerely, as if he truly meant every word. And then he was looking at her, his eyes laying siege to hers, with an indefinable expression, and then he gently but firmly slipped the gold wedding band on her finger, the same finger that, until she had become betrothed to Lucas, had worn Andrew's ring.

When the cleric pronounced them man and wife, Lucas leaned forward to place a light kiss on Eve's lips as a seal to the marriage. Apart from taking her hand occasionally to hand her in and out of the carriage when they attended some event and to place the wedding band on her finger, it was the first physical contact there had been between them since he had kissed her on their engagement. His mouth was gentle on hers, as befitted the formal occasion in front of witnesses. The time for passion between these two would not come just yet.

His duty done, the cleric mumbled congratulations and watched the bride and groom depart in the waiting carriage to the groom's house for the wedding breakfast.

At the house Henry bent and kissed Eve's cheek. 'Congratulations, Eve, and to you too, Lucas. I sincerely hope you will be happy together.'

'My dear Eve,' Beth enthused, rushing forward to embrace her as others began crowding round the newly weds. 'You make a lovely bride and I wish you both every happiness.'

'Seconded by me.' William pecked her cheek and shook Lucas's hand.

William didn't sound quite as certain as Eve would have liked. She knew he had qualms about what she had done and didn't fully approve. But he respected her decision, for which Eve was grateful. With Mrs Coombs ushering the servants about their business while telling them that their new mistress would make his lordship an excellent wife, Estelle came to give her a hug, her pretty face shining with excitement as Eve lifted her off her feet and hugged her back.

'You look lovely, Mama,' she whispered, her mouth against her ear.

'And so do you, Estelle—and you, too,' she said, drawing Sophie and Abigail towards her with her free arm and placing an affectionate kiss on each of their cheeks while Sarah Lacy, holding a wide-awake Alice in her arms, looked on fit to bursting with happiness. Unable to resist this lovely addition to her growing family, Eve gently kissed her plump baby cheek. 'All of you look like fairy princesses and I couldn't have wished for prettier bridal attendants. Now off you go. I think Thomas and David are waiting for you to show them the house, but don't be long. We will be sitting down to eat very soon.'

When they had scampered out of the room, with a strange sense of unreality Eve went to take her place beside her husband. Already so perceptive of his mood and able to read every nuance in his light blue eyes, she knew he would be feeling right now that he would rather be anywhere than here. Drawing her closer, he put his hand over hers, covering her wedding ring. He looked deeply into her eyes and she felt her heart turn over. Never before had she seen such a tender expression on his proud features. But both of them knew this was a business arrangement and should not be treated as something romantic.

Lucas had watched the tender scene with the children and was moved to an emotion he hadn't felt in a very long time. Eve seemed to have a talent for motherhood. She was warm and loving and physical and never afraid to show her feelings. He felt a pang of regret. He didn't have any memories of anyone kissing his children, or seeing their faces light up with joy as they did whenever they were with Eve.

Lucas looked at his bride as if he were seeing her for the first time. He smiled, his pleasant thoughts bringing a warmth and humour to his face, which had been lacking so far this day, and he was surprised at the answering response. Her mouth was full and a luscious shade of deep pink. He noticed too she had an unbelievable small waist and a long, lovely neck. Her eyes were the most brilliant, incredible shade of dark blue to be almost violet and were quite extraordinarily wide with a slight upward slant that emphasised her high cheekbones. Her skin was creamy smooth and rich with a translucency that had him wondering whether it continued beneath the ivory satin of the gown she wore. He speculated and the thought put a covetous gleam in his eyes.

In fact she was exquisite, this wife of his, and put all the pale, simpering, overeager English roses who came out each Season in the shade. When she had approached him with her outrageous proposal of marriage, wishing to know all there was to know about her before he committed himself, he had sought William out at the Foreign Office on the same day that he had spoken with Eve's solicitor.

William had told him that as soon as her period of mourning had ended, Eve had received proposals from several gentleman of note—a French count, an Italian millionaire—and had been showered with admiration from every eligible male in New York society, and yet she was neither spoilt nor pampered, and her father had seen to it that she had not been cushioned against all the vicissitudes of life. She was also so accustomed to wealth that fortunes meant nothing to her.

And if he were honest, Lucas would have to admit that he had admired her from the moment she'd taken him on in the park and then in his own home, a courageous, stubborn young woman, who did not fear him, and on being confronted by Maxine was scornful of her attitude. She was aware of the risk she was taking in marrying him, yet she was prepared to trust him, to risk every-thing her father had worked for. Suddenly he felt the weight of the burden she had placed on him and he knew it was up to him to make sure that Eve was always safe.

Ignoring everything else for the moment, there might have been only the two of them in the room as she met his gaze, and suddenly Lucas found himself actually looking forward to his future for the first time in a long time. In the beginning, as part of their arrangement, he was prepared to wait as patiently as it was in his nature to be for Eve to become his wife in the full meaning of the word, which, now he'd had time to reflect, if he had anything to do with it would not be long in coming.

'Well, here we are—married again, both of us.'

'But we were not married to each other.'

'Then we shall have to learn how to live together,' Lucas said gravely.

Eve looked down to where their hands were still joined, his strong fingers wrapped around hers. 'Which I hope will not prove too difficult—given your unpredictable temperament, my lord.'

'I promise I shall try to be patience personified in the future.'

Perhaps it was the occasion and all that it implied, or perhaps it was the odd combination of gentleness and solemnity in his light blue eyes as they gazed into hers, but, whatever the cause, Eve's heart quickened its pace.

'However our marriage came about, whatever differences there are between us, could we put them aside, do you think, and behave like any normal, newly wedded couple at their wedding feast?'

Mesmerised, Eve stared into his fathomless eyes while his deep, soft voice seemed to caress her, pulling her under his spell. For some reason, his request did much damage to her resistance. She nodded finally and softly said, 'As you wish.'

'You look very lovely, Eve,' he said, smiling crookedly and handing her a glass of champagne, 'or perhaps I should say Lady Stainton. How does it feel to be a titled lady?'

'No different to what I was fifteen minutes ago.'

'Plain Mrs Brody?'

She wrinkled her face. 'I would like to think Mrs Brody was never plain.'

That made Lucas chuckle, which went a long way to making Eve relax. It was the first spark of humour she had seen from him since the evening of their engagement.

'You're right. She was courageous, warm and kind and she had a beautiful smile.'

Her laughter bubbled to the surface like fresh spring water. 'Now you flatter me—and coming from you, that raises my suspicions and warns me to be wary.'

The blue eyes lightly swept her and catching her own, held them with a smiling warmth. 'Don't be. I never say anything I don't mean. You have many qualities I admire, Eve, and in particular I am delighted that you like children so much.'

'It's very hard not to when blessed with one of my own and three adorable stepchildren—if you count Alice. You have no idea how happy it has made Estelle having sisters to play with.'

He cocked a handsome brow as he gave her a knowing look. 'And in time a brother.'

Perhaps Eve should not have been standing so

close. It was most difficult to subdue the deepening blush of embarrassment while appearing nonchalant, for her thoughts had become tangled in the fact that while she insisted on keeping her side of the bargain they had made regarding the terms of their marriage, he was reminding her of his side of the arrangement.

'I—I hope so. I know I am bound by my word, and I have every intention of fulfilling my part of the vows, but I asked for time and you granted my request.'

'I did, and be assured that you have nothing to fear from me. I accept the way things are between us, but you cannot blame me for hoping for a turn of fate. I want an heir, and I can think of no greater satisfaction than for you to bear my son.' His look through narrowed eyes was one of wicked mischief. 'You are now my wife. Have you not vowed to love, honour and obey me, sharing your life with me—as well as all your worldly goods?'

'And must I remind you that you have done the same, Lord Stainton?' An impish smile played on her curved lips.

He grinned. '*Touché!* Although I consider that I have come out of it with the best deal.'

'In monetary terms, maybe you have,' she murmured, her attention drawn to the door as the three girls entered, their faces rosy and shining with the pleasure of the day. 'But I am satisfied with my side of the bargain. The girls really do look lovely. It's the first time Estelle has been a bridal attendant.'

'And Sophie and Abigail. They've never had so much excitement in their young lives.'

'I have a feeling that all this excitement will wear them out and that by tonight we are going to have three tired children on our hands.'

The wedding breakfast had been prepared by Mrs Coombs. The long table was festooned with flowers and there was a wealth of food and champagne for the thirty or so guests. It would have been a subdued affair had the children not been present, which Lucas did not approve of but Eve had insisted upon. Their excited chatter and laughter lightened the atmosphere, coiling itself warmly about the adults.

All too soon it was over and the guests had left. The children were in the nursery and Eve was alone with her husband. They were about to partake of a glass of champagne before going to their separate beds when one of the footmen informed them that a Mr Edward Barstow had arrived to see them both.

'I've put him in the study, my lord.'

Lucas became thoughtful. 'Barstow?' He looked at Eve. 'Isn't he your solicitor?'

A shadow of apprehension crossed her vivid features. 'Yes. I wonder what he wants.'

'Let's go and find out.'

Mr Barstow was seated at the desk. When the study doors opened he rose swiftly to his feet, stealing a quick, appraising look at the dark-haired Lord Stainton and his beautiful new wife. With a pair of penetrating ice-blue eyes levelled on him, Mr Barstow swallowed nervously as Lord Stainton walked round the desk and gave him a curt nod, waiting for him to speak.

Eve, in whom patience had been a lesson painfully learned and not always completely, waited for Mr Barstow to speak. There was a hard knot in the centre of her chest, and try as she might she could not get rid of it.

Mr Barstow cleared his throat. 'Good evening, Lord Stainton—Lady Stainton. I apologise for presuming to call on you without first making an appointment—and today of all days—but I felt my news could not wait.'

Eve returned the greeting, finding it strange that he did not offer them his congratulations. 'Good evening, Mr Barstow. Will you take some tea?'

'No—no, thank you.' He glanced at Eve, then quickly away again, the weight of what he had to tell her heavy indeed. Placing his valise on the desk, he extracted a sheet of paper. 'I received this letter earlier today—from a Mr Pilger, who as you know is working on your father's affairs in New York.' He handed it to her. 'I thought, seeing the gravity of its contents, I should show it to you and Lord Stainton at once.'

Eve glanced at it in puzzlement.

'Please read it, Lady Stainton?' Mr Barstow urged as she gazed questioningly at him.

Eve began to read, and the more she read, the colder she became. Even when she had finished reading she couldn't comprehend the words so she read them again. Then she took a moment to stare down at the letter through horrified, disbelieving eyes, still unable to assimilate what she had read.

Concerned by the sudden pallor of her face, Lucas went to her. 'Eve? What is it?' Watching her intently, he held out his hand for the letter.

Eve's hands were trembling as she gave it to him. 'Please read it, Lucas. Perhaps you can make some sense of it.'

Lucas did. Other than the merest tightening of his expression, there was no visible reaction to the staggering news, or to all its serious and terrible implications. Regarding Mr Barstow in dispassionate silence, he handed him the letter.

Biting off an expression of sympathy he knew

Lord Stainton would reject, he looked at his wife. 'I—realise what a dreadful shock this must be to you, Lady Stainton. I am so very sorry.'

'But—this cannot be right, Mr Barstow. There must be some mistake. There has to be. My instructions were simple. I informed you that my financial affairs were to be transferred to my husband on our marriage. He is now legally entitled to every penny I have.'

'You no longer have the money at your disposal—at least not nearly as much as you hoped there would be.'

Eve was aghast. 'But—my father was a wealthy man. He amassed a fortune. It—it cannot be gone.'

'It would seem a substantial amount of his holdings have folded, Lady Stainton.'

'But it cannot have disappeared overnight.'

'His assets have been dwindling steadily for some time, and, as you will know, all branches of the American economy have suffered grievously in recent months—which I feel is the reason why you have been unable to access his money. In its battle to save itself, the bank called in its loans so ruthlessly that many concerns, not to mention individuals, your father was one of them—are ruined.'

'Did he know of this before he died?' Lucas asked, surprised at the calmness of his voice.

'I believe so. He sold off some of his investments

when things began to go under. Perhaps if he'd lived, being the kind of man he was, in all probability he would have recovered, but as it was—'

'He died,' Eve whispered. She looked at Lucas's taut features. 'Lucas, I had no idea. You must believe that. Are—are there any debts—creditors to pay?' she asked as Mr Barstow closed his valise.

'Not to my knowledge. Mr Pilger is winding down your father's affairs in America and will let me have the paperwork in due course.'

Lucas looked at him. 'Is there anything else?'

'No, sir. I'll see myself out.'

His retreating footsteps could be heard going through the hall. Not until the outer door banged to did Eve move towards Lucas. He stood with his back to her, his hands resting on the mantelpiece, his head bowed, his shoulders taut. Nothing could be heard but the rustling of her skirts. She came to a halt a few feet from him, pausing to gather her wits before she spoke. She tried to think how to begin, and because she was so overwhelmed with emotion she said the first thing that came into her head.

'You're angry, Lucas, and you have every reason to be.' She saw his shoulders stiffen at the sound of her voice and when he brought himself up straight and turned and looked at her, his expression gave her no reassurance. His eyes were slits of explosive rage in his grim face, and she could almost feel the effort he was exerting to keep it under control. His gaze snapped to her face, his pale blue eyes turning an icy, metallic silver.

'You're right,' he bit out, his mouth set in a bitter line, his black brows drawn in a straight bar. 'It would appear that you married me under false pretences, Lady Stainton.'

Eve flinched at his enunciation of her new title, which rang with a hollow note. 'It does look like it. I promised you a fortune. I can't believe there isn't one. That it's virtually all gone. You had no reason to marry me after all.'

'Right,' he snapped, striding to his desk, and dragging out the chair sat down. 'No reason at all. Why in God's name did I take your word regarding your wealth?' Why had he been so naïve? After everything that had happened with Maxine, had he not learnt his lesson?

'Lucas, you have to believe me when I say I had no idea and I do not understand how it could have happened.'

'What is there to understand? It's simple enough. Your father lost his money. Whether it was bad management or the state of the American bank makes little difference.' His lips twisted in a bitter, cynical smile. 'It would appear your father and I have much in common, my sweet. Before I met you I had only myself and my daughters to take care of. Now, with a wife and another child foistered on me, I find I have extra responsibilities I could do without.'

The vicious meaning of his words cut Eve to the heart. With a surge of genuine anger her jaw jutted with belligerent indignation and tension twisted within her as she quickly came to the defence of her darling daughter. 'Since you see us as pitiful nuisances—'

'Your words, not mine,' he interrupted harshly.

'Nevertheless,' she seethed, her voice like splintered ice as she took up a stance in front of him, 'that is what you mean—and as I was saying, if that is how you see us, then I shall remove myself and Estelle from your house forthwith.'

'Like hell you will. I will give you a warning, Eve, and heed me well,' Lucas said in a terrible voice. 'Do not even consider leaving this house with the intention of leaving it for good. You are my wife and you will not leave without my permission. You will remain here with me until such time as we go to Laurel Court, and do not dare disobey me.'

Fury was quick to flare in Eve's eyes. Moving forwards, she planted the palms of her hands on his desk and leaned towards him. 'How dare you, Lucas Stainton? I do not need your permission to do anything and if I want advice I would not ask you, and how dare you actually remind me of my vows—would you like me to remind you of yours, my lord?'

His eyes narrowed and a murderous glint shone out at her. No woman had ever dared to speak to him so defiantly or look at him with sparks shooting from her eyes. There was a deep and dreadful silence, a silence so menacing, filled with an unwavering determination of the two to hurt, to destroy one another, that the tension was palpable.

Lucas scraped back his chair, but Eve did not flinch. Their eyes locked together in awful combat. Neither was about to concede.

'Do not goad me, Eve, and do not defy me, because you won't like what will happen if you do, believe me,' her husband said perilously.

Eve's voice held nothing but contempt. 'I am not your chattel and I will not be treated as such. What has happened is unfortunate, but it does not necessarily have to be the end of the world.' The expression on her husband's face was difficult to read, but some new darkness seemed to move at the back of his eyes.

Combing his fingers through his hair in frustration, he turned from her as if he couldn't bear to look at her or be close to her and strode to the window where he drew a long breath, striving to get control of his temper. When he spoke again he seemed more composed.

'The damage, whatever it may be, has already been done. I'm to blame for this. Being fully aware of the state of the American economy, I should have investigated more thoroughly into your father's affairs before committing myself to this marriage. I can only hope that my banker will take a more understanding view. You may not care a damn about my feelings—'

'But of course I care,' Eve cried, wishing there was something she could do, something she could say to make things better.

His lips twisted scathingly. 'Do you realise what will happen if this ever gets out? It will cause the biggest scandal in London since my divorce from Maxine. It will bring further disrepute to my family.'

The utter helplessness of being a woman totally at the mercy of her husband struck Eve with full force. Then her dormant self-respect flared into life. His manner and his deliberate cruelty riled her. Did he think this was easy for her, that she wasn't suffering too?

'Your family is now my family, Lucas, so it affects us both,' she flared, her cheeks burning with anger. 'Dear God in heaven, what do you want me to do? What do you expect me to say? I didn't know how bad things were. Have you any idea how hard all this is for me?'

'Yes—yes, of course I do.'

'Lucas…' she began, taking a step closer, then stopping when she got nothing from him but a blast of icy contempt from his eyes. 'I realise,' she began again, her voice trembling with emotion while she tried to think how to reach him, how to diffuse his wrath and keep her own at bay, 'that you must despise me for this, but do you think I could have stood by your side this very day and promised the things I did if I had known any of this—if I had even suspected this would happen? I would have told you.'

'I don't despise you, and I don't blame you. I blame myself.' Lucas saw little good in lashing out at her. She was feeling just as devastated as he was, but with all the qualified people her father had employed to take care of his affairs, why the hell hadn't she been informed that he was facing financial ruin?

Eve drew a shaking breath and braved another step closer. 'I know I've hurt you terribly and I am sorry, but there is nothing I can do about it. If you're expecting me to shout and weep, then you're wasting your time. I am not given to hysterics.'

Lucas looked at her, seeing the hurt and despair in her eyes. Feeling something inside him, some strange emotion that was unrecognisable to him just then, unconsciously his hand went out to her. His expression became one of mixed emotions, strangely gentle, and his light blue eyes softened and were filled with sorrow and compassion, telling her of his regret that this disaster should give her pain. But Eve would have none of his pity or of his concern and her cold, narrowed eyes told him so.

'Eve, I do know how distressed you must be feeling—'

'Do you, Lucas? Do you really? I don't think you do. This is not just about you, and if this is the way it has to be between us then I suppose I will endure it. The deed is done and we will have to find a way to live in harmony with it, because the only alternative is to have our marriage declared null and void or to divorce.'

Lucas froze, his eyes pinning hers as cold and hard as steel. He moved slowly towards her like a dangerous predator. 'Eve, let me make one thing perfectly clear. I will say this once and once only and you will listen to me and never, ever, mention divorce to me again. First, our marriage such as it is, will not be nullified, and, second, we will not get divorced. Divorce, as I found to my cost, is an expensive business and only undertaken by those who are wealthy. I am not. That aside, Eve, if I were the richest man in Christendom I would not put myself through it—or sully my family name further—by embarking on the enterprise again. Do I make myself clear?'

'Yes. Perfectly.'

'Good. Now go to bed,' he said between his

clenched teeth, and while Eve was willing to stay and argue the matter further, Lucas's cold anger told her there was no point.

Eve tossed her head proudly and, turning from him, marched to the door. 'While you're in this present state of mind I think that would be for the best,' she threw back at him. 'We can discuss this whole thing reasonably and rationally in the morning. Goodnight, Lucas.'

Usually, her terrified mind reminded her, Lucas's temper was explosive, and he was so infuriated by the fact that the fortune he'd expected was not forthcoming, that instead of raging, he'd been coldly, murderously silent and that alarmed her more than his outburst would have done.

She felt physically ill when she left him. She went up to the bedroom that was to be hers on the first floor. Lucas had given her the choice of any of the rooms and she had chosen this one because it was close to where the children slept.

Passing the night nursery she looked in, relieved to see they were fast asleep. In helpless misery she entered her room, relieved there was no one there. It had been a long day and seeing the covers turned back on the bed and her nightdress draped over a chair, together with a fire burning in the fireplace, it all looked suspiciously inviting.

She was still in a state of shock as she began to

undress, tugging at the innumerable hooks down the back of her dress and then unpinning her hair. She shook it out with both hands so that it tumbled like a thick dark snake down to the small of her back, and then climbed into bed.

Overwhelmed with the alarming news she had received and unable to believe it, she squeezed her eyes closed and held back her tears while her mind tormented her with more pressing problems.

In bed she lay awake for a long time, tortured with doubts about the future and with the awful fear that, despite what Lucas had said about not wanting to end their marriage, after he had considered it in the cold light of day, he might see it as the best option and do just that.

Lucas downed the glass of liquor in his hand and poured himself another, but no matter how much he wanted to drink himself into oblivion, there wasn't enough liquor in the world to douse the fury that was burning inside him like an inferno.

After all his experience, and what had happened with Stephen, he'd been taken in by a woman he'd thought would bring him a fortune, when, in fact, she was worse off than he was. Dear God, he thought, wanting to smash the glass into the hearth, if it weren't so serious he would laugh at his own gullibility. He took another swallow of his drink.

If he'd had any sense at all, he would have thrown Eve out of his house before she made that damned proposition.

Rage boiled inside him like acid, destroying any tender feelings he had for her. Damn the woman. Damn her conniving female heart. She had brought nothing to the marriage, and to add insult to injury she was denying him the pleasure of her body until she felt like submitting to him. The hell with what she wanted, he thought, tossing back the rest of his drink. Since she couldn't keep her side of the bargain neither would he, and if she didn't bend to his will he would damn well break her to it.

He could think of nothing but his need to possess her, intent only on the conclusion of his own desire, to crush her, to hurt her, to claim her body in any way she chose to give it.

Eve was drifting on the edge of sleep when she had a strange feeling that someone was in the room watching her. Her eyes snapped open. A man—Lucas—was standing quite still at the bottom of the bed, the glow from the embers of the dying fire behind him. With his black tousled hair and dressed in shirt and trousers, his shirt open to the waist and the sleeves rolled up over his forearms, he was strangely threatening as he stood motionless as a dim statue, all his attention riveted on her.

With a gasp of indignation she sat up and got out of bed, grasping a blue silk bed-gown draped over the back of a chair close to the bed.

'Lucas! What are you doing here?' Her mind was in complete turmoil. She couldn't imagine why he had come to her room. Without answering he moved towards her. Tall, lean of waist, belly and hips, with strong muscled shoulders, Lucas Stainton was undoubtedly a handsome man, but his face in the mellow light was too strong, his mouth too stubborn and his chin too arrogant for Eve's liking just then. In fact, the sheer power emanating from him brought a fluttering to her stomach. She could smell brandy and his eyes were piercing bright. He stopped a few inches from her, a mocking smile curving his lips.

'Why, Eve, who else did you think it would be on our wedding night?' he drawled. 'A prowler, perhaps?'

'I really have no idea. Lucas, it is very late and time you were in bed.'

His smile became a leer as his smouldering, insolent gaze swept over her, turning to amazement at the heavy mass of the auburn fox pelt that rippled down her back to her buttocks, crackling and alive in the light from the fire.

'I know—which is the reason I am here.'

Unconscious of the vision she presented in her

clinging robe and her hair tumbling over her shoulders in loose disarray, Eve's cheeks flamed, but at the same time her heart missed a beat. The meaning behind his words was only too clear. She felt her modesty, intact for so long, was being invaded by this man, her husband, who was beginning to alarm her nervous, awakened senses.

'I meant in your bed, not mine.'

'I know what you meant, but I decided that your bed will be far more comfortable than mine, so here I am.'

His cool mockery snapped Eve's fragile self-control. Planting her hands in the small of her waist, she glowered at him irately. 'Aye, Lucas, and fortified with a considerable amount of your fine brandy and a good deal of natural stubbornness. Now please leave. You are drunk.'

'So I am—and with good reason. Now get into bed, and stop playing the outraged virgin when we both know you're not. You have been married. You have a child, so you are not uninformed about these things. Besides, it is customary for marriages to be consummated on the wedding night.'

A small knot of tension began to form in the centre of Eve's chest. 'But you said—'

'Forget it,' he ground out. 'A wife's vows require that she submit to her husband in all things, and that includes satisfying him in bed.'

'You? And what about me?'

His grin was salacious. 'I am confident of my ability to satisfy you too, Eve.'

'Must I remind you of our arrangement?'

He cocked a dubious brow. 'Ah—the arrangement. And are you still absolutely certain this is how you want it to be between us?'

She nodded. 'Positive.'

'And if I refuse?'

'Then I'll do as you ask and submit to you.'

'Submit?' he repeated, furious by her choice of word. 'I don't want you to *submit* to me—to give yourself with reluctance.'

Eve's eyes locked on to his and her response was emphatic. 'Then don't pressure me,' she flared on a note of desperation. 'You promised you would give me time. We made a bargain and I thought you were gentleman enough to keep it.'

'I'm no gentleman and that was before today's unfortunate events. Things have changed,' he told her coldly. 'The arrangement, my sweet, is off.'

'And you obviously think I am compensation for an unpaid debt,' she threw at him angrily.

'Precisely.'

He raised his head and Eve was alarmed by the predatory gleam in his eyes, which looked dark in the dim light. He took a step towards her and then another, and Eve retreated step for step, until the backs of her legs bumped the bed. Unable to go forwards and adamantly unwilling to fall back on to the bed, she stood in mutinous silence, her heart pounding in her chest. He paused and his dark brows pulled together.

'Now, suppose you tell me why the prospect of going to bed with me seems to frighten you?'

'I'm not frightened. I don't fear you—truly I don't. I just don't want you to touch me,' Eve uttered, uneasy with his boldness. Tendrils of alarm wrapped themselves round her heart. 'You are drunk, Lucas. Please go away. Don't do something you will have cause to regret in the morning.'

She turned to move away from him, but in sheer frustration as she continued to deny him, Lucas reached out and, with his hands on her waist, roughly spun her around and jerked her into his arms, drawing her against his hard, muscular length.

'Enough of this nonsense,' he murmured shortly, his male senses aroused and eager to get on.

Eve's heart crashed terrifyingly as he bent his head and took her lips in a hard, silencing kiss. Pressed firmly against him, she was a mass of quivering rebellion. She was aware of nothing but the vigour of him, the power of him, the faint scent of his cologne and the aroma of brandy on his breath that fanned her cheek. Bracing her hands against his chest, she tore her lips from his and averted her face, offended by the effrontery of him.

'Stop this,' she said, breathing hard, deeply shocked by his assault. 'Don't, Lucas, please, please don't, not like this—not this way. I don't want you to.'

'Be still,' he muttered, taking her chin between his strong fingers and turning her head back to his so that she was forced to meet his eyes. He met her wary gaze beneath the long curving sweep of her lashes and admired the soft blush on the creamy skin of her cheeks, the slim, straight nose, and the delicately formed lips, which seemed to beckon the touch of his own.

'I know only one way to kiss a woman, Eve,' he whispered silkily, his fingers becoming gentle on her jaw, sliding his parted mouth along the smooth satin fire on her slender neck, 'and I've never had any complaints before. I'm beginning to think you enjoy baiting me, for you do it better than anyone I've known before.'

The room was hushed and dark and still around them. His hands glided restlessly, possessively, over her. Her struggles excited him further, his hands going at once to her breasts, the small nipples quivering against his hard palms, sliding his hands down her back and over the gentle swell of her buttocks, aware that her trembling body was naked beneath her flimsy nightdress and desiring nothing more than to strip it from her and push her down on to the bed and lose himself in her.

Unable to relax her rigid body, still she struggled against him, jerking herself away, trying to fend off his inquisitive hands. She was becoming increasingly afraid, her natural reserve and modesty in the face of so much male aggression turning her cold and resistant, for what he was doing, without any thought to how she might be feeling, was a stark reminder of Andrew's cruelty and made her feel that history was about to repeat itself.

And yet even now something told her that, given time and patience, for him to allow her senses to become accustomed to this powerful being invading her female world she had protected for so long, she would become as he wanted her to be, and as gratified as he appeared to be.

'Lucas—I can't…' she protested, only to have the words silenced by his mouth.

As his passion built, so did his conscience and the awful, guilty premonition that what he was doing was wrong. As some semblance of reality returned, abruptly he dragged his lips from hers and stepped away from her, seeing that her face was a mask of tortured anguish. Deeply shocked, he flinched with pain and remorse. How could he have done this to her? How could he ever hurt her? Raking his hand through the side of his hair in angry self-disgust, unable to look at her one second more, he spun round and strode to the door. He paused for a moment before he turned and studied her in silence.

After a moment he said in a quiet, almost apologetic tone that startled Eve, 'The fault for what happened just now was mine and I apologise. It had little to do with your baiting me. The contents of Mr Barstow's letter cancelled out our arrangement and merely gave me an excuse to do what I've wanted to do for some time.'

'Lucas—if I've hurt you…'

'Eve, the only wound that's been inflicted tonight is to my pride. The failure of our bargain infuriates me, and it galls me beyond measure to occupy an empty bed on my wedding night. It doesn't have to be like this between us. Is your own pride so great that you can't set it aside for just a few hours—just this once?'

A lump of nameless emotion constricted her throat, and although she had not forgiven him for coming to her room and trying to force himself on her, she was moved by the way he had stepped back and apologised. She felt something stir in her breast, the feeling moving down to the pit of her stomach where it lay, warm and comfortable. Looking into his face, she was unable to look away, held by something she was unable to name, but which her female body instantly recognised.

She had seen the look once before when a man had wanted to take her to bed, but then she had feared the look—and with good reason. However, she felt it strange that she did not fear the way Lucas was looking at her—quite the opposite, in fact, for she found herself unprepared for the sheer force of the feelings that swept through her and she knew that she was in grave danger, not from her husband but from herself. The prospect of pretending for just a few hours that she was a beloved bride and he an amorous groom seemed not only harmless but irresistibly appealing and she was tempted to ask him to take her to bed, but something deep inside stopped her.

Finally, drawing a long, steadying breath, she said, 'Yes.'

The single word, spoken with such quiet conviction, hit Lucas in all its finality. 'Then I will bid you goodnight.' He turned from her and left her room, his heart twisting in agony at what he had just done—coldly forcing himself on her like the wretch that he was.

Like a sleepwalker, numb, stunned by what had just happened, Eve turned to the bed. Still in her robe, she crawled beneath the covers and curled herself in a tight ball, hugging her knees. Yet the haunting pressure of Lucas's lips and body pressed close burned in the depth of her being.

Chapter Nine

The following morning Eve dressed and went down-stairs. The house was surprisingly quiet considering four children lived in it—so very different to the Seagrove household, where children's voices and laughter could be heard for most of the time. When she reached the hall she was informed by one of the footmen that Lucas would like to see her. As she crossed towards the study, she realised it was going to be more difficult than she anticipated greeting him with just the proper degree of casualness after what had transpired between them the night before.

When she had visited the nursery earlier, although Sarah had given her a quiet look, Eve was relieved that she was sensitive enough not to employ any indelicate talk concerning her wedding night—although what Sarah would think were she to tell her that both she and Lucas had slept in their own beds she really had no idea.

Lucas was working at his big desk amid a pile of folders and papers and did not look up, not even when she closed the door. He was freshly shaved, groomed and sober, but his handsome face was unreadable.

'Please sit down,' he said, his voice terse, cold and impersonal. Keeping his eyes lowered, with a wave of his hand he indicated a comfortable winged chair to the side of the desk. 'I'll be with you in a moment.'

Doing as he bade and perching straight backed on the edge of the chair, Eve wondered how he could look so utterly casual and composed after last night. He seemed able to dismiss it entirely. She sat quite still, hardly daring to move, practically holding her breath, the swift scratching of his pen across the paper invading the silence in the room. After a full two minutes he suddenly threw down his pen and looked up. Whatever thoughts of revenge and wounded pride had driven him to seek her out in her bed were forgotten, while she was struggling to look even a little normal in the aftermath of his assault.

On the other hand, she realised he no longer looked cold or cynical or angry, and that was a relief.

'You wanted to see me, Lucas.'

'Yes,' he replied blandly, shoving his chair back and standing up. 'You look pale, Eve. Did you not sleep well?'

'I did—eventually.' He offered no word of apology for having intruded on her privacy, even if he didn't mean it, and though his lips smiled, his eyes did not. Not that eager to refer to the matter, standing up, she said, 'What is it you wanted to see me about?'

'To tell you that I intend leaving for Laurel Court tomorrow morning. I intend to keep this house for the time being. With no one living in it, the upkeep will be minimal. Please see to it that the children are packed up and ready to leave by nine o'clock.'

For a moment, surprise left her speechless. This was the last thing she had been expecting. 'Laurel Court? But—shouldn't servants be sent on ahead to get things ready?'

'There isn't time. We shall travel together. You liked Laurel Court, as I recall, so I don't suppose you have any objections.'

'There is nothing I would like better. But surely a few more days to prepare wouldn't go amiss.'

'No, Eve,' he said abruptly, 'and please don't argue. I have urgent business in the north-east and I don't want to leave you and the children alone in London.'

'But you are suggesting that we are to be left alone in the country.'

'Why not? You will be perfectly safe. Laurel Court is a hell of a lot better for the children than living in town.' When she didn't respond, he said in a bored drawl, 'At least at Laurel Court you will be spared my presence. Please tell me you didn't expect me to remain and play happy families. Tell me you aren't that naïve.'

Flinching from the chilling bite of his tone, Eve looked at the hard, handsome face. Mr Barstow's arrival yesterday had successfully destroyed any hope she might have had of meeting Lucas on any sort of common ground, confusing her and seriously diminishing her own sense of worth. Swallowing convulsively, she shook her head and answered him honestly.

'After the events of yesterday I didn't know what to expect, but I did not expect you to ignore what happened.'

'Good. At least we are in agreement on that. There's been enough deceit and misunderstandings between us.'

Suddenly Eve felt a burning annoyance at his attitude and all her resentment toward Lucas and the circumstances that had changed her life so immeasurably welled up inside her in a fierce anger.

'I did not set out to deceive you, Lucas. So if you are to continue punishing me for something that was beyond my control, then do so if it makes you feel better. For myself, I am relieved you are to put some distance between us. I only hope the northeast is far enough away.'

Lucas's eyes darkened in anger. 'I am not,' he

insisted with straining patience, 'intent on punishing you and nor do I place the blame for what has happened at your door. I am doing my damnedest to come to terms with the unfortunate circumstances that have brought about this débâcle, while trying to work out what to do to save us from complete ruin.'

'And you think you can do that by going away?'

'It is possible.'

She put up her chin. 'Very well. If you will excuse me, I will go and inform Sarah there is some packing to do.'

Lucas watched her go with grudging admiration. The situation for her must be devastating, he realised suddenly. She too had lost everything and now she was forced to face a new way of life at the side of a husband who had made it clear he didn't want her.

But then, that wasn't entirely true. He did want her, that was the trouble. One part of him wanted nothing to do with her. And yet another—by far the greatest part—wanted to take her in his arms and awaken all the exquisite, undiscovered passion in that lovely body. She aroused carnal feelings in him that he had no business feeling if he meant to keep his distance from her, yet he knew how fragile his control was whenever he was near her.

* * *

Lucas got to his feet as Eve swept into the dining room on their first night back at Laurel Court. He had a glass of wine in his hand and had been swirling the deep red liquid round as he stared broodingly into the fire. He turned slowly towards her, placing his glass down while he poured her some wine and handed it to her.

'So, Eve, are you happy to be back at Laurel Court?'

'Yes, I confess I am. I have developed a fondness for it, and the children are excited about being back.'

The look he gave her was sharp and meaningful. 'You do realise that I am in danger of losing it if nothing is done to recoup my losses,' he reminded her, deliberately sowing the seeds of discontent.

Holding on to her temper with superhuman effort, Eve managed to speak calmly. 'The collapse of my father's finances have come as a bitter blow to you, Lucas. I do know that without you feeling that you have to remind me of it all the time.'

'And never fails to stir your temper,' he remarked, admiring the way anger turned her eyes to a deep midnight blue.

'And you have a talent for raising my temper to boiling point more than anyone else. As mistress of this beautiful house I will do everything to help in any way I can.'

'You will find plenty to do over the days and weeks you are here. The staff is small and we can't afford to set on more, so your duties will be many. Do you ride, by the way?'

'Yes,' she answered stiffly. 'I love riding.'

'Then I'll show you the whole of the estate in the morning—such as it is.'

'I'd like that. When do you intend leaving?'

'In two or three weeks. I want to make sure you are all settled in before I go.'

'And will you be away long?'

'As to that, I have no idea.'

He led her to the table when their food was brought in. Their places had been set together, Lucas at the top of the table, Eve beside him, so that they might talk without the length of the table between them. The candlelight gleamed on the polished surface and shimmered on the crystal glasses.

Eve ate in uneasy silence, but as the wine and the delicious chicken and onion soup began to have a softening effect on her, and looking forward to the braised beef and lemon soufflé to follow, she began to relax.

'With so few provisions, Mrs Coombs has excelled herself,' Eve commented as she spooned the soup into her mouth.

'Mrs Coombs is very much aware that we are dining alone together for the first time as husband

and wife and she has gone out of her way to make this a memorable meal. So even though we both know it will not have the desired effect, enjoy it and be sure to thank her afterwards.'

'I do not need reminding of my manners, Lucas,' Eve told him tartly, 'but I think I should remind you of yours. Where I come from, it is considered ill bred to argue at the dining table.'

Her sharp reprimand filled Lucas with amusement, and, duly chastened, he said, 'You are quite right. I should know better and I apologise.' Having finished his soup, he put his spoon down. Leaning back in his chair, he looked at her speculatively. 'What is to become of us, Eve? Nothing between us is going as planned, is it? We have both lost a great deal and are paying the price. But there might be other options.'

Eve raised both brows, a little smile quirking her lips. 'You aren't, by any chance, thinking of robbing a bank?'

He grinned. 'Nothing so dramatic.'

'Has it got anything to do with your going to the north-east in such a hurry?'

He nodded. 'I shall be travelling to Newcastle. I've inherited a parcel of land up there. The land itself isn't worth much, but then again it might be. You see, there is a disused mine on it.'

Eve stared at him in amazement. 'A coal mine?'

He nodded. 'When it was brought to my notice shortly after my brother died, I employed the services of a mining engineer to take a look at it. He has surveyed what he can of it, although it is much flooded and the pit-head buildings in disrepair, as is the pumping system, he assures me there are still rich seams of coal to be got out.'

'But without the necessary capital to modernise, to make it safe and operative, how can it be reopened?'

'I shall go cap in hand to every banker and every businessman I can think of who might be willing to lend me the money, and don't forget I have this place as collateral.'

'But do you know anything about coal mining?'

'Not a thing, but I can learn. As fortune would have it, Henry's family home is close to Newcastle. He has kindly offered me his hospitality. He is to come here the day before I leave and we will travel together.'

He continued speaking of his journey north, falling silent when the next course was brought in, and not until they were alone did either of them speak.

'Have you selected rooms for yourself?' Lucas asked, slicing through the succulent piece of beef.

'Yes—a lovely suite of rooms overlooking the gardens. One of the reasons I chose them is because they are close to the nursery. Do you approve?'

His eyes narrowed and gleamed across at her and the semblance of a salacious smile curved his lips. 'Most certainly,' he murmured softly.

Lifting a brow, Lucas regarded his wife for some time until she chafed at the unsuppressed humour she saw dancing in his bright eyes. Discomfited, Eve watched him narrowly, suspiciously. A queer feeling settled in her stomach as she wondered what he found so amusing about her selection of rooms.

'You clearly find my selection of rooms entertaining, Lucas. Would you care to share it with me? If you don't think they are suitable, then perhaps you would suggest something else.'

'I would not deprive you of the rooms you have chosen. They are the ones I would have selected for you myself. It suits me very well having you so close.'

With belated perception she realised what so amused him and she gritted her teeth at the thought of her own foolishness. 'Do you mean to tell me that of all the rooms in this huge house, I had to pick the ones next to yours?'

'Correct. And there is a door connecting your apartment to mine, so it is—convenient.'

She glanced at him sharply. 'Not too convenient, I hope. I sincerely hope there is a lock on the door.'

He paused in his eating and surveyed her dispassionately. 'There is, when I choose to use it. I do fear the nearness of you might completely destroy my good intentions—although if that should happen, I hope you would not object as strongly to my actions as you did last night. The last thing I want is for you to submit to me, but I don't think it would be too difficult to make you want me, Eve.'

Eve's colour deepened. The quiet emotion in his voice startled her and she looked away. It was a challenge, softly said, and Eve found herself gripping the napkin in her lap to keep her hands from trembling. His intention was to put on a grand front, and he expected her to do the same. But how easy it would be to let appearances slip into reality—if only this were not an arrangement between them.

Lucas was so attractive and she was drawn to him in a way she had never thought to experience. Even if none of the gentler emotions such as love were present, could they not have a good marriage? Yet the arrangement and Andrew's past callous indifference to her as a woman and his wife had set a barrier between them and her pride refused to let her cross it. She could only hope that Lucas's restraint would continue and her resistance would not be tested as it was last night.

Aware of her confusion, Lucas was unable to suppress a smile. 'When you have need of my services, feel free to knock on the connecting door.

You will find your husband more than willing to share your bed.'

'I have no intention of doing any such thing.'

'Why? Would it be such an onerous duty?' His smile widened, which she found infuriating. 'Your cheeks are flushed, Eve. Are you unwell?'

'I am perfectly well, Lucas,' she snapped, 'If it is your intention to try and batter my defences with another assault similar to the one you tried last night, then please don't.'

Lucas smiled inwardly. He had got the measure of his lovely wife and knew that her demeanour was no indication of how she was inside. She was a clever woman, granted, but she had not yet learned that resistance, or indeed any kind of opposition, only turned Lucas Stainton in the other direction from the one which Eve wanted him to take.

'This is foolishness, you know, Eve.'

'Foolish?'

'To keep yourself apart from me. You are my wife and one day you must bear my children—however distasteful the idea appears to you now. Resisting the inevitable is like swimming against the tide. Some day you will have to abandon your resistance and let the tide take you where it will.'

'Then when that day comes, Lucas—whether it be tomorrow, next week or next month—I will be sure to let you know.'

Eve continued to eat in silence. Lucas had given her much to think about and the fact that he had such easy access to her worried her considerably.

Gazing at her as he ate his meal, Lucas was struck afresh by her loveliness. It was easy to forget he hadn't wanted to marry her. What was difficult was controlling his physical reaction to her nearness. An exercise in fortitude, he thought wryly, that was going to be exceedingly trying.

Eve's mind was working on similar lines. She too was experiencing a similar physical reaction to the one Lucas was experiencing. His dark green coat and close-fitting light grey trousers hugged the contours of his muscled torso and long, well-defined legs, making her fully aware of his overwhelming mas-culinity. She was finding it harder and harder to retreat into cool reserve when she was near him, es-pecially when memories of his kiss, hot, wild and sweet, kept swirling around in her mind.

Chastising herself for allowing her thoughts to suggest what her body wanted to experience again, Eve was relieved when the meal was over. Pleading tiredness, she declined the coffee and excused herself. She hurried up the stairs, gaining the safety of her bedchamber. Only then did she pause to catch her breath. Whether it was from relief at having escaped her husband, the exertion of her climbing the stairs, or simple fear, her heart pounded in her breast, seeming to jolt her entire body with ever beat.

One of the maids was turning down the covers on the bed and stayed to help Eve out of her clothes and into her nightdress. She was discreet and went out quietly. Silence filled the room. Left alone in her apprehension, Eve stared at the offending door. Going towards it, she turned the knob. It was for all its ominous presence locked, but she had no doubt at all that the key was on Lucas's side of the door. Stepping away from it, she prayed desperately for the strength and fortitude that would be required to face whatever lay before her should he decide to exercise his husbandly rights and unlock that door.

If Lucas should find his way into her room and seek to finish what he had started last night, she was absolutely certain that she could not withstand his persuasive, unrelenting assault. What she had experienced in his arms had been new to her. He had aroused feelings and emotions Andrew never had, and she had no idea how to deal with them.

After a while she got into bed, her ears attuned to every sound in the great house. She heard Lucas enter his room and, holding her breath, she lay as stiff as a statue as she listened to his slow footsteps moving about, fully expecting him to come through the door at any minute. Eventually there was silence, but her husband was as easily dismissed from her mind as a wolf at her throat.

When Eve awoke, glistening bright sunlight filled the room in abundance as the maid drew back the heavy drapes. Rousing slowly, she blinked and huddled deeper into the covers, not yet ready to rise until she glanced at the clock on the mantelpiece and saw it was nine o'clock.

When Lucas came striding through the connecting door, bathed and attired, no evidence of her sleepless night remained. Seated at her dressing table brushing her hair, she stared at him in horror and disbelief that he should take such liberties as entering her room without knocking. In an immaculate white shirt, buff-coloured riding breeches and gleaming black boots, he looked incredibly handsome and at ease with himself. From somewhere in the depth of her momentary panic, indignation seized her.

'Good morning, Eve.'

'Good morning, Lucas,' she replied, tossing him a cool glance as the maid made a hurried departure. 'Don't you ever knock?'

His brows lifted derisively. 'On my wife's bedroom door? Never, so you'd better get used to it.' He grinned leisurely as his perusal swept her.

'Very nice,' he murmured, perching his hip on her dressing table and watching her in fascination as she brushed her magnificent wealth of hair. 'That colour suits you.'

Lucas's eyes captured hers and held them prisoner, until she felt warmth suffuse her cheeks. 'What do you want?' she asked bluntly as she continued to concentrate on her hair, trying to ignore the effect his presence was having on her heart rate, and not to look at the lean, hard muscles of his thighs as they flexed beneath the tight-fitting breeches.

'I came to see if the sights were better in here than they are in my room.' The corners of his lips twitched with amusement and his eyes gleamed into hers as he added, 'I am happy to report they are.' Idly he reached out and took a heavy lock of her hair, twining it around one of his long, lean fingers. 'You have beautiful hair, Eve. 'Tis a crime to confine it in knots and coils all the time.'

'Lucas, do you mind?' she snapped, snatching it from his finger and proceeding to twist and coil the rich mass and secure it with pins in her nape. 'It's just not practical to have it hanging loose all the time.'

'You seem to have suffered no ill effects from your first night as mistress of Laurel Court.'

'I slept very well as it happens.'

'Despite the presence of the big bad wolf on the other side of the door.'

'Yes, Lucas, despite that. It must be a long time since the house had a mistress.'

'It is. Stephen might have made free with my wife here, but as you know he never married her. My mother was the last mistress.' He smiled, 'She would have liked you. She set great store by family and would have seen in you a hope for its continuation. Indeed, she would have been anxious for us to produce an heir.'

Eve had the feeling he was laughing at her, but she was not amused. The subject was one she dearly wished to avoid. Her silence spoke for itself.

Lucas's mouth quirked in a half-smile. 'As I am. Of course every man wants a son and you seemed to fit the requirements of my son's mother admirably. You have beauty as well as brains, Eve. Our son will be well blessed.'

Incensed, Eve shoved a final pin into her hair. 'And is that supposed to be a compliment? Is that all you see me as—as some kind of—of brood mare?'

'That you should bear my son was part of the arrangement. With three children between us, I have no doubt of our ability to produce more offspring.'

Flushing furiously, Eve avoided his eyes. 'We have three daughters, Lucas, and your brother produced Alice, don't forget. Producing a son might prove to be another matter entirely. I shouldn't think you would want another girl.'

'On the contrary. I happen to like little girls. My self-esteem has need of consolation, of a sort, and I can think of no greater comfort than for you to bear my child—boy or girl.'

As quickly as it rose, the colour drained from Eve's face. 'I know I am bound by my word, and I will abide by it, but I ask that you give me a little time.'

His eyes held her gaze. 'Providing that's all it is. Things change, Eve—like the conditions to our…arrangement. I am sure your father would have wanted you to have a full, rich life and that is what I intend to give you.'

He spoke so seriously that Eve turned her startled gaze on him. 'Do you really mean that?'

He shrugged, lightly fingering her hairbrush. 'Why should I not? A marriage of convenience need not be doomed to disaster.'

'I hope not, although I doubt I shall ever be able to forget that this is exactly what my union with you is, and that you see me in less than a romantic light.'

'Do I detect a note of regret?' Gleaming whiteness flashed as he grinned down at her. 'Despite your American upbringing, there is a strong sense of the English in you. If you feel you have missed the incessant tradition of wooing before rushing into marriage, then we could pretend we are not yet married and begin the wooing process right here and now.'

Suspicious of everything he said and did, Eve stared at him, unsure if he was teasing or not. 'I don't think so, Lucas. I agree a civilised relationship would be very agreeable, but I am not yet willing to forgo our arrangement.' She smiled sweetly. 'Now, shall we go down to breakfast and afterwards you can show me the wonders of Laurel Court.'

'I believe, my sweet,' he said solicitously, following in her wake, appreciatively watching her hips as they swayed with a natural, graceful provocation, 'that you have a penchant for testing me and my ability to withstand you. I shall be delighted to show you the estate, and the fact that you refuse to forgo our arrangement only spikes my interest— so I warn you to beware, Eve.'

Eve turned her head and looked at him, and she did not miss the meaningful sparkle in those pale blue eyes.

Eve was not disappointed in her expectation of Laurel Court, the ancestral home of several generations of Staintons, comprised of woods, parkland and fertile fields. This was Lucas's home, the place where he was born and where he'd grown to manhood.

When she was mounted, Lucas brought his horse alongside her dancing mare, eager to be off.

'Shall we go?'

The day was pleasant and warm with gusts of wind that billowed out the skirt of Eve's jade-green riding habit and loosened tendrils of hair about her face. Her horse was spirited and eager and needed a firm, attentive hand on the reins. She was deeply conscious of her companion as he rode beside her, letting his body roll easily with the surge of the powerful mount beneath him.

Lucas stole an admiring glance at his companion. He stared at her profile, tracing with his gaze the classically beautiful line of her face, the sweep of lustrous ebony eyelashes, the delicate curve of her cheek. She represented everything most desirable in a woman. She rode well, assured, elegant and in control, apparently unconscious of his gaze. He felt a familiar quickening in his veins. How vital and alive she was, with the sun bringing out the vivid lights in her hair exposed beneath her fetching hat set at a jaunty angel, a white feather curling up from its shallow brim.

They stopped to rest the horses by a small lake beyond a grassy slope, dismounting and leaving their mounts to graze on the tender tufts of grass by the water's edge. The tranquil lake with willows draping their heavy branches in the water was a peaceful, perfect setting. Two swans went gliding by and water lilies rode the stillness of the water like white boats. They strolled along the bank, the warmth of the sun beating down on them.

Eve breathed deeply, soaking up the atmosphere. 'This is a lovely place. You were so lucky having all this on hand while you were growing up. New York was so very different. In the summer we used to go and stay with friends on Long Island, but it was nothing like this.'

Lucas turned his head and glanced at her. She looked lovely with a flush of health beneath her flesh and her eyes clear and vivid blue, the snapping colour of them brought about by the joy of being at Laurel Court.

'I suppose I was fortunate, although I suppose I took it for granted. I haven't been here for some time—it was difficult when Maxine left me and came to live with Stephen. It seems strange being back. There is much to be done but, until I can grasp back some of the capital I lost, things will have to wait.'

'I can understand how difficult it must have been for you. You say you inherited the land in the north-east. Do you have relatives up in Newcastle?'

'Not that I know of. The deeds to the land were found in my brother's papers when he died.'

'Won't you tell me about him?' she asked quietly.

'You don't want to know, believe me.'

'As a matter of fact, I do.'

'You must already have heard what he was like.'

'I have heard things that have been said about him, but I cannot form an opinion about someone I didn't know. Was he much older than you?'

'Ten years.'

'And was he never married?'

'He was too busy pleasure seeking. We were not close. Years of heavy drinking did not deal kindly with Stephen. His health suffered and the poor condition of his liver often reflected itself in quick and severe changes of mood. Long periods of elation when he was drinking were followed by a slow decline into discontent and remorse to the depths of black depression. Yet for all his faults he still possessed his share of irresistible charm. The easy lopsided smile and twinkling blue eyes were capable of melting even the coldest female heart— and there was none colder than Maxine's.'

'What is she really like, your wife?'

'You've met her. You must have seen for yourself what she's like. I would spare you the more unsa-voury details,' he answered, followed by a curt, impatient question of his own. 'Eve, are you always so inquisitive?'

It was a thinly veiled reprimand and a warning not to come any closer, but Eve couldn't accept that. 'I'd rather you didn't—and, yes, I'm inquisi-tive by nature,' she said, much to his surprise. 'But it's not just that. I would like there to be truth and honesty between us.'

'Very well. Maxine's attitude to marriage did not include the concept of fidelity. She succumbed to Stephen's charms, turning to him for the excitement she craved after the birth of two children in the mistaken belief that as the older brother he had no shortage of money in his pocket or his bank.'

'Was Stephen her only lover?'

He shook his head. 'I believe there were others.'

'I—thought that in most aristocratic houses adultery was taken for granted, always provided, of course, the affair is conducted with discretion.'

'Not in my house, and not when the other party was my own brother. Neither of them took the trouble to conceal the affair.'

'And—the children?'

'They are both mine. I am sure of that. When Maxine failed to provide me with a male heir, she ignored the two she had given birth to and thought she was free to amuse herself as she pleased. She walked out before Abigail was out of the cradle.'

He fell silent and Eve dropped her eyes in shamed remorse for forcing him to speak about his brother and his wife, reopening old wounds. 'I'm so sorry for asking,' she said quietly, 'but thank you for telling me.'

They continued to walk in companionable silence,

watching a rather splendid kingfisher skim the surface of the water and hearing the cry of a curlew overhead.

'Tell me about your husband?' Lucas said after a while. 'Who was he?'

Eve turned her head and looked at him sharply. She was very conscious of him studying her, deliberately and at some length, and her new consciousness of him made her avert her eyes. She was taken off guard by the question, but it was asked politely and with a subtle interest, and she saw no reason not to appease his curiosity. In fact, she was surprised he had not asked about Andrew before now.

'Andrew? Our families had been friends for as long as I can remember. He was older than me— almost ten years—and famous for his charm and good manners.'

'And how old were you when you married?'

'Seventeen.'

'A naïve and virginal seventeen,' Lucas murmured softly, his gaze on her flushed face.

'Yes, I was. I think he thought of me as a child.'

'And you loved him, of course?'

She turned her head and looked at him in helpless consternation. 'Why of course?'

'Isn't passion supposed to be characteristic of seventeen-year-old girls? Aren't all young ladies supposed to be in love at that age?'

'Passion, maybe. Clear thinking isn't.' She gave a rueful smile. 'I remember that very vividly. I didn't love Andrew. We were—friends. I respected him—but love? No.'

'Then why did you marry him?'

'Because our families were friends. It—was expected of us.'

'And did you always do things to please everyone else?'

'Yes, but where my marriage to Andrew was concerned, I should have listened to my head.' She smiled wryly. 'I don't suppose you can call six months a proper marriage, but at the time it felt like a lifetime. We were in New Orleans at the time with his business. He went out one night and was shot in a bar-room brawl with some Englishmen. Like your brother, Andrew liked to gamble—but he didn't like to lose. He couldn't take it. I realised afterwards how little I knew him.'

'And he was not entirely the charming man he seemed to be.'

'No. He was quick to anger—and—not very nice.'

Unexpectedly Lucas's expression darkened into a thoughtful scowl and he felt an unexplainable surge of anger at Andrew Brody. He stopped and gently took her arm, forcing her to look at him. A suspicion had entered his mind and, once it had, the rage he felt at the suspicion was so powerful he couldn't rest until he'd proved or disproved it. In her dark blue eyes he detected a terrible anguish.

'Eve, did Andrew physically abuse you?'

The light was harsh on her face, but she turned it up towards Lucas. It was as if he had seen through the very bones of her head into the secret places of her mind. 'No—he—he didn't hit me or anything—but abuse doesn't have to be physical,' she said quietly, turning from him and walking slowly on, wondering what he would say if she told him the truth, that in her experience, the ugly and humiliating way men and women expressed their love physically was agony.

Lucas glanced at her profile. Now her face tightened and shut, as if a door had been closed. Quite obviously her brief marriage had been a horrendous crisis in her life, and he wasn't sure that even after five years she had been able to surmount it. If not, it went a long way to explaining things about her that had puzzled him from the beginning. Had the physical side of marriage she had endured married to Andrew been so bad that she had been reluctant to enter into marriage again—with anyone? If so, there was little wonder she had insisted on the proviso that they slept apart.

'It's all right, Eve. I see I've embarrassed you.'

His voice was so gentle. Gentle and yet positive. 'My marriage to Andrew is in the past and belongs there, but one good thing came out of it—Estelle. She has made everything worthwhile.'

'I can see that, but there is something I would like to ask you. The question is of a sensitive nature, but if we are to proceed with our marriage it is one I shall have to ask you some time.'

'What is it?'

'Do you still have nightmares—problems—call it what you like, about what happened with Andrew?' Lucas asked. 'Because if you do—'

'No,' Eve interrupted quickly, embarrassed heat consuming her face. 'Of course I don't—at least…'

Once again Lucas stopped and she turned to face him, his expression grave, his gaze refusing to relinquish hers. 'The truth, if you please, Eve. We have to get to the heart of the matter. It is important to both of us.'

She swallowed audibly, suddenly nervous about talking about something that had lain dormant for five years. 'I know it is, but…well—I don't think so—at least I hope not. Afterwards, when Andrew died, having no one to confide in—not that I could ever talk to someone, however close, on such a sensitive matter—I tried seeking explanations in my own mind about what…you know, and I thought about it in such a way that reduced it to proportions my young mind could understand and accept.'

'And what conclusions did you reach?'

'That sexually I was illiterate. Perhaps if I'd had someone to guide me, to show me what being a woman meant, then I would have been aware of what was to happen and it would not have been so bad. My mother died when I was quite young, you see, and although my governess was a good teacher and a fine woman, there were things she couldn't teach me because, being a spinster, I don't think she ever learned them.'

'And when you came to me with your proposition, insisting there would be no sexual contact between us if I accepted, did you honestly think I would meekly comply to your suggestion?'

'Yes,' she replied simply, 'if you were desperate enough for the money.'

'And you didn't think I might become sexually frustrated, spending the rest of my life close to a beautiful wife and being denied any contact?'

She sighed and moved to stand by the edge of the lake, looking out over the water. 'In truth, I don't think I thought about that side of it very much.'

Lucas moved to stand beside her. Eve forced herself not to turn towards him. 'Your trouble,' he said thoughtfully, 'is that you don't know what you're missing.'

Eve did look at him then and her eyes sparked. 'Yes, I do. Andrew saw to that.'

'It sounds to me as if Andrew was a bit of a bully

who only thought of his own gratification. Your governess may also have been at fault, but on the other hand, maybe it would be better if I showed you what you have been missing.'

Before she could move, he had pulled her into an embrace that brought her right up against him so that her breasts were against his chest and his hips leaned hard and flat against her skirts.

His powerful, animal-like masculinity was an assault on her senses. 'Lucas! What are you doing?' she demanded.

An explicable, lazy smile swept over his face. 'Preparing to give you a lesson.'

'Please let me go, before you do something you will regret.'

'I won't. Neither of us will. I'm a good teacher. Relax,' he whispered when she struggled against him, relieved to see a look in her eyes that was not quite fear and not quite anger either. 'Despite how you perceive what happened when you were married to Andrew, marriage to me will not be the same. We are both adults and we both know exactly what this is leading up to. Do you want me to spell it out so there's no mistaking my motives?'

A heated blush stained her smooth cheeks and he deliberately pushed the point. 'My motives aren't noble, Eve—they're adult and they're perfectly natural, and it's already a foregone conclusion that

I'm going to kiss you,' he murmured, lowering his head, his eyes fixed securely on her lips. 'This is a preliminary demonstration, not a full-scale initiation, I promise,' and before Eve could make any further protest he'd claimed her lips in a long, shuddering kiss.

Eve stiffened within his arms and tried not to jerk away from him, for there was nothing she wanted more than to be loved by this handsome, challenging husband of hers, to be loved as a woman should be loved by a man, but she wanted to give her love freely, not to have it taken. But when he deepened his kiss, her heart began to hammer like a wild, captive bird.

Shyly she slid her hands up his chest and around his neck, holding him close and shyly kissing him back. The kiss was disturbing, and it induced in her a whole new range of uncontrollable feelings. Her eyes, which had been wide open to begin with, slowly fluttered closed. All she was conscious of was Lucas's mouth and his body pressed to hers and what he was doing to her, and she wanted it to go on for ever. She had no thoughts, only feelings, and they filled her with such a sense of languorous pleasure that she seemed to be floating.

Lucas told himself to go slowly, to stop before he forced her down on to the grass and behaved like the sex-starved male he was instead of the leisurely lover he'd promised to be, but when her hands slid into the hair at his nape, her mouth yielding with tormenting sweetness to his intimate kiss, he felt a burgeoning pleasure and astonished joy that was almost beyond bearing.

Dragging his lips from hers and brushing a kiss along her jaw and down her throat, where a little pulse was fluttering with all the wild panic of a trapped butterfly, Lucas again sought her mouth, passing his lips over the soft contours. He traced the trembling line between her lips with his tongue, urging them to part, insisting, and when they did he plunged his tongue into the soft sweetness of her mouth and kissed her long and deep.

Long minutes later, Lucas finally forced himself to lift his head, and gaze down into her eyes. 'I think we're going to have to stop.'

Eve thrilled to the sound of his voice, the words he uttered and the touch of his fingers filling her with conflicting emotions. She struggled to free herself from the trance-like state induced by his intoxicating kiss, the heat of the sun, and by the glittering waters of the lake. She glanced around, suddenly conscious that they were in an open place and easily watched.

'I think so, too. Someone might see us.'

He chuckled lightly. 'Be at ease. Your virtue is safe with me. Who could be more concerned than your husband?'

She smiled somewhat shyly. 'Who indeed?'

'Do you still fear what will happen when you are in my bed, Eve?' Lucas questioned huskily, watching intently the myriad of emotions flit across her face.

It came with a slow dawning that in his arms most of her apprehensions had fled. Though the barrier of not knowing how it would be between them remained, it no longer worried her like it did and hopefully would soon be removed, but still she resisted on the strength of her old fear. 'We shall have to wait and see.'

'For what? You no longer have an adequate excuse to avoid my bed. The sooner you realise that, the better it will be.'

He continued to look at her, his eyes clearly expressing his wants. The bold stare touched a quickness in her that made her feel as if she were on fire. Her pulses raced and her heart took flight. She could feel his nearness with every fibre of her being, and she was less shaken by the sight of him than by his slow perusal.

'I—I think we should be getting back,' she said hesitantly, turning from him.

They walked back to where they had left the horses, moving more quickly than before and without speaking. Lucas cupped his hands for Eve's booted foot and hoisted her effortlessly into the saddle. Hooking her knee round the pommel and arranging her skirts, she tried avoiding his eyes, but her gaze was irresistibly drawn to them. He stood beside her, looking up at her, holding her eyes in a wilful vise of pale blue. His voice was soft as he continued, but it held a note of determination, which in a peculiar way both frightened and angered her.

'In the beginning when our bargain was struck I trusted you. I have had a taste of what you have to offer, the sweet warmth of your lips, and I am impatient to sample the rest of you, which is mine by right of wedlock. And I will have it.'

With a cluck of her tongue she reined the horse about and cantered off without waiting for Lucas to mount. With a satisfied smile parting his lips to reveal a flash of white, he was soon riding in her wake, her mare chafing against the control of the bit, her tail arched high and her full mane flowing. And on her back a vision of loveliness, cool and relaxed and controlling the horse with a practised hand, the full riding skirt covering both herself and the side of the horse.

Their pleasant interlude by the lake had given her much to think about, that he knew, and he sincerely hoped she would resolve her dilemma before it was time for him to leave.

Of late he was ever conscious of her, and whenever

he was close to her he was aware of all her womanly attributes and he wanted her. The scent of her lingered on the perimeter of his mind. She was like a fire burning in his blood, a fire that was unquenchable, for the thought of other women became soured in his mind when he compared them to his lovely wife.

Chapter Ten

For the rest of the day Eve was noticeably quiet. When Sarah asked her advice about a matter to do with the children, she gave it, but without real interest, which brought a frown of consternation to Sarah's brow. That something was on her mistress's mind was obvious, but considering her recent marriage followed by a hurried departure for the country, it wasn't surprising.

Every time Eve thought of Lucas and the feelings he had stirred in her, she could feel the blood rushing to her cheeks. In frustration she put her hands to her heated face. This is ridiculous, she thought, furious with herself. If I'm going to blush every time I think of Lucas, I'm in terrible trouble. Ever since she had returned from their ride she had been fighting common sense and dreaming about what could be—that the roots of their marriage were beginning to take hold in the barren soil of their unfortunate beginning. For goodness' sake, she told herself scathingly, all he did was kiss you. Oh, if only there was someone she could confide in. If only she could talk to Beth, with her good, rock-solid sensible composure and sound advice.

In an attempt to calm her frustration and bring some semblance of normality to her thoughts and the problem her marriage was posing, she went out into the overgrown garden to pick some flowers to fill the empty vases. She was so absorbed in her task and her thoughts that she failed to notice the man observing her.

Lucas stood casually watching her through the open window of the study as Eve snipped some rampant white roses and placed them carefully in the basket she carried on her arm. His eyes passed over her shapely figure with warm admiration. The light breeze teased the rich locks of her hair tumbling about her shoulders. Her arms reached forward to snip a rose almost out of her reach, and for a moment the bodice of her gown stretched tight across the slim back. He enjoyed watching her. Despite her earlier marriage there was a graceful naïvety about her that intrigued him, and he thought he would greatly enjoy instructing her in the ways of love.

Eve suddenly paused, arrested by the intruding suspicion that she was being watched, and straightened up. Her eyes were drawn like a magnet to the mullioned windows of Lucas's study on the ground floor, catching sight of the tall, jacketless onlooker calmly watching her, and the shock that went through her made her catch her breath.

The evening meal was a strained affair. When Eve swept into the dining room she found her husband already there. Seated in front of the fire with his long muscular legs outstretched in front of him and crossed at the ankles, he looked disgustingly at ease as he sipped a glass of wine. At the elegantly set-out dining table he was far too close for her peace of mind, for he sat at the head of the table and she close on his right. His gaze never wavered from her.

He was bronzed from the sun, and in contrast his light blue eyes seemed to shine like bright gems. Why did his presence always affect her? Why didn't he just go away and let her be reconciled to his leaving? Why did he have to prolong her agony? There was a long night to be got through, when her self-control would be tested to its limits.

'You were watching me this afternoon, Lucas.'

'Do you mind?'

'How long were you standing there?'

A slow smile touched his lips. 'Long enough.'

Eve was in no mood for a game. 'For what?'

His smouldering gaze passed over her. 'Long enough to come to the conclusion that you're worth much more than any bargain.'

Eve stared at him in surprise, unconscious of the vision she presented in her gold-coloured gown, cut low to reveal her white shoulders, and wearing her hair loose, which was the way Lucas liked it. She shrugged casually. 'Oh, I don't know. A fortune for my companionship seems like fair trade to me.'

'I'm partial to more than companionship, Eve. Much more.'

'I suspect your interest is partial to a great deal of female companionship, Lucas. No doubt you've had plenty of ladies to choose from in your time.'

His smile was as smooth as his voice. 'I'm a gentleman, my sweet, and a gentleman never tells.'

Eve lifted her head haughtily. 'You rate yourself too highly, Lucas.'

He grinned. 'I've always held myself adaptable to the circumstances.'

'I think what you mean is that you're a cad,' she said with firm conviction.'

'If a cad is a man who likes a woman to warm his bed, then I agree. I'm a cad.'

'And proud of it, too.'

His chuckle was low and deep. 'At this moment there is only one woman who interests me—only one woman that I want in my bed.

After sharing a kiss, I think we should progress to the next stage, to something more intimate— in my bed.'

Eve flushed crimson. 'Lucas, we are having dinner. Please behave and control your lustful cravings.'

'That is becoming an impossibility, my love. We are husband and wife. How else should I behave?'

'With restraint. Now, if you don't mind, I think we should direct our attention to something less provoking.'

'What do you suggest?'

'You are to leave shortly. I think for the time that is left we should discuss what is to happen while you are away. The enormous task of running this house and employing more staff, doing what is best for four children and dealing with people I have never met I find daunting. So, if you don't mind, Lucas, I would be grateful if you would instruct me on matters before you leave.'

Lucas agreed and the rest of the evening was spent discussing less amorous issues, but when Eve left him to his brandy to go to bed, she knew it was still at the forefront of his mind and that he was not yet done with her.

With her new found duties as mistress of Laurel Court and living in a constant whirl of activity, Eve was kept busy from dawn until dark. Lucas was out for most of the time, reacquainting himself with his tenants and checking on the general order of things.

Laurel Court was a beautiful house and tastefully furnished. A long gallery hung with family portraits ran along the front on the first floor. Rooms entered into more rooms—bedchambers and withdrawing rooms and a vast study with book-lined walls and soft leather chairs. Impressive paintings—oils and watercolours, some painted by masters—adorned the silk-lined walls. When Eve thought about Lucas's struggle to revive his fortunes, she thought that a mere fraction of the contents of this house alone would solve his problems overnight, but she could understand why he was loath to part with any of the treasures Laurel Court housed.

After the first week word had spread that Lord Stainton was in residence with his new wife and neighbours began calling and invitations were issued for them to attend various affairs.

The children were blissfully happy and Eve was gratified that Estelle, a bold child with great charm, had adapted to her new life with her stepsisters better than she could have hoped. But Eve was concerned about both Estelle's and Sophie's education and made her concern known to Lucas on returning from church one Sunday morning.

'Estelle and Sophie are growing fast. They're

both five years old and very bright. It's time they had a governess.'

Watching his eldest daughter fly up the stairs after a giggling Estelle, Lucas frowned and nodded. 'I agree. We'll have to look for someone suitable.'

'Can we afford it?'

He grinned down at her. 'I'll sell one of the paintings to cover her wages. It won't be the first. But you are right. I want to give them the kind of upbringing every child should have. A governess will bring some order to their lives.'

'I would like to start some foundation for us, too, as a family—for the children's sake, you understand, so they can grow up secure in an orderly environment. They are bewildered, you see. Neither Sophie nor Abigail can understand what happened to their mother and it must be explained to them as gently as possible—not the whole of it, since it will only bewilder them more—so they will not be hurt by gossip in the future.'

'I agree,' he said, his tone bitter, 'but when is a child old enough to be told that its mother abandoned it when it was in the cradle?'

'Like I said, they must be told as gently as possible. In the meantime, I'll begin finding a governess—someone reliable, kind and pleasant.'

'Who will not be too indulgent—'

'Like Sarah, you mean.' Eve smiled. 'She does

tend to indulge them, but that's her way and I cannot fault it. She is so good with them and loves them dearly.'

Lucas looked at her, his expression soft. 'And that's important to you isn't it, Eve, that all the children are loved?'

'Of course, although the new governess must instil discipline. That is important too.'

'And she must also be intelligent,' Lucas added, happy to leave this side of his children's upbringing to her.

'That goes without saying. I'll write to Beth to see if she can help.'

Alice, who was assured of her welcome into this new environment, had been emaciated when she had arrived into the Stainton household. She had now acquired the glossy good health and plump contours that came with nourishment. Her hair was a fluff of dark curls. She was a pretty baby and what a delight she was turning out to be, smiling and laughing at everything that moved.

Sarah, who was thrilled to be living at Laurel Court with her beloved Mark, thought Alice was an absolute treasure and no trouble to anyone, she remarked fondly. There was a brightness and sweetness in her that was endearing, drawing members of the household to her like pins to a magnet. Whenever Miriam took her for a walk in the gardens, there was always one of the gardeners Lucas had set on—local men who had worked at Laurel Court in the past—hanging over the perambulator for a sight of her, and to tickle her tummy, which never failed to make her chortle happily.

Riding home after visiting one of the farms to see how the haymaking was progressing, on hearing the babble of children's voices and a high-pitched yell, Lucas had his attention drawn to a merry, colourful gathering beneath a giant horse-chestnut tree and beside a shallow brook that ran into a large pond in a dip just beyond the house's gardens. It was a particularly lovely day, one of those soft drowsing days of midsummer. Lucas turned his horse in the direction of the happy people.

Miriam was gently rocking Alice's perambulator; seeing Lord Stainton, she bobbed a respectful curtsy. Miriam was very much in awe of her employer and usually scuttled into another room when he came to the nursery—which was often since they had come to Laurel Court. Sarah said it was odd that he should suddenly start taking an interest in the children, and was quite baffled by it—although Sarah also said that maybe Lady Stainton had much to do with that, for she spent a great deal of her time in the nursery. Lord Stainton was even-tempered with his daughters, sitting them on his lap and listening patiently to their little troubles, so that they gladly accepted their papa into their childish world.

Now, as Miriam looked up at him shyly, the warm glow of the sun turning his face to a deep amber and his eyes piercingly blue, she thought Lord Stainton was perhaps the most handsome man she had ever seen. His dark hair tumbled by the breeze curled vigorously, falling over his forehead. His gaze settled on his wife, who was standing on the bank watching Estelle and Sophie paddling in the brook, his eyes took on a hungry look and his teeth gleamed in a bold buccaneer's grin.

'Can anyone join the picnic?'

Until that moment Eve had been unaware of his presence. She froze into stillness, her back towards him. It was as if she was afraid to turn to see who intruded on their simple picnic. After a moment she turned and looked up at him, a smile on her lips and a warm welcome in her eyes.

'Of course, Lucas,' she said, remembering the last time he had seen her picnicking on the day the balloon had gone up in Hyde Park, and how different his attitude had been that day.

Springing athletically from the saddle, he let his horse loose to nibble the grass. His gaze was drawn to the two girls in the water, their skirts tucked into their drawers, squealing with laughter as they held on to each other for support on the slippery stones. The brook was placid, the reeds on the far side reflected mirror-like in its calm surface.

'They're obviously enjoying themselves,' Lucas remarked. 'Where's Abigail?'

'Over there.' Eve pointed to the little girl earnestly picking daisies and clutching as many as she could in her small fist. 'She insists on picking enough daisies to make a chain to go right round the tree. Now you're here you can watch Estelle and Sophie while I help Sarah set out the picnic.'

Lucas had no objections to this and, removing his jacket, he sat beneath the tree, leaning his back against the trunk and draping one arm over his raised knee. He was content to do as Eve asked, but, try as he might to concentrate on the two girls, his gaze was constantly drawn to his wife, and his thoughts had a habit of turning to lust whenever he looked at the woman who insisted on keeping him from her bed.

As he listened to the friendly drone of a browsing bee as it busied itself in a clump of sleepy dandelions, his heavy-lidded gaze feasted on the vision of the lovely creature in a pale sprigged summer dress. The richness of her loosely brushed back hair emphasised the creamy whiteness of her fine skin and her brilliant blue eyes. She looked enchanting. Eve was warm, loving and giving. She was made for love and having children and everything else a husband and wife could contrive in a successful marriage.

The restraints she had forced on his nature were in danger of breaking, and the force between them had grown powerful and impatient in its long captivity. Tonight would be his last night at Laurel Court for some time, and perhaps with a little candlelight and champagne—and that way he knew he had with a lovely woman, he would succeed in luring her into his bed. He would be his most charming, he decided, and hopefully he might recapture that passionate moment they had shared when they had ridden together the day following their arrival at Laurel Court.

Placing plates on to the shining white cloth spread out beneath the spreading canopy of the tree, Eve could almost feel her husband's eyes burning into the back of her neck and she turned slightly. The source of her discomfort sat smiling and unconcerned with Abigail, who had clambered on to his lap, as she did at every opportunity. His sensual mouth was curved in a soft smile, and his light blue eyes were speculative. Feeling the blood warm her flesh, she quickly looked away, hearing him chuckle softly, fully aware of the effect his presence was having on her.

Eve poured some lemonade into a glass and turned and handed it to him. 'Here. You look as though you need it. It's very cold and might go some way to...'

He lifted his brows, deeply amused. 'What? Cooling my—?'

'Lucas,' she whispered harshly before he could say 'ardour'. 'Remember where you are. This is a children's picnic, not a—'

'What? A—' In the face of her scowl warning him not to utter anything unmentionable, he laughed out loud. 'Worry not, Eve, I am fully aware of where I am and that little pigs have big ears.'

Abigail, her interest pricked, looked up at her father. 'Am I a little pig, Papa?'

'No, my pet. You are a little angel.' Ruffling her hair playfully, he laughed, lifting her off his lap and moving closer to Eve.

The picnic was all laid out and Eve called to the children to come and eat. Immediately they gathered round and like hungry monsters began tucking in to anything they could lay their hands on. To Sophie and Abigail it was a novelty seeing their authoritative father sitting on the ground joining in their picnic and seemingly enjoying the experience. At first his presence disconcerted Sarah and Miriam, who kept as far away from him as was reasonably possible, but his relaxed manner and the ease with which he joined in the laughter and light-hearted banter put them at their ease.

Lucas sat cross legged next to Eve, watching Sophie munch in a most unladylike manner on a chicken leg and Abigail break pieces of bread into her napkin to feed to the ducks on the pond.

'How very uncivilised,' he remarked, amazed that not so very long ago he would have upbraided his daughters for their lack of manners.

'No, it isn't,' Eve was quick to retort. 'The children are having fun. I can see nothing uncivilised in that.'

'You spoil them.'

His tone of voice made her look more closely at him. She detected some indefinable, underlying emotion in it as his eyes gleamed beneath the well-defined brows. 'They should be spoiled now and then. They are children for such a short time. Did you never have fun when you were a boy, Lucas?'

His eyes danced with the joy of memory. 'All the time—in this very brook as it happens. And if the girls were of the opposite gender, I could show them some of the finest trees on the estate to climb.'

'And what, may I ask, is so very wrong with girls climbing trees?' Eve remarked with mock indignation, laughter lighting up her eyes. 'I will have you know that as a girl I climbed some very impressive trees.'

'And fell out of several, I'll wager.'

'I did too,' she confessed, not too proud to admit it, 'and I had the bruises to prove it.'

'That doesn't surprise me in the slightest. From the very first I could see you showed none of the restraint implanted into young ladies of my acquaintance. You do not tread with caution, more with an air of one who suspects that delightful danger lies ahead, but you are prepared to enjoy it nevertheless.'

Eve stared at him. 'Is that how you really see me?'

He nodded. 'I also see you as courageous and that you have a sense of adventure and a rebellion that strains against any chains that try to bind you against your will. You must have presented a nightmare to your father while you were growing up.'

'I did—often—but he was so lovable, like an old bear, and he didn't seem to mind.'

Estelle and Sophie returned to the brook, screeching with laughter as they splashed each other with complete abandon. Lucas went to bring some order to the antics of these helplessly laughing young girls, but, unable to quell their exuberance, he found himself drawn in instead, becoming the recipient of a shower of water. Unable to swallow his laughter and oblivious to his trousers and shirt front soaking up the spray, he knelt on the bank and splashed them back.

Smiling, Eve watched him. For the first time she saw her husband indulging in riotous fun and behaving with complete impetuosity with his children. She felt some exquisitely painful emotion squeeze her heart. She could deal with a morose Lucas, an angry and temperamental Lucas, but this was a new side she was seeing to her husband and harder to deal with.

How attractive he looks, she thought, conscious of some unwitting excitement. Her body was taut, every muscle stretched against the invisible pull that was for ever drawing her towards him. He hadn't told her in so many words what he expected of her tonight, but it was there in his eyes every time he looked at her, and she would have to be strong indeed to withstand him—if she wanted to.

The hour was late when Henry arrived. Eve was contemplating going to bed.

'I'm sorry I'm late. I was unavoidably delayed,' he said, shaking Lucas's hand and affecting a fine courtly bow to Eve. Taking her hand, he bowed over it in the best of old-world tradition while smiling broadly at her. 'It's a pleasure seeing you again, Eve, and may I say you are looking lovelier than ever.'

'You may,' she said, smiling graciously. 'In fact, you may say anything you like to me, Henry, if it's complimentary.'

'I'm happy to see you've survived marriage to my good friend here without scars.'

'So far, but it's early days. I'm sorry your visit is to be brief. You should have been staying a few days at least.'

'Next time I will.'

Henry followed them into the drawing room, feeling a deep admiration for this lovely woman who had taken on his friend in his hour of need. Pity about her inheritance, though. That was bad luck, losing it like that. Lucas had told him about it before he'd left London, and Henry had been worried about how his marriage to the young American widow would stand such a set-back. But now, seeing them together after just a few short weeks, they seemed to be getting on well enough.

'Your husband is anxious to get to Newcastle to survey his land—is that not so, Lucas?'

'Absolutely,' he answered, handing Henry a much-needed brandy. 'But not so much the land as what's beneath it.'

Henry winked at Eve good humouredly. 'We'll make a colliery owner out of him yet. This is just the start. He'll soon be taking up the reins of his business empire again, Eve, with all his old shrewd-ness—manipulating his investments, weaving his way through the intricacies of the stock market and buying shares in this and that. You'll see.'

Lucas glanced at him, a fierce gleam of anticipation in his eyes. He was excited about his trip to
Newcastle and eager and determined to tackle his
responsibilities, to take what he might find in the
industrial north by the scruff of its neck and force
it to his own will as he had done in the past.

'That is exactly what I intend to do, Henry, and
I don't intend hanging about. You're right, this is
the start of my recovery and I refuse to mess it up.
The steam-engine has created an unprecedented
demand for coal, which may become the main
source of my income, but I shall soon have interests in other concerns.'

'Such as?'

'The railways—which, you mark my words, will
eventually put the coach out of business. Every
day miles of new track are covering various parts
of the country, linking towns, cities and ports as
never before. If a boom is coming, I mean to be in
on it, Henry, and any other form of trade, be it
glass making, copper-smelting—indeed, all the in-
dustries that go on in the north, in Manchester and
Liverpool and anywhere else.'

Eve looked at him with admiration. She liked to
hear him talk like this, to see him fairly snapping
and crackling with energy, ready to attack whatever
it was that came his way, to cast off the brittle,
restless shell that had encased him since he had

been stripped of his wealth, to smooth the sharp edges that had once cut not only those he dealt with, but himself. He would recover, she had no doubt, for was he not the most dominant, hard-headed, stubborn man she had ever met?

Henry raised his glass. 'I will drink to that, Lucas. I wish you every success.'

Suspecting the two men were about to fall into an in-depth discussion about coal mining, Eve said, 'If you'll excuse me, I'm just going to check on the children and then I'm going to bed. I hope you don't mind, but it's been a long day. Lucas will entertain you, Henry.'

She turned at the door and looked back. Lucas was watching her leave, and in his eyes was a look that told her he was not done with her yet.

Wrapped in her pastel dressing gown in the privacy of her bedroom and curled up in the chair by the hearth, Eve felt a deep contentment, believing that at last things might be starting to go Lucas's way and that their future would be secure.

Her thoughts wandered away from the subject of coal mines and industry that occupied her husband's mind, and her own became no different to what Lucas's had been by the brook. Her face was soft and wistful as she gazed into the glowing embers. Her arms hugged her slender waist, as if they sought to simulate a lover's embrace, which was but a memory of their kiss, which seemed more like it had occurred today instead of almost three weeks ago. Breathing deep and closing her eyes, she felt again the ache in her breasts when they had been crushed against Lucas's hard chest and the warmth of his breath against her lips, and once again she saw the urgency in his gaze as he lowered his lips to hers.

Suddenly a sound from behind the door intruded into her thoughts. Her eyes snapped open and she listened to the footfalls that were familiar to her now. She had listened to them every night and not since the morning following their arrival had Lucas entered her room through the connecting door. The warmth of the fire relaxed her body, and as she continued to listen to him moving about, again she felt the awakening of pleasure deep within her. It was strong and disturbing, flooding her body with a pulsing warm excitement.

Dear God, what was the matter with her? Why was she so afflicted? She had been Andrew's wife and had found no softening in her heart in his bed, yet now her mind envisioned the dark, handsome face of the man behind that door. She resented the hold he had over her so that she didn't know what to think any more, and she withdrew in horror from the bold, unmistakable urging of her body. She knew she would not be free of this torment until she had given him what he wanted from her.

What she wanted?

With each day he grew bolder and on each encounter he confronted her more openly.

This was no chaste marriage she had with Lucas, not with the outpouring of passion that had already been displayed between them. The footfalls fell silent, but a light still shone from beneath the door. Her husband was waiting for her on the other side like a big black spider intent on luring her into his web, this she did not doubt. He was challenging her, testing her, wanting her to go to him.

It was as if some mystical presence were embodied within that room, for she was caught for a moment by a yearning so strong and physical she found it hard to draw breath. Uncurling her body, she stood up and padded to the door. She looked at it long and hard before putting her hand on the brass knob and slowly turned it.

Was it locked?

Her heart lurched when it yielded. For a moment she wanted to turn and flee to her bed, but somewhere in her tormented mind, she knew Lucas was right, and that their marriage should be more than in name only. Gently she pushed the door and it opened silently into a room of large proportions and dimly lit.

Eve saw the shadowy shape of a huge bed on a raised dais, and there, very much at ease, seated in a large armchair by the fire was the room's inhabitant. The image of relaxed elegance, Lucas was calmly watching her, supremely confident in the hold he knew he had over her. He had discarded his coat and waistcoat and neckcloth, and his fine white linen shirt was open at the throat to reveal a firm, strongly muscled throat. His sinewy arms showed below his rolled-up sleeves. His eyes smiled at her, touching her everywhere, and the mocking grin gleamed with startling whiteness against his swarthy skin—in fact, there was a health and vitality about him that was almost mesmerising.

With her gauze dressing gown draped about her like a diaphanous cloud, and with her hair unbound in a single great fall down her back, Eve stood staring at him, her eyes dark and huge in her pale face, burningly aware of the reasons that had brought her here. All at once she knew there would be no going back, for the figure, which was already rising with a cool nonchalance that did not seem appropriate to greet her with a deep, profoundly mocking bow, had succeeded in luring her into his bedchamber.

'Come in, Eve. I was expecting you.'

'I know.'

'Although I did not expect you quite so soon. I

thought the struggle with your inner self would have taken longer.' He met her expectant gaze with a cool, crooked smile of mild amusement. 'Thankfully Henry was quite worn out from his journey and eager to seek his bed—as I am, but for different reasons. I'm glad that you've decided to see sense. The law does not recognise chaste marriages.'

'My state of abstinence I intended to diligently pursue as my only means of escape from…'

'What happens in bed between husband and wife,' he stated calmly when she faltered. 'And yet here you stand, confronting your husband in his lair—a man you bought under false pretences, I might add.'

'Do you have to keep reminding me?' she snapped, her concern more with her own response than with his lingering, hungering gaze.

He smiled, leisurely, infuriatingly—sure of her. 'Do you recall me saying that it would be interesting to see if the agreement we made would outlast the testing of the flesh?'

She raised her head haughtily, tossing back her glorious mass of hair. 'What of it?'

'We have been married a mere three weeks and already you are showing signs of weakness.'

'And no doubt you think because I let you kiss me that day that you have found a chink in my armour?'

His chuckle was low and deep. 'No, my love, not a chink, but a massive hole.'

Purposefully he reached out and loosened the belt on her dressing gown. Eve put up no resistance. She met his gaze directly and her body tensed as his hands worked it off her shoulders and it fell to her feet, revealing a sheer white nightdress. One soft and lovely shoulder was temptingly bare. Her body was covered and yet revealed everything, and Eve saw the quickening of passion spark in her husband's eyes as they slowly perused her from head to toe. Stripped naked by his bold gaze, every bit of the courage she had strived so hard to erect was shattered in an instant. She was too close to that muscular chest, too close to the scent of him, of everything that was masculine.

For a moment she was assailed by the memory of Andrew and what he had done to her. Her flesh went cold. Then a darker fear pierced her terror. Had Andrew mentally scarred her, left her unable to respond to a lover's touch? Her mind rebelled, but a trembling set in. Seeing her hesitation, Lucas sensed it and questioned it with a frown. Reaching out his hand, he caressed her cheek with feather-like fingertips.

'You tremble. Do you fear me?'

Eve waited for the screaming denial to come from the dark recesses of her mind—and this time she was determined to quell its intrusion and the trepidation that had arisen and surged within her.

Lucas was not forcing her as Andrew had done. He was awaiting her consent. The knowledge stilled her panic. When she met Lucas's eyes, she suddenly realised the moment was rapidly approaching that she had dreaded, and that it was too late to withdraw.

'It has nothing to do with fear.'

He drew his finger gently down the bare flesh of her slender neck. 'The time for talking has ended. Now it is time for loving.'

'It is my intention to be your wife in every way, but I have had little practice, so I ask you to show patience, Lucas.'

He raised a quizzical brow. 'And you won't run scared and change your mind?' She shook her head, but he could see the uncertainty in her large dark eyes. His expression softened, understanding more about what was going on in her mind than she realised. 'I am not like Andrew. You will not find what we do either distasteful or undignified. This I promise you. You will find pleasure, not pain in my arms. Making love is a time for giving and sharing, not taking. I will not hurt you. But I must warn you that what happens between us—that what you will find and experience here in my bed—may bind you more eternally than anything else in your life.'

Lucas's long-starved passions flared high.

Disposing her of her clothing and his own, he swung her up into his arms and carried her to the bed, his need to possess her paramount to all else, to claim her body and make her his own in every sense, to seduce her before the shuddering, rapturous invasion, making sure with his experienced hands and mouth that her climax would be as devastating as his own would be.

His eyes revelled in their freedom as they feasted hungrily on her naked body, on her beauty stretched out alongside him—her swelling, full ripe breasts, pink tipped and tantalising, the inward curve of her narrow waist, the seductive roundness of her hips, and the long, lithe grace of her limbs. He had already realised that beneath her clothes Eve was what every man dreamed of, but he was unprepared for this vision of incomparable beauty, of the soft, creamy satin lustre of her skin that contrasted against the darkness of his own. He wanted to look at her, to explore every inch of her, to taste and smell, to satisfy his male curiosity in the soft curves of the woman who was now his wife.

Nervous now and feeling like a child in a woman's body, Eve was unable to avert her gaze from her husband's splendid, naked body. It was powerful, lean and broad in all the right places, the gleam of his skin darkened by the generous covering of hair on his chest. She felt devoured and found it difficult to remain pliant beneath his probing eyes, but as his fingers and lips began their assault, she forgot everything.

Andrew's rough, careless handling of her on their wedding night and the subsequent months, had left her scarred, this she knew, but ever since she had met Lucas Stainton, ever since she had met the physical flesh and bone of the man, she had felt there was more to it than what Andrew had done to her. When Lucas had taken her in his arms he had made her breathless and aroused feelings inside her in the most startling way, just like he was doing now. But she was no starry-eyed girl. She was cautious now, wiser.

She found her lips entrapped with his, and though they tasted of brandy and were soft and gentle, they flamed with a fiery heat. She felt herself falling slowly into a dizzying abyss of sensuality and awakened passion. With a silent moan she slipped her hands around his waist, clinging to him for support, aware of the sudden increase in his ardour in each of his searing kisses. She shivered as his mouth left hers and traced a molten path over her cheek, her brow, and he nuzzled the sweet-scented tresses beside her ear, touching it lightly with the fiery tip of his tongue.

Hearing her soft moan and her faint inhalation, Lucas was satisfied and encouraged by her reaction.

Purposefully he tightened his embrace, feeling her body shudder against his, and he realised with a surge of desire that her demureness and reserve hid a woman of intense passion. He wanted her, wanted to fill his mouth with the taste of her, to have those inviting hips beneath him, to have those long, lithe legs wrapped around him.

His eyes were translucent in the subdued light, his lean and handsome features starkly etched. A strange feeling, until this moment unknown to Eve fluttered within her breast, and a flood of excitement surged through her.

Lifting her heavy auburn hair aside, Lucas slid his warm parted lips to the point of her shoulder and along to the flesh of her throat, his mouth, hot and wet, searing the intoxicating ripeness of her breasts, his white teeth lightly nibbling the smooth silken skin of her belly. He felt her tremble at the intimacy of his touch, but instead of pulling away, as he expected her to do, she nestled closer. He turned her to him and they came together naturally, like two beings forged together by a common bond. His hand trailed down her spine, pressing her hips tighter against him, where the fire, a throbbing pressure growing in his loins, was already raging. He had played out his hand with patience, but now it was waning.

He knew he must be gentle lest her fear destroyed

the moment, and so he held her and stroked her, and when he entered her he was ready to be as patient as she needed him to be, since he had won.

Eve's body reacted to his intrusion, to this indescribable, splintering feeling that built pulsing beats deep within her, with a mindless pleasure that mounted to such an all-consuming intensity she did not believe she could bear it. She became helpless with desire, allowing it all to happen, wanting it with primitive ferocity. She felt the thunderous beating of her heart. What Lucas was doing to her was stunning, expanding to a rapture that made her arch beneath him, the wild, soaring ecstasy fusing them together and sending her up in flames.

A shimmering bliss erupted in an explosion that tore a gasp from her throat, and together they were joined in sweet oblivion. Time seemed to verge on eternity before everything drifted back into place. Lucas raised his head and looked down at her. She was flushed and satiated with loving. Driven by a mindless compulsion to have her, he had taken her with a determination and hunger that stunned and aroused him. Her hair was spread out in shimmering waves across the pillows, and she was staring up at him with wide, searching eyes that had taken on a strange, deep hue, amazement etched on her flushed face.

The whisper of a sigh escaped her as she lifted

her face to meet his, wanting to hold on to this moment in time lest she lose some portion of it to the oncoming forces of normality. Her trembling lips parted as his mouth possessed hers with a gentleness that was nothing like the fierce kisses of a moment ago.

'My God,' he murmured, his eyes smouldering. 'You are wanton beyond belief and quite magnificent, Eve.'

Completely captivated by the intimate look in his eyes, the way the hard planes of his face had smoothed out and the way a stray lock of crisp, dark hair fell across his forehead and the compelling gentleness in his voice, Eve swallowed and said, 'So are you.'

His hypnotic gaze held hers as his fingertips stroked her cheek seductively, sliding along the line of her jaw to her lips. From the first moment he had taken her in his arms he had known they were a combustible combination, and what had just passed had been the most wildly erotic, satisfying sexual encounter of his life. Whatever Eve had felt had been real and uncontrived, and, as he now knew, she was totally uninitiated.

'Would you like me to tell you what I like most of all?'

'Please.'

'I like the way your body fits into mine so perfectly, and that it is attuned to what I want. Are you regretful, my sweet?' he questioned huskily, his warm breath caressing her cheek.

Eve shook her head, and strangely it was no lie. All the doubts she had expected, all the qualms of gnawing shame she imagined would torment her, were not there. More unnerving and frightening to her was the strange sense of contentment, of rightness she felt being in his arms, as if it were where she was meant to be.

She thought how little comparison there was between what had just happened to her and her unpleasant experiences with her first husband. It was more than simply that Lucas could touch her heart while Andrew had meant almost nothing to her. The man to whom she had just given herself so spontaneously, with whom she had just shared the most intimate of experiences, had really become her lover in every sense of the word. Lucas's love making and not Andrew's clumsy, painful fumbling had made her blossom into a woman.

'Are you content now I have fulfilled my word?'

'Nay, Eve, far from it,' he murmured, nuzzling the hollow in her throat where a pulse was beating a tantalising fast rhythm beneath her soft flesh. 'The night is far from over. Tomorrow I must be away early and I intend to make the most of you while I have you in my bed.'

He moved against her, his body rousing, responding again to the softness of hers, and then she was his again, and he revelled in the sweetness of her, touching and kissing her with all the skill of a virtuoso playing a violin, as if he had all the time in the world.

When he finally raised himself from her, her slumberous, love-filled eyes gazed up at him adoringly, and that look, along with the way her arm was slung possessively around his waist, set alarm bells ringing. Gently he pulled away from her, feeling his blood run warm when she stretched with the suppleness of a cat and sighed with contentment, and the way her dark eyes were watching him languorously brought desire surging through him all over again.

She had a body that was created for a man's hands, and a mouth that positively invited his kiss. The woman in his arms had fire and spirit and she was also charming and innocent. She had given him exquisite pleasure, and when the moment of his release came, he couldn't have said who clung to the other most desperately. It was as though the very life source was being wrung out of him. He had turned her into a passionate, loving woman, a woman to fill his arms and warm his bed and banish the dark emptiness within him, a woman to fill his life with love and laughter and to help him fulfil his youthful dreams.

What more could a man want? What more, indeed?

What he didn't want was what she was capable of doing to him, and this thought brought him up short and restored his sanity. He was beginning to care for Eve in a way he was not comfortable with. He was furious with himself for wanting her, hating himself for that weakness, that same weakness that had almost destroyed him when he had married Maxine. How stupid he was being, how incredibly gullible to let himself fall into the same trap twice.

Sensing a change in him and that he had withdrawn from her, suddenly anxious, Eve propped herself up on her elbow, the covers slipping off her shoulder to reveal her pink-tipped breasts that still throbbed from his kisses. 'Lucas? What is it?'

'Nothing,' he replied, trying not to look at her loveliness readily available to him for the taking. But he could not help himself, and, as his eyes devoured her, Eve felt the heat in her face, and then it spread, filling every part of her body at that nakedly desirous look, a need, and a certainty, telling her he was sure of her, as sure as he had been that she would want him when he had finally succeeded in luring her into his bed. 'Eve, if you don't mind I think you should return to your own bed. Tomorrow will be a long day, and as you know, I have to make an early start.'

Suddenly Eve's passionate lover had turned into a civil stranger. Bewilderment clouded her eyes. It was replaced by humiliation on being reminded of how things stood between them and being so casually dismissed from his bed. The passion, the magic they had spun in the privacy of his bed, had delighted her and it had seemed satisfying to Lucas. But in the full knowledge that Lucas did not love her, she did not deceive herself—they married for convenience, and this she must not forget. He had taken her only for her money and was trying to make the best of what they had—a man who might need his wife to warm his bed from time to time, but who would purposely and effectively keep her at arm's length and lock her out of his heart and mind as if she didn't exist.

Without a word she got out of bed and, self-conscious of her nakedness, slipped her nightdress over her head, wondering how he could look so absolutely casual after what they had just done. Picking her dressing gown up from the floor, unable to conceal the hurt she was feeling, she turned and looked at him.

'Shall I see you before you leave, or is it your intention to sneak away without saying goodbye?'

Overwhelmed with guilt, Lucas swung his long, lean body off the bed and strode towards her and caught her to him, his eyes alive with mirth at her obvious outrage. 'Oh, Eve, I apologise if my request sounded dismissive and I don't blame you for being furious, but it was never my intention to offend. But such is your allure, my love, that if you stay I shall be in no mood for sleeping and I shall be so worn out that I may have to delay my departure for another day.'

'Then why don't you?'

'Because you know very well that Henry has come here so that we can travel north together.'

Unconvinced by his excuse, Eve disengaged herself from his embrace. 'Of course. You are right. I should hate to be the cause of any discomfort you might feel in the morning.' Stepping away from him, she looked at his hard, handsome face. 'And you need not worry, Lucas. I did not know what to expect of anything that we did, but I did not expect you to make any undying declarations of love.'

Lucas read her every reaction in her expressive eyes and he was satisfied that he'd done his utmost to kill any romantic illusions about love she might have.

'I'm not that stupid or naïve.'

'I'm glad I haven't misread you. Eve, there is no reason why ours cannot be a happy marriage. You won't find me a cruel husband, and when I have made it back to where I was before, you will find me a generous one.'

It was a strange thing for a man to say, when such thoughts should never need to enter a wife's mind. Eve gazed up at the cool, dispassionate man. 'How cold you make what is between us sound, Lucas. How matter of fact. Do you feel nothing for me at all?'

His features tightened and his eyes hardened. 'Of course I do. I have grown extremely—fond of you. Eve, I told you in the beginning that love is a romantic notion that has no place in my life, that I have no love to give—at least not the kind of love I think you are looking for—but there can be affection between us and who knows? After this night you may already be with child—my son— and if that is the case then after the birth you can do whatever you please. That is part of the arrangement we made that I will adhere to.'

Eve stared at him. His eyes were hard and uncompromising, watching her steadily. There was no doubt he meant every word he said. She was suddenly angry. All the happiness she had felt at the prospect of their future together and bearing him a son was quenched in outraged pride. What he had said enraged her and she looked at him with contempt.

'You haven't learned anything about me at all, have you, Lucas? How can you speak in such a callous manner, without feeling or emotion, as if loving someone and having a child can be settled with cold logic? I told you then and I will tell you again. I will never abandon a child of mine. Ever. So if that means having to live here with you for the rest of my life, then so be it.'

'I am glad, because I cannot think of anything that would please me more than having you in my bed whenever we are together.'

Eve was appalled. Was that all he was going to say? She waited, beginning to feel uncertain and more than a little afraid, because she now realised with cruel certainty that she was in love with him— in love with her own husband—and she would glory in it if she thought he felt the same, but if all the love was on her side, she wouldn't humiliate herself by telling him so and seeing the mockery in his eyes. She was hurt and disappointed, for she had wanted what had happened to have changed him as much as it had her, but she could see it had not and never would.

'Goodnight, Lucas. In the morning I shall make sure the children are up and ready so you can say goodbye to them.'

Closing the door on him, she walked to her bed like a sleepwalker. She was too numb to feel and full of pain. Shock had formed a merciful cushion around her which, as it melted, would give way to suffering in all its sharpness.

Chapter Eleven

Lucas didn't see Eve alone again. The following morning he breakfasted early with Henry. When it was time to leave, as she had told him, the children were assembled to bid him farewell. Eve stood holding Abigail's hand. His eyes were drawn to her and he took a step towards her as though to put a hand on her, but she stepped back, her face blank, her eyes empty, a hard blue emptiness that told him nothing of what she felt, and at once his eyes hardened as he turned away from her.

In the coach bearing them northward, Henry gave his friend, who lounged morose and uncommunicative in the corner, a searching look. Sensing all might not be well at Laurel Court and he hadn't yet found connubial bliss, he enquired after Eve and asked how Lucas was settling down to married life again. Unsurprisingly his enquiry was met with a blank stare.

'Fine,' Lucas replied curtly, before fixing his gaze once more out of the window.

'You're a fool, Lucas,' Henry reproached harshly, feeling heartily sorry for Lucas's wife. 'Eve is an extraordinary young woman—ravishingly beautiful, too—and it is obvious that she adores your children. You should think yourself damned lucky to have her. I pity you—ignoring the one woman in a million who could make you truly happy.' He turned and looked at his friend. 'Are you listening?'

Lucas sent him an impatient look. 'To every word,' he drawled, remembering the moment when Eve had left his bed and how cold he had felt without her presence, and that when he'd driven away from Laurel Court he had suddenly felt totally bereft. 'How can I not when you are bombarding my ears. And if it's of any consolation to you, Henry, I agree.'

It was three weeks following Lucas's departure that Eve suspected she was pregnant. The thought pleased her and a smile of quiet joy lightened her face and her step. A baby was one good thing to come out of the night she had spent in her husband's bed that had been both wonderful and appalling. Of course, she thought wryly, Lucas would be delighted, especially if it turned out to be his much desired son, and if she provided him with a daughter she would have to go through the whole procedure again.

She tried not to dwell too deeply on that night and how much she missed him, the pain of their parting having seeped into her very bones. During daylight hours when she had the running of the house and the children to distract her, she succeeded, but when darkness came and the children were tucked up in the nursery and she was in her bed, the memories would come creeping out of the corners of her mind and she would relive all the glorious things Lucas had done to her and the dreams would pursue her all the way into wakefulness.

Beth responded quickly to her letter enquiring about a governess for the children and told her she had asked a Miss Fraser—who was working in Bath with a good family and was seeking a new position now her charges had been sent away to school—to contact her. She was well liked, reliable and extremely knowledgeable about most subjects, and Beth thought she might be just the person Eve was looking for.

Beth was right. Miss Fraser was everything Beth had said of her and was eager to take up residence at Laurel Court and begin teaching Sophie and Estelle—and very soon Abigail—as soon as possible. More importantly, the children liked her, which meant a great deal to Eve.

She had letters from Lucas telling her of his progress in the north and she was touched that he could find time to think of her and write to her, although she was disappointed that there were no endearments in the letters. His news was about re-opening the mine, which, according to his mining engineer, was rich in coal reserves and when it was up and working in the near future, promised to be a thriving concern.

He told her he had managed to secure the necessary finance without difficulty and went on to tell her of a new pumping system that would benefit the mine, what it was like down on the coal face, the people—hewers, hurriers and trappers he would have to employ to work the mine, viewers and under-viewers—and that he had already found a reliable manager, a Mr Christopher Dunlop who was married with a young family. Mr Dunlop also had an engineering degree in mining and a good head for business. Lucas was confident that he could leave him to oversee everything during his absence, for he had no intention of moving to the north-east.

One piece of news that delighted Eve and was so uplifting was in a letter from Mr Barstow concerning her father's affairs. It would seem that her father had assets not affected by the decline in the American economy after all and she was still a wealthy young woman—perhaps not as wealthy as she might have been, Eve thought, but with that and the colliery in the north-east, it would go a long way to helping Lucas back on to the road to recovery.

Apart from the dark cloud her relationship with Lucas had created, Eve was content at Laurel Court. It all seemed so unchanging, so safe and secure and immune to the changes of the outside world, so much nicer than London. So that when a carriage came bowling down the drive one day and stopped outside the house, she had no premonition of what was to come.

She had just taken a turn around the garden in mellow morning sunshine and, returning to the house, went to receive her visitor. Every vestige of colour drained from her face as she stopped in a shock of recognition. It was Maxine, and, whatever it was she wanted, Eve was sure she was not going to like it. Never had she needed Lucas more than she did just then.

Desperately trying to crush the apprehension that had stirred restlessly at her first sight of the woman, struggling to remain calm and composed and pinning a smile to her face, she crossed the hall towards her.

'Lady Maxine. This is a surprise.'

'And not a very pleasant one, I'll wager. I expect I'm the last person you want to see—and I am Lady Hutton now,' she informed Eve haughtily.

'Alfred and I were married last month—about the same time as you and Lucas, I believe.'

'Then congratulations are in order. Do come into the drawing room.' She smiled tightly at the hovering servant. 'Have refreshment sent in, will you, Tilly? Please, Lady Hutton, come this way.'

'I do know my way. I lived here long enough,' she retorted drily.

'Yes, I know.' When they were alone and seated opposite each other, Eve was aware that an atmosphere of disturbing, inexplicable hostility had entered the room that until a moment before had been filled with mid-afternoon quiet. Folding her hands sedately in her lap, she looked at her visitor squarely. 'Lucas is away just now, so you'll have to make do with me, I'm afraid.'

'I know. He is in Newcastle. It is you I've come to see.'

'Oh?'

'I would like to see my daughters. I have a right to see them, wouldn't you say, having been kept from them all this time?'

'I don't think that is correct, Lady Hutton,' Eve said coldly. 'No one has kept your children from you. You chose not to see them.'

'Do they ask about me?'

'Sophie does occasionally. Abigail—I believe was very young when you went away.'

'And Alice?'

'She is thriving.'

'Good. And you have become fond of them?'

'Extremely fond. They are adorable, lovable children. I have a daughter of my own who is Sophie's age. They have become good friends.'

'And you would not like to see my three girls removed from here?'

An icy tremor of alarm trickled its way down Eve's spine. Her heart skipped a beat as she met Maxine's eyes steadily, seeing something she did not care for glowing in their depths. 'Certainly not. There has been enough sadness and disruption in their young lives. At last they have some stability and they are happy with things the way they are.'

Maxine raised her head haughtily. 'Are they? We shall see about that. I would like to see them.'

Eve could feel a gathering of concentration, like shadows entering the bright, elegant room, like dark forces of will being directly focused on her. 'I'm afraid I cannot allow that—not without Lucas. Besides, your sudden arrival might—upset them. If you wish to see them, you must contact Lucas first. Where are you staying?'

'At the King's Head in the village—with my husband. But how dare you refuse to allow me to see my own children? I am their mother. Do not try to stop me seeing them.'

Eve straightened on the edge of her seat and looked Lucas's first wife in the eye. 'I'm afraid I must. But let's not play games, Lady Hutton. I find using children as pawns in adult games distasteful. Why don't you tell me the real reason that has brought you here? Lucas is away. You knew that before you came. You have asked him for money in the past and he refused to give you more after the divorce settlement. Perhaps you thought I would be more amenable—although now you are married, surely it is your husband who should provide for you.'

Maxine betrayed her exasperation with a sound of disgust. Getting money out of Lucas's new wife was going to be more difficult than she'd imagined. 'I do need money—but unfortunately Alfred is…financially embarrassed at present.'

'As you say, Lady Hutton, it is unfortunate, but that is not my concern.' Eve's tone was frosty. Maxine's blonde hair was exquisitely coiffed and her well-endowed body was gowned in costly good taste, which belied the impoverished state she was constantly pleading. 'Do you really expect me to give you some money?'

'Of course.'

'And if I don't?'

'Then I will have no choice but to take my daughters with me.'

Eve blanched and her body stiffened. 'If you intend to blackmail me, then you can think again. When I married Lucas, my wealth was given over to him—which is how things are done in England. You must know that.'

'Don't tell me you can't get your hands on it if you want. Your father was reputed to have been an extremely wealthy man. Are you refusing my request?'

'You seem to have the general idea. You will not get a penny out of me. Threaten me all you like, but it will not change a thing. I cannot allow you to see the children and I will certainly not let you take them out of this house. Lucas has left them in my care, and that is where they will stay. When he returns, the two of you can discuss in a civilised manner what is to be done with your daughters, but while he is away they are my responsibility, and I take my responsibilities very seriously, Lady Hutton.'

Feeling the sting of defeat, a wave of maddened colour washed over Maxine's face and her lips twisted contemptuously. 'Is that so? Well, we shall see about that. Obviously Lucas feels indebted to you for getting him out of a fix, but how does it feel knowing you hold a man by playing upon his indebtedness to you?'

Eve met the trembling rage of the other woman with assurance. She stood up. 'I don't have to discuss my feelings with you, Lady Hutton. I don't think we have anything else to say to each other, so I think you had better leave.'

The servant came in with refreshment. 'I'm sorry, Tilly. Please take it back to the kitchen. Lady Hutton is leaving.'

Maxine's face hardened to a frightening malevolence and her eyes narrowed to slits of pure loathing. 'You'll regret this, I promise you,' she hissed, her head high, her expression contemptuous.

'I don't think so. Good day, Lady Hutton.'

Without another word Maxine swept out of the room and the house. Not until Eve heard the carriage drive away did she realise she had been holding her breath. She was much shaken by what had transpired and sincerely hoped she wouldn't have to set eyes on Lucas's former wife again, but deep down inside her she knew Maxine wasn't done with her yet.

It was mid-afternoon the following day when Abigail was missed. The three girls had been in the garden with Miriam walking Alice. After playing their favourite game of hide and seek, Abigail failed to be found.

Miriam went to the nursery to see if the little girl had returned to Sarah, but she hadn't. Deeply concerned, Sarah asked everyone if they had seen the child, only to be met with shaking heads. Instructing everyone to search the house and gardens, she went looking for Eve, finding her in her room lying down after suffering a bout of nausea, which was one of the discomforts of her pregnancy.

'We can't find Abigail,' Sarah blurted out, breathless after running up the stairs. 'I thought she might have sneaked in here for a cuddle or something, knowing how attached to you she has become.'

Eve stared at her, stunned by her words. 'No, I haven't seen her, Sarah,' she said, sharing Sarah's concern for the missing child. 'Who was the last to see her?'

'Sophie and Estelle. They were playing hide and seek in the garden. Oh, Lady Stainton,' she cried wretchedly, wringing her hands, 'I am so worried that something terrible has happened to her. I've asked everyone to look for her—to search all the places they know she likes to go.'

Eve felt a peculiar hollowness developing in the pit of her stomach. Immediately she went to question Sophie and Estelle, and by the time she had finished Sophie was sobbing tears of distress.

'She—she might have fallen or sprained her ankle or something,' she cried. 'You will find her, won't you? She can't be lost.'

Eve gathered the little girl to her and tried to be patient, speaking as softly as she could manage. 'We will find her, Sophie. Like you said she might

have had a little accident. Was she upset or
anything when you last saw her?'

'No, she was looking forward to going to see the
kittens in the stable when we'd finished playing.'

'I see. Then we'll start by looking there. Now
you and Estelle stay with Miriam while Sarah and
I go and look for her. I'm sure she isn't far away.'

The hollowness inside Eve deepened as she left
the nursery. She almost knew where Abigail had
gone—been taken. Fear and doubt and then anger
flared in her eyes, and suddenly she was all action.
Grim faced, she turned to Sarah, giving orders in
a confident and sure voice.

'We must be calm, Sarah. Get the staff together
and search every inch of the house and outside,
anywhere a little girl might hide—beginning with
the stables. She might have gone to look at the kittens
by herself. In the meantime, I'll have Mark take me
in the carriage to the King's Head in the village.'

Sarah stared at her as though she'd taken leave
of her senses. 'The King's Head? But—why on
earth would you want to go there?'

'Abigail's mother—Lady Hutton as she is now—
called to see me yesterday on the excuse of wanting
to see the children. I think you know why she really
came, Sarah. When I refused to give her what she
wanted, she threatened to take the children. It's
too much of a coincidence that Abigail should go

missing now. I think Lady Hutton has taken her in the hope that I will pay handsomely for her return.'

Sarah was horrified. 'You mean she has kidnapped her own daughter?'

'I wouldn't put it past her, would you?'

Sarah shook her head, no longer knowing what to think.

'She is staying at the King's Head with her husband, so the sooner I get there the sooner I can find out what she's playing at and hopefully bring Abigail home. The poor mite must be so distressed. But just in case I'm wrong, see that every nook and cranny is searched.'

It took Eve half an hour to have the carriage made ready and to travel to the King's Head. It was a large and busy coaching inn, with a wall enclosing its huge yard. Stepping down, she hurried inside, oblivious to the stares she drew from ostlers and patrons alike. Her heart sank when the proprietor told her that Lord and Lady Hutton had left for London an hour ago.

'And the child? Was there a child with them?'

He nodded. 'Aye, and I thought it queer at the time—seeing as they didn't arrive with one.'

Eve thanked him and returned to the carriage, instructing Mark to take her back to Laurel Court and to saddle her a horse. Hurriedly she changed into her riding habit and woollen cloak as she told Sarah that her fears were confirmed, that Lady Hutton had taken Abigail and that she was going after her.

Sarah tried to argue, telling her it was madness to embark on such a mission when it was almost dark and that a summer storm threatened to break the long spell of hot weather. The wind was already rising and black thunderclouds gathering overhead.

'I have to, Sarah,' Eve said, pulling on her gloves as she hurried down the stairs.

'Then at least take the carriage.'

'I will make better progress on horseback. They have taken the road to London, so at least I know which direction to take. They'll probably pull in for the night somewhere so I'll stop at every inn I see.'

'But you might come to harm,' Sarah cried, hurrying after her as she strode across the hall.

Eve spun round, her face white and her whole body trembling. 'I have to do this, Sarah. I will never forgive myself if anything happens to Abigail. My husband left his children in my care and it's up to me to get her back.'

Sarah watched her gallop off with a terrible sense of foreboding. In desperation she picked up her skirts and ran to the stables to speak urgently to her husband. 'Mark, you have to go after her,' she cried in frantic haste. She was relieved to see he was already saddling a horse and that he intended doing just that.

Darkness shrouded the land and the wind rose viciously as Eve made the headlong journey after Lord and Lady Hutton. As the miles rolled past, above the noise of the wind she listened to the pounding hooves and terrifying pounding of her heart. Every inn she came to she stopped to enquire if Lord and Lady Hutton were staying, but to no avail.

Fear instilled itself into Eve's heart, fear and desperation. What if they had taken a different road and they weren't going to London at all. They might even have stopped to stay with friends. Just when she thought she would have to turn back, she struck lucky.

At the same time that Eve, pursued by a concerned Mark, rode in search of Abigail, Lucas burst into Laurel Court with all the turbulence of the threatening storm. No one was ever unaware when Lord Stainton had arrived, was present or had just left, such was the forceful vigour that went with his make up. Buoyed up with the success of his Newcastle trip and impatient to see Eve, rather than spend the night in Oxford he'd hired a horse and ridden the short distance to his home.

Home! He savoured the word with relish. He had not thought of Laurel Court as home since he was a youth, and now he did, and his beautiful wife waiting within its walls had made if feel so. Dear Lord, how he'd missed her. When he remembered the unforgivable way he had treated her on the night before he left, shame and self-disgust tore through him. How could he have done that? She was the dearest, the sweetest, most magnificent woman he'd known, and he loved her. Yes, he loved her so much he ached with it, and he meant to tell her tonight.

How long had he loved her? he asked himself curiously as he went inside, and the truth was that he didn't know. From the first moment he had seen her, probably, and he desperately wanted her love. He was greedy for it. Nothing made sense when he thought of her—of Eve, in all her audaciousness, defiant and brave, her eyes blazing as she prepared to do battle with him, and those same eyes docile and brimming with contentment after making love.

Glad to close the door on the dreadful weather, he strode briskly into the hall. Surprised to see everyone standing around, he stopped, looking from one to the other. Sarah, her face a frozen mask, was the one who moved towards him.

'Good evening, Sarah,' he said, smiling broadly. 'Where is my wife?' He looked around, expecting her to materialise at any second.

'Lord Stainton. Something has happened.'

Lucas looked at her hard. Something was wrong. Very wrong. The suspense hovered thickly and ominously. 'Tell me.'

The smile vanished as he listened. He was as calm as though Sarah was telling him about the weather. When she had finished, he looked over his shoulder to one of the footmen. 'See that my horse is saddled.' His voice was decisive. He expected to be obeyed at once. 'Which direction did she take?'

'The London road,' Sarah provided.

No more than a minute or two later, at the same moment that thunder rumbled overhead and lightning streaked across the sky, Lucas was racing after Eve and Mark. The thought that something dreadful had happened to Eve and his daughter tortured him. It consumed him and filled him with a torment worse than any soul could.

Eve was shown into the private dining room Lord and Lady Hutton had requested. They both looked towards the door when Eve entered. Maxine smiled slowly, unsurprised to see their visitor, and her husband—a nervous, quiet man of few words—rose, wiping his mouth on his napkin.

'Lady Stainton! Why, how delightful to see you.'

'I believe you are expecting me,' she said, her eyes on Maxine, noting there was an alertness about her, an interested, expectant gleam in her eyes.

Lord Hutton laughed uneasily. 'Expecting you? Why should we be?' Confused, he looked at his wife, his manner suddenly turning from confusion to suspicion. 'Maxine?'

Maxine raised her head in an imperious manner. 'Yes, I knew you'd follow when you missed the child,' she said impassively, her eyes taking on total uninterest as she calmly continued to eat her meal, as though Eve were a stranger who had somehow got past the proprietor and invaded her privacy.

Eve glared at her accusingly. 'I hope you're proud of yourself. Where is she?' she demanded, hardly able to contain her fury.

'Where every child should be at this time. In bed.'

Eve stared at her in shock and disbelief. 'In bed? Are you telling me you have put her to bed and left her alone?'

Maxine shrugged. 'What is so very wrong with that?'

Eve was incensed. 'I would like to see her. My first concern is for Abigail and I want assurance that she is all right.'

'She'll be asleep,' Maxine said coldly. 'I don't want her disturbed.'

Lord Hutton was looking from one to the other, scowling darkly. 'Maxine, what is this? Lady Stainton is clearly quite distressed. I was under the impression that she agreed to you taking the child.'

Eve drew herself up, her face set and white. 'I did no such thing. My husband left the children in my care. How dare you calmly come along and kidnap one of them?'

'Kidnap? I would hardly call claiming one's own daughter kidnap,' Maxine stated coldly.

'When someone abducts a child demanding money for its return, I think the word is appropriate,' Eve threw at her, so angry she had to clench her hands to keep herself from slapping the supercilious face of this silly, selfish woman.

'Maxine,' Lord Hutton chided harshly, 'is this true? What have you done?'

She glared at her husband, suddenly irate. 'Alfred, I would be grateful if you would learn to keep out of what does not concern you.'

'Not concern me?' His face became suffused with anger as he prepared to assert himself, which, being a man who wanted nothing more than a quiet, uninterrupted life, was a rarity. 'You think not? Listen to me, woman. You are married to me now. You live in my house and I shall say what goes on in it and who comes and goes.'

'I need no one's permission to take my own child,' Maxine flared, throwing her napkin on to her dinner and getting up forcefully from the table.

'Be that as it may,' Eve retorted, outraged, 'but you forfeited any rights you had over your children

when you walked out on them. You abandoned
Abigail when she was still in the cradle. You aren't
fit to be a mother,' she seethed, unable to conceal
her disgust. 'Have you no shame—no sense of responsibility, no idea what Abigail is going through
at this very minute? Dear sweet Lord, what you
have done is the cruellest thing. I am deeply concerned about Abigail, who, because of your greed,
will suffer for it. Will you tell me where she is, or
do I have to ask the proprietor?'

Lord Hutton stepped forward, glowering darkly
at his wife. 'There is no need to do that. I will take
you to the child myself.'

'Do that, Alfred,' Maxine hissed, 'but I will not
allow Lady Stainton to take her.'

'We shall see about that,' Eve seethed, turning
her back on the woman and following Lord Hutton
out of the room and up the stairs. The inn was full,
noisy and so smoky her eyes smarted.

Lord Hutton pushed open a door into a softly lit
room. It was quite small. The covers on the bed
were ruffled, as if someone had been lying on it,
but the bed and the room were empty. Something
inside Eve shattered and she began to move her
head slowly from side to side in denial.

'She must have been so frightened and confused.
Where can she have gone? I must find her,' she
cried frantically.

'I'll have the inn searched.'

When no sign of Abigail was found, Eve ran outside to search the inn yard and stables, questioning ostlers and anyone she saw, but no one had seen her. Panic and fury rose in her breast as she ran from the inn. It was dark and raining, the moon appearing now and then between breaks in the cloud. The wind caught and swirled her hair about her head. She looked about her in desperation, wondering which way a little girl in her distress would be likely to take. Seeing a path leading away from the inn, she ran towards it, calling Abigail's name as she went.

Running on, she went into the woods beside the track, going deeper and deeper into the interior, still calling the little girl's name as she zigzagged in and out of the trees, branches and thorns tearing at her face and clothes. It was very dark. Fear dissolved into chilling terror when above the noise of the storm came the sound of rushing water—a river in full flow—and it sounded very close.

'Oh, no. Dear Lord, please don't let her have come this way.'

She ran on, losing all sense of direction, and then miraculously she saw a white, frightened face staring up at her. Eve's heart almost burst with relief. Falling to her knees beside the diminutive and forlorn little girl, she pulled the sobbing child to her breast, smoothing the wet hair from her face and shushing her and rocking her. Abigail was in such a distressed state she could scarcely get her breath.

'Hush, sweetheart. I'm here now. You're safe. No, hush…'

Eve's heart ached for the bewildered terror of this child who had been taken from her own safe and protected world into one that was an alien, frightening place by complete strangers. Hugging Abigail's trembling little body close beneath her cloak, she wrapped her in compassionate arms. After a while Abigail's sobs were reduced to hiccoughing. Sensing the river was very close and afraid to venture back to the inn in the dark in case she fell into the water, she decided to stay where she was—to wait out the night if necessary. Her clothes were damp, but it was reasonably dry under the trees and it was not particularly cold.

She bent her head, unable to stem the tears. She was exhausted and she wanted—wanted what? Lucas. At that moment she wanted her husband more than she had ever wanted anything or anybody in her life. She wanted him to take away the fear and dread, for him to tell her what to do, to feel his strength and his arms about her and his voice telling her that everything would be all right.

The noise of wind and water was so loud she didn't hear her name being roared in the darkness of the night.

* * *

When Lucas reached the inn he was met by Mark. The young man was pacing about, as though in a quandary as to what he should do. His relief on seeing Lucas was immense.

'Thank goodness you're here, Lord Stainton.'

'Where is my wife?'

'I wish I knew, sir. As far as I can make out, she's gone looking for Miss Abigail, who's wandered off and is goodness knows where.'

Lucas stopped short, horrified, as another rumble of thunder shook the ground. 'In this?'

'Aye, sir. Lord Hutton is quite beside himself. I've been out with others with lanterns from the inn looking for them, but—nothing.'

At that moment an extremely distraught Lord Hutton came outside. 'I can't tell you how terribly sorry I am about this, Lord Stainton. I had no idea what Maxine was up to. None at all. You have to believe that.'

'Oh, I do,' he ground out.

Lucas's eyes went to Maxine hovering in the doorway. At the sight of her he felt ice-cold anger settle in his chest, then spread to every part of his body, and yet it felt as though his thoughts were so maddened they would set fire to his mind. Quickly he strode towards her and looked directly at her, and she felt the need to recoil from the expression in his eyes. They were as hard as rock. They were narrowed with what looked like venom, and his mouth snarled in a cruel twist.

'You heartless, selfish, stupid bitch,' he hissed when he finally stood in front of his former wife. His eyes, narrowed to ice-blue slits, were alive with some dreadful emotion he could not keep hidden. Almost demented with anxiety, he could barely stand, the pictures of Eve and Abigail wandering about in the dark somewhere he could not shut out.

'After everything, you won't let me be, will you, Maxine? Not content with bleeding me dry, you try it on Eve—who is more of a mother to Sophie and Abigail, and Alice, than you ever were—and when she refuses to give in to your demands you take one of your children to blackmail her into giving you what you want. Well, I hope you're satisfied. God alone knows where they are.'

'They—may not have wandered far. The river—'

'River? There is a river?' He stared at her in horror. Combing the wet hair from his brow with his shaking fingers, he stepped away from her, hating her. 'Eve is the bravest, most generous-hearted woman I know, and by God, Maxine, if anything happens to either her or Abigail, I swear I will…'

'Enough,' thundered Lord Hutton. 'Lord Stainton, hurling insults at my wife—although God knows she deserves it—will not help find your wife and child.'

Lucas looked at him, trying to control his rampaging fury and dread. 'No, you're right. She's not worth it. I must go and look for them myself.'

Lord Hutton watched him turn, but not before he had seen those piercing eyes glare one last time at Maxine, the flame in them shrivelling her so that she fell back in alarm. What kind of woman, Lord Hutton wondered, was Eve Stainton, that could render a man to such a passion, to such a deep belief in his own conviction that she was alive somewhere out there in the dark with his daughter, and that he would not rest until he had them back?

Lucas stumbled about in the dark, turning this way and that in his desperation to find his wife and child. He stood on the edge of the wood calling her name, the words whipped from his mouth and borne away high on the wind. He searched for most of the night, before turning back to the inn. The sound of the river played ominously on his mind, but he refused to even contemplate that Eve or his daughter might have fallen in and been swept away.

He lowered his forehead on the trunk of a tree, his muscles in his throat working convulsively as he called her name one more time. This time it came out as a hoarse whisper, as waves of agonising pain exploded through his entire being. The appalling devastation of what her loss would mean to him was too dreadful to contemplate. He could not bear to lose her. Eve stirred his heart, his body and his blood to passion, to a love he could not have envisaged, and given the choice it would be eternal.

He could not face a world without her in it, without that special blend of humour and wit, of fearless courage and angry defiance, that passion he had experienced in his bed, her lips smiling at him, her deep blue eyes challenging him, the compassion and understanding she had for his children. All these things made up Eve, his wife.

Dawn was just beginning to break and Lucas was sitting by the fire in the tap room, his elbows on his knees, his head in his hands. Lord Hutton, who had fallen into an uneasy doze, was seated across from him. They were both about to resume the search.

Standing in the doorway holding Abigail's hand, Eve couldn't believe her eyes when she saw Lucas. As if in a trance, slowly she moved towards him.

'Lucas? Lucas?' she said again, her voice dwelling on his name.

She stopped short. Everything seemed to happen in slow motion as she watched his body stiffen. Slowly he raised his head and turned and looked at her, his face a ravaged and tormented mask, his eyes haunted. Eve was appalled at what she saw. Gone was the cynical twist to his strong mouth and the arrogant tilt to his head. He stared at her as if she were some kind of apparition. She stood there, her hair a tangled mass hung to her waist. She was almost unrecognisable to anyone but him.

'Eve?' He mouthed her name, his gaze going from her to his daughter and then back to his wife. 'Eve?' It was louder now and Eve watched him unfold his long lean body and then he was striding across the room and she was in his arms. He crushed her to him, his anguish so great, so tearing, that it carried him beyond all boundaries, as tears poured down her cheeks.

'I have been driven out of my mind. I thought you were dead and I could not bear it. I love you. Oh, God, I love you so much. I can't tell you what I thought. I looked everywhere but I couldn't find you—and the river… Oh, God, the river.'

'I know, I know, Lucas, but I am all right, truly.'

With her cheek resting against his chest, Eve smiled. Her suffering really had been worth it, just to be here in his arms, she told herself, feeling the fast beat of his heart beneath her cheek, and the rise and fall of his chest as he breathed, and to hear him say such wonderful things to her, things she had despaired of ever hearing from his lips. Her heart began to beat with such joy it quite alarmed her, that she could feel so elated after her terrible ordeal. It was just too incredible for words. She was safe now and nothing could touch her again.

Raising her head, she looked at him, loving him. 'I found Abigail and, not knowing where we were, was too afraid to move. It was dark and I was terrified that we might fall into the river, which seemed to be rushing all around us, so I waited until it was light enough to make our way out of the wood.'

He continued to hold her, trying to absorb her body into his. Placing his hands on either side of her face, he kissed her with a hungry violence. A shudder went through his tall frame as she arched into him and kissed him back. Only when she felt a tug on her skirt did she remember Abigail. So did Lucas and, releasing Eve, he swung the child off her feet and held her to him, kissing her cheek and murmuring soft, soothing words of comfort.

'Thank God. Thank God,' he murmured hoarsely, overcome with emotion. 'Everything will be all right now, my darling.'

'And I won't be sent away again? It was very dark and I was frightened and it made me cry,' Abigail mumbled, her soft cheek resting against his.

'I know, sweetheart, and I'm sorry I wasn't there, but no one is going to take you away ever again. I promise.'

'I want to go home now,' she murmured tiredly.

'And so you shall.'

Lord Hutton took Eve's arm. 'Come, Lady Stainton, sit by the fire. I'll summon the landlord and have him prepare you some sustenance. You look quite worn out. It must have been an ordeal.'

She nodded, sitting wearily in the chair Lucas had vacated a moment before. 'One I would not wish to repeat.' She glanced about her. 'Lady Hutton? Is she…?'

'In bed. Although I have to say she sees the error in what she has done and is—remorseful.'

'I'm sorry, Lord Hutton, but after everything Abigail has suffered at her hands—and my own harrowing ordeal—I doubt she knows the meaning of the word.'

A tired Abigail came and climbed on to her lap and Eve kissed her head, wrapping her arms around her protectively. 'At least she doesn't seem to have suffered too much from what has happened to her. A hot bath and a nap will do her good, although I don't want her to be left alone.'

Lucas looked down at them, unable to believe they had returned without mishap. 'A hot drink for you both, Eve, and then we must get you home. Mark should be here at any time with the carriage.'

'Mark?'

'He followed you last night and spent most of it searching for you. I sent him back to Laurel Court for the carriage.'

'And you, Lucas? Why didn't you let me know you were coming home?'

He grinned. 'I wanted to surprise you. Instead I was the one to be surprised when I arrived and found you were not there. Sarah told me what had happened and I came after you.'

Lucas turned and stiffened when he saw Maxine hovering in the doorway. Elegantly arrayed, tilting her chin in her usual proud manner, she slowly moved into the room. There was something new in her eyes, a hint of pleading—and, yes, remorse. But Lucas's first wife was not one to relent easily, and her gaze met his a little defiantly.

Tightening her arms about Abigail, who had her face buried in Eve's cloak, Eve looked at Maxine a little uncertainly. She was rather pale and the lack of colour made the small veins in her cheeks more visible, making her look older than her thirty years. Eve had not seen Maxine since she had left the inn last night and she did not really want to, but this matter had to be resolved before they left.

'Maxine,' Lucas greeted her in a chiding tone laced with sarcasm. 'I trust you slept well.'

'As a matter of fact, I didn't sleep at all, you see—I know it was a terrible thing that I did and I thank God that Abigail has been found unharmed. I admit I have not always thought in such terms, but there have been reasons for that.'

'Forgive me if I have difficulty believing you,' Lucas ground out. 'The reason you turned your back on your children was that you couldn't stand having them around you.'

'I know what I have done is wrong. All I could think of was myself. You were right, Lucas. I am not a fit mother. I never wanted children, you see.' She shrugged. 'Unfortunately, within marriage, one cannot prevent these things happening.'

'Too damn right you can't,' Lucas bit back, 'but when they do such things are dealt with reasonably and one does not evade one's responsibilities. It didn't take me long to realise you married me for my money and nothing else.'

'Money!' Lord Hutton cried, his face suffused with wrath. 'Why is there all this obsession with money?'

'It's a very useful commodity, Alfred,' Maxine stated coldly.

'Of which I have precious little, so you will have to get used to it, just like you will have to get used to living in Devon, Maxine, for I have lost all interest in London's pleasures. In fact, to be absolutely honest they sicken me. We will leave within the week.'

Maxine stared at him in alarm. 'No—no, Alfred, you cannot mean that. I have no liking for the country—I will suffocate and you know it.'

'Madam, after what you have done you will do as you are told.' It was said calmly, but there was no mistaking the steel beneath the words. Lord Hutton was a down-to-earth man who found it hard to show emotion, but he was overwhelmed by the enormity of what his wife had done. 'You took a child against the wishes of Lady Stainton—that she is your own child is beside the point, since you have not clapped eyes on her in God knows how long. To my thinking it was a criminal offence that caused immense and unnecessary distress to all concerned.'

Maxine paled and looked strangely meek and humble as she held out her hands to him in beseeching appeal. 'Stop it, Alfred—please. Do not speak to me like this.'

'If you say one more word, Maxine, I shall knock you senseless. You greedy, vindictive—' He took a shuddering breath, fighting to control his temper. 'Dear God, had I the means I swear I'd divorce you myself.'

Maxine blanched, horrified at the thought that she would be so humiliated twice. 'Alfred—you wouldn't.'

'Yes, madam, I would, but as it is I am stuck with you, so we will have to make the best of what we have.'

'Stop it, both of you,' Lucas interrupted. 'It's too late for any of this and I do not want to argue in front of Abigail. What is done cannot be undone, and I for one am sick of it. Maxine, I do not intend to see you again in the foreseeable future. Feeling as you do about your children, nothing can be achieved by it. But if you try anything like this again, I swear I will be the one to knock you sense-less.' He looked at Lord Hutton 'Take her to Devon, Lord Hutton, and keep her there. And be sure to lock away your family silver, otherwise in the blink of an eye she will find a way to divest you of it.'

Lord Hutton nodded. 'Oh, I shall, Lord Stainton, most certainly. I have the full measure of my wife, and you may rest assured that this will be the last time she will come pestering you for money.'

Chapter Twelve

Arriving back at Laurel Court, Mrs Coombs and Sarah took charge, but when they tried to get Eve to go to her room and rest she refused and went to sit with Abigail, seeing that she was given a soothing drink and put to bed. The child napped fitfully and finally slipped into a peaceful sleep, confident that if she woke in terror she would be comforted by Eve's presence.

Not until Abigail had woken and was being fussed over by Sophie and Estelle and a doting Sarah did Eve go to her own room for a much-needed bath.

The early evening breeze stirred the curtains and in the silence of the house Eve could hear Lucas moving about in his room as she stepped into the warm scented water prepared by Tilly, and relaxed in the luxury of it.

Lucas let himself into Eve's rooms. His eyes did a quick sweep; on hearing a splashing sound coming from her bathing chamber, his smile was lascivious. Padding across the carpet in his stocking feet, he was met by a wave of rose-scented steam. Having just taken a bath himself, stripped to the waist he leaned against the door post, his eyes aflame. All he wanted to do was feast his eyes on her.

Eve was in a big brass tub with her back to the door, her head resting on the high rim. Her freshly washed hair was secured in a wild untidy knot on the top of her head, with damp tendrils curling and clinging to her neck. One slender leg suddenly emerged from the water and was raised skyward, sleek and glistening with droplets of water as her hands reached out to lather the firm white flesh.

An amused smiled twisted his lips. It was his most fervent desire to join his wife in the tub, but it was highly likely her maid would return at any minute and her embarrassment would be excruciating if she were find the master and mistress indulging in such antics.

Believing she had heard Tilly return, Eve said, 'Hand me the towel, will you, Tilly?'

Seeing a towel draped over a chair, Lucas shoved himself away from the doorframe, reached for it, then held it out. Without turning, Eve arose from the tub and stepped out. She started to turn and reach behind her for the towel—that was the moment she saw Lucas.

'Lucas!' His heated gaze seared her and in a moment of alarm it was in her mind to flee, but then her eyes warmed and her smile welcomed him. 'How silently you came. Are you here to share my bath or to tempt me with your own nakedness?' she whispered, wantonly trailing a finger lightly down his bare chest. 'It is obvious you have no excuse for spying on me.' She allowed him to drape her in the towel and, turning her back on him, she sauntered into the bedroom.

Lucas watched appreciatively her hips moving with an undulating grace beneath the towel, then followed her. His eyes devoured her when she dropped the towel and reached for her dressing gown, exposing her body to the full—the full, ripe, swelling breasts and the luscious roundness of her hips and long shapely legs.

Knowing full well the effect her nakedness was having on him and that she was rousing his senses to full awakening, and in no hurry to cover herself, still smiling, she slowly put her arms into the flowing sleeves and tightened the belt around her slender waist, but not before she had seen the hard glint of passion strike sparks in his pale blue eyes.

Her bare feet seemed to glide over the carpet, and her lips were curved upwards in a totally wicked smile. She gave a deep throaty laugh and placed the flat of her hands on his chest, sliding them upwards over his ribs, feeling the heavy thud of his heart beneath her questing hands.

'When are you going to tell me what it is you want?' she purred as his hands came round her waist. Slowly, deliberately, she leaned into him, the peaks of her thinly clad breasts pressed to his chest, rousing his blood to boiling as the heat of her touched him.

'Dear God, Eve, you know damn well what it is I want without me having to spell it out,' he rasped, his long-starved passions flaring high as he folded her in his arms, crushing her to him and covering her soft reaching mouth with his.

Her arms snaked around his neck and she returned his kiss with all the passion and longing that had been gathering force inside her since he had left her. Placing his hands beneath her knees, he swung her up into his arms and carried her to his bed, kicking the connecting door shut. Placing her on the covers, he leaned over her, untying the belt of her robe and removing it, before divesting himself of his trousers and revealing the naked male beauty of his body in its arrogant readiness to make love to his wife.

Eve waited for him, her breasts and her insides quivering in hot anticipation.

Lucas leaned over her, his hand leading her with purposeful intent, bold in his knowledge and gentle in his regard of her. There was a radiance about her he had never noticed before, something different, but he could not name it.

'How lovely you are,' he breathed. 'You have grown even more beautiful in my absence. Is it some kind of sorcery you practise, my love?'

She laughed softly. 'This is no sorcery, Lucas. Your eyes do not deceive you. You have been absent too long, that is all,' she murmured, pulling his head down to her lips.

There was between them a storm of passion that deafened their ears as greatly as the crashing of thunder. Each kiss and touch was fire, each word a caress, each movement in their union a masterpiece of music, a rhapsody of passion that played on their heart strings and united their souls, combining to become a consuming crescendo that left them sated and warm and pulsating with pleasure.

Eve lay exhausted and drowsy in her husband's arms, her breath softly stirring the furriness of his chest. How she loved him, and she gloried in being able to respond to him in their bed. Lucas, his dream fulfilled after the long, tortured weeks of being without her, turned his head and buried his face in her loosened hair, savouring the sweet scented fragrance of it.

A warm and gentle breeze stole in through the open windows and cooled their heated bodies. Some moments later Eve rolled on to her stomach and, leaning on his chest, looked up at him, her gilded tresses spread in thick waves of silk over him, her deep blue eyes dark and sultry.

'Did you mean it?' she asked softly.

His mouth twitched at the corners. 'Mean it? Mean what?'

'Earlier you told me that you love me. And don't you dare insult me by telling me you can't remember because I won't believe you. Was it said to placate me, in the heat of the moment—or what?'

His gaze met hers without wavering, promising everything. 'The answer to that is that I meant it. I do love you, Eve, beyond all else. I love you so much that it hurts.'

The relief was so painfully exquisite that Eve thought she would die of it. 'What? I have to ask myself is this the man who told me that love is a silly, romantic notion that has no place in his life, that you don't want to be loved and that you have no love to give.. What has happened to change your mind, Lucas?'

'You, Eve. You have changed my mind. I was a complete ass. Can you ever forgive me for saying those things to you?'

'There is nothing to forgive, Lucas. I know why

you said them and why you couldn't accept my love. Until you made love to me I had not realised the full extent of how much your marriage to Maxine had damaged you emotionally. Now I fully understand. But things change, people change—and I believe Maxine has changed— as you have changed, Lucas. In fact I think you are rather wonderful and very clever.'

'No, I'm not,' he declared solemnly. 'If I had even the slightest intelligence, I would have taken you to bed on our wedding night—or before.'

'When was the first time you wanted to do that?'

'The day you arrived at my house and gave me a severe dressing down for shouting and cursing and doing all the things every bad-tempered, temperamental gentleman does when things aren't going his way,' he admitted, smiling at the memory. 'No one had dared do that since I was a child. I think I fell in love with you then—when you were holding Estelle with one hand and trying to hold on to a wriggling puppy with the other. It was when I went to Newcastle that the depth of what I felt was driven home. I missed you—Lord, how I missed you. You have no idea how much. But what of you, Eve? How do you feel?'

'Like your wife—your wife who loves you very much,' she said, her eyes aglow with love, 'you and your children, and one day I will give you a son.'

'Suddenly that no longer seems important. You see, I have come to realise that as much as I want a son, I want you more. So, my love,' he murmured, rolling her on to her back and beginning to plant tantalising, rousing kisses on her lips once more, 'feel free to fill the nursery with as many daughters as you wish, providing they all look like you.'

Nothing touched Eve more than this, which was all the proof of his love that she needed.

'The children have missed you,' she murmured between kisses. 'They are thrilled to have you back.'

Breaking off nuzzling her ear lobe, he looked at her from beneath hooked eyes. 'And the new governess? Is she suitable?'

'Miss Fraser. She's worth her weight in gold. You'll like her—and the children adore her.' She smiled teasingly. 'Have you decided which painting you'll have to sell to pay her wages?'

He gathered her close, his kisses urgent, warm and devouring as he continued with his seduction. 'It will no longer come to that, my love. Very soon we shall have enough money to employ a thousand governesses.'

She laughed softly, feeling the bold urgency of him once again. She pushed him away and he looked down at her in puzzlement, his eyes questioning. 'You must learn to be more gentle, Lucas.'

'Why,' he murmured, shoving back her hair and

proceeding to kiss her gleaming shoulders, her breasts, his lips warm, devouring, fierce with love and passion, 'are you in danger of breaking, my love?'

'No, Lucas. I am strong enough to withstand our lovemaking, it's just…'

'Just what?' His mouth went lower, kissing her belly and becoming bolder still.

'You might hurt the baby.'

He stopped what he was doing and slowly looked up at her. The silence grew. Very slowly he brought himself up to lean over her. 'What did you say?'

'I said you might hurt the baby.'

He smiled. 'So that is what is different about you. I knew there was something, but I'm damned if I could put my finger on it.'

'Do you mind?' she breathed, watching his face.

'Mind? No. I am ecstatic. I love you. We love each other. Everything is as it should be.'

Lucas stood on the terrace gazing over the magnificent grounds at Laurel Court, which had been tended, pruned, planted and nurtured by an army of gardeners and brought back to its former glory. Things were going well for him. After all his determination and hard work, his business ventures were thriving and he was beginning to reap great rewards. The money bequeathed to Eve by her father as yet remained untouched in the bank. They had discussed at length what was to be done with it and they were in accord that it could be used to set up a trust for the children, in particular for Alice, since there would be nothing forthcoming from her mother.

Attired in a simple gown of lavender silk and lace trim, Eve came to stand beside him, linking her arm through his.

Master James Stephen Stainton was one year old. It was his birthday, a momentous day, and Eve wasn't going to let it go by without a party. Not that her son was aware of it, but he was enjoying all the attention that was being showered on him.

'Penny for them?' she murmured, following her husband's gaze.

Placing his hand over hers, he smiled down at her. 'I was just thinking what a lucky man I am— to have you and the children and all this. Don't they make a charming picture?'

Looking at their joint offspring scampering about with Beth and William's boys—the family having come on an extended visit—she agreed.

The gardens seemed to be full of children running wild on this lovely spring day, and Miss Fraser, a harassed expression on her face, was inclined to blame Miriam for that. The young nursemaid seemed to delight in encouraging them, even joining in their game of hide and seek, which entailed a great deal of activity and laughter and tumbling about.

Master James was sitting on the grass, his face rosy and smiling, and then he rolled onto his hands and knees and began crawling after Alice, who was toddling after Abigail. James was a beautiful child and there was very little of Eve in him. As young as he was, he even had the same arrogant jut to his baby jaw as Lucas, the same scowl, the same light blue eyes and an air about him of masculine fierceness.

Postponing his decision to go to the children and join in their games, Lucas slid his hand round Eve's waist, drawing her possessively close. He smiled and touched the deep red curls at her neck and then he bent his head and kissed her gently on the lips.

'What a fine sight. Do they not make you feel proud? Are you happy, my love?'

The kind of happiness he spoke of began to spread through her until she ached from it. 'Very.'

'Are you certain?'

'Absolutely.'

'For the first time in my life I finally know what it feels like to have a home and a family. It is you I have to thank for that. The bargain we made

turned out to be a good one. You are a fine woman, Eve Stainton—an exceptional one.'

His wife tipped her face up to his and laughed. 'You are not bad yourself, Lucas—and I love you.'

* * * * *

HISTORICAL

LARGE PRINT

MARRYING THE MISTRESS

Juliet Landon

Helene Follet hasn't had close contact with Lord Burl
Winterson since she left to care for his brother. Now Burl
has become guardian to her son she is forced to live under
his protection. He has become cynical, while Helene hides
behind a calm, cool front. Neither can admit how affected
they are by the memory of a long-ago night…

TO DECEIVE A DUKE

Amanda McCabe

Clio Chase left for Sicily trying to forget the mysterious
Duke of Averton and the strange effect he has on her.
However, when he suddenly appears and warns her of
danger, her peace of mind is shattered. Under the
mysterious threat they are thrown together in intimate
circumstances…for how long can she resist?

KNIGHT OF GRACE

Sophia James

Grace knew that the safety of her home depended on her
betrothal to Laird Lachlan Kerr. She did not expect his
kindness, strength or care. Against his expectations, the
cynical Laird is increasingly intrigued by Grace's quiet
bravery. Used to betrayal at every turn, her faith in
him is somehow oddly seductive…

◉™ MILLS & BOON®
Pure reading pleasure™

HIST0609 LP